The
FIRE ARTIST

ALSO BY DAISY WHITNEY

Starry Nights

The
FIRE ARTIST

DAISY WHITNEY

BLOOMSBURY
NEW YORK LONDON NEW DELHI SYDNEY

First published in the United States of America in October 2014
by Bloomsbury Children's Books
www.bloomsbury.com

Bloomsbury is a registered trademark of Bloomsbury Publishing Plc

For information about permission to reproduce selections from this book, write to
Permissions, Bloomsbury Children's Books, 1385 Broadway, New York, New York 10018
Bloomsbury books may be purchased for business or promotional use. For information on bulk
purchases please contact Macmillan Corporate and Premium Sales Department at
specialmarkets@macmillan.com

Library of Congress Cataloging-in-Publication Data
Whitney, Daisy.
The fire artist / by Daisy Whitney.
pages   cm
Summary: As an elemental artist, Aria can create fire from her hands, stealing her power
from lightning—which is dangerous and illegal in her world—but as her power begins
to fade faster than she can steal it she must turn to a modern-day genie, a granter,
who offers one wish with an extremely high price.
ISBN 978-1-61963-132-8 (hardcover) • ISBN 978-1-61963-392-6 (e-book)
[1. Fire—Fiction.   2. Magic—Fiction.   3. Family problems—Fiction.
4. Genies—Fiction.   5. Love—Fiction.]   I. Title.
PZ7.W6142Fir 2014   [Fic]—dc23   2014005596

Book design by Nicole Gastonguay
Typeset by Westchester Book Composition
Printed and bound in the U.S.A. by Thomson-Shore Inc., Dexter, Michigan
2 4 6 8 10 9 7 5 3 1

The Fire Artist *is dedicated to my amazingly talented writer friends C. J. Omolulu and Courtney Summers. Thank you for helping me shape this story every step of the way.*

The
FIRE ARTIST

1

Lightning Strikes the Heart

A plume of flames erupts from my fingertips and rises high above me. As I widen my arms, the fire curves in a brilliant arc. More flames burst into the inky night at my command.

I call them down, luring them back into my scarred and hardened palms, like scarves of silk being pulled back into a magician's top hat.

Then, with a graceful bend, I grasp a pair of arm's-length chains I've left on the ground for this moment. I raise my arms above my head, wirelike whips in my hands now. A quick flick of my wrists and sparks race to the metal on the wires. A crack, then molten drops rain over me, a willowy canopy of sizzling hisses that light up the faces of the crowd. They are packed tightly into every inch of the bleachers, their bare arms glistening with sweat in the muggy night.

My fireworks hail down from the cloudless sky, falling gently at first, then quickly, like bullets and gunfire. Another snap and sparks leap higher. And another, until I can no longer distinguish the crackling sound of the fire from the gasps and cheers of the crowd.

On summer evenings like this, the metal bleachers are jammed with the young, old, and everyone in between, clasping tight their crinkled, hastily printed flyers advertising our lineup of fire, ice, earth, and wind. I'm the final act, and I'm nearly done, so I drop the chains to the ground and show my palms to the audience. I'm not the only one who can do this. But no one in or around Wonder, Florida, is tired of coming here to watch flames fly from human hands, with fire that flies higher, burns brighter, and curls tighter than any other fire artist's in a long time.

This is the big one, when I extinguish all the fire, the park goes dark for one long, silent moment, then a spectacular torch flares from me high into the sky. I glance at the onlookers. They are tense, jaws tight, bodies hunching forward in the stands. I look away, and it's then that a pair of phantom fingers pinch a corner of my heart. My shoulders pull in as my chest constricts. My throat tightens for a moment.

Like a glass being knocked off the corner of a counter, I've spilled fire all over the ground. I can't blame it on stage fright. I'm not nervous.

I'm losing my fire again. It's not the first time. It won't be the last.

The fire skitters away from me, racing over the hard grass and packed dirt, hell-bent on the front row. I fall to my knees to coax the sparks back to my hands, before they burn off the feet of the girl with the ratty pink sneakers who has been kicking the ground absently as she watches. Now, fear fills her eyes, and she leaps up onto the bench. Her mother grabs her and holds her tight.

My heart sputters, like it's gasping for a last breath. There's a hole in the show, a patch I must fill in. Like an actor forgetting a line and covering it up with an ad lib that doesn't quite fit, I grasp the long ribbon of blazing orange and tug it back into my hands.

As if I meant to nearly roast the audience.

To maintain the illusion I jump back onto my feet, thrust my arms high in the air. I'm a gymnast who's expertly dismounted, covering up the broken bone inside her. The little girl has tucked her head against her mother's chest, but the mother is softening. It's a show, after all, and I have shown them that my little stumble must have been scripted.

Now there is clapping, and hollering, and so much whistling too. Fingers inside mouths making the sounds that draw taxis to the curbs in cities I've never been to. The audience is swallowed in cheers. They got their money's worth and then some. Our shows don't cost much, not at this level or this venue, a part-time ballpark a few miles from swampland and a few blocks from the abandoned amusement park that used to be Wonder's greatest draw. Had this night been two years ago, we might have also heard the cranking of the roller-coaster cars chugging up tracks, or the groans of the circling Ferris wheel nearby. But the Eighth Wonder of the Modern World amusement park has since closed down, and all that's left are the skeletons of the rides that peer over the wooden fences.

Together, the ten of us in this latest cast of performance artists—including my best friend, Elise, who can harness the

3

wind—lower our heads in unison, all while my heart thumps against my chest as if it has a repetitive injury, an insistent hiss in the pipes. My heart is not like the others'; it's not whole.

It's missing parts.

I walk inside to the locker rooms that house ballplayers on other nights, guys with big, broad chests and beefy arms and mouths that chew gum or spit tobacco. I slow down, waiting for Elise, and I pull her aside into a quiet corner.

"It's time for another renewal."

Her eyes are sad. "I know. I could tell when the fire jumped away."

"Will you do it for me again?"

"You know I will. You don't even have to ask. I always will," Elise says, and I can hear the heaviness in her voice. "I'll start tracking the morning storms for tomorrow."

The weather forecasters were right, but we're behind the first flash storm. We catch a glimpse of a streak of lightning far off, and Elise jams the gas. But the thunder comes nearly forty-five seconds later.

"It's at least nine miles away!" I shout, even though I'm next to her in the front seat of her brown hatchback that used to be painted pink. "But there's more coming. There has to be."

We fly down the Wilderness Waterway, sprinting past mangrove islets.

Elise points. "There."

Lightning pierces the sky, ripping it apart with a bright

4

scratch. We count out loud, reaching thirty seconds before the thunder rumbles toward us.

"Closer," I say, and Elise nods. She is pure determination now, focused and instinctual as we race toward the brewing storm. We cross into the curtain of rain, and she barely slows her car at all, cruising over the soon-to-be-slick highway as raindrops turn heavy and hammer the car. Elise's parents gave her this car when she turned sixteen, a pink hatchback, since pink has always been her favorite color. She drove it in all its girly glory for a few months until she realized it would be far too conspicuous on days like this. She and I painted it brown one afternoon, and I bought her cherry ice cream when we finished. Her parents simply shrugged and figured her change of heart was the capriciousness of a teenager, when the truth is she changed it to protect me.

To protect us. If she's caught helping me, the consequences for her and her family could be dire.

The rain pounds harder into the windshield, and Elise grips the wheel, her arms like steel cables as she steers through the wet onslaught.

Another flash of lightning. Seconds later, a clap of thunder. She slows down and squeals to a stop on the side of the road, empty beach alongside us. She looks around, scanning the deserted beach to make sure we're alone. Then she throws open her door, and I do the same, following her as she rushes across the sand, still glancing behind and around in case there's someone who'd see us. But we're all alone here. The air is electric. I keep pace with her, ankles digging into the sand as we run closer to the storm. There's an outcrop of rocks near the edge of the water, and Elise races to it, giving us a shield in case anyone driving by can make out what we're doing from a distance.

I'm battered with rain when Elise stops short, breathing hard. She plants her feet firm and holds out her hands. Her palms are open wide, and, like a switch turned on, gusts of air burst forth from her, powerful blasts that stir the sand into swirling gales at our feet. She lifts up her hands, bringing them over her head, the squalls rising with her. I squint, trying to keep the sand out of my eyes.

The wind she weaves intensifies. Her arms move as she fortifies her elemental creation, layer by layer. Some air artists can execute beautiful flips and twists in the air, can contort their bodies in strange and gorgeous ways through wispy blasts of air, but Elise's gifts have always been more blunt. Her true ability is in the sheer strength of the air she can make, the way she can guide it with the precision of an atomic clock. Soon she's crafting a miniature tornado around us, the wind a creature that bends at her command.

She peers up at the gray and crying sky, then turns to me and gives a quick nod.

All I have to do is stand and wait.

When the next jagged needle rends the sky a few hundred feet away, she yanks her man-made air with the strength of an Olympic weight lifter. Her cocoon of wind tugs the lightning bolt into her orbit. With the control that I wish I had, she sends the razor edge of the bolt into my heart.

In an instant, my nostrils fill with the smell of burning flesh. All the nearby air heats up, roaring up hundreds of degrees for a split second or more, and Elise runs out of the line of fire. There's a choking in my chest as my heart digests the electric current. And just like that, it's done. My heart is a ravenous beast, blind and hungry and needy as it gobbles a force of nature.

Then comes the thunder. It howls in my ears, the sound wave vibrating through my molten insides.

The crack deafens me, and everything goes dark as I collapse to the ground.

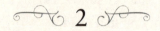

2

Monsters and Makers

My chest caves in and back out. Hands shake my shoulders hard, the back of my head hitting the sand. I cough and gasp and flip to the side.

Elise falls off me, panting, her own chest heaving too.

She pushes her soaking wet hair away from her forehead. "You were unconscious for a couple minutes this time. I was shaking you. Trying to get you to come to. That's the longest, Aria."

I cough a few more times, then rub a hand against my chest. It's burning, like a fever. My toenails are toasty. My kneecap is broiling. Even my eyelashes are hot.

The rain has slowed; it's merely drizzling now, and the clouds are breaking, making way for the sun.

"Sorry," I manage to say as I pull myself up, sitting now. I'm always knocked unconscious after a lightning strike. No big surprise there.

Elise drapes an arm around me. "Don't say sorry. Are you okay?"

I nod.

"God. I'm a wreck. My heart is beating fifty thousand miles an hour. Do you have any idea how awful it is to strike your best friend with lightning?"

I laugh weakly, making a wheezy sound. "Can't say that I do."

"It's totally traumatizing. I'm going to be in therapy for life, you know. I'm going to have some shrink when I'm old, and I'll still be talking about you and how it was like killing you each time I replenished your fire."

"I'm sorry I made you do this. But you're not killing me. It's just a blackout for a few minutes."

"You didn't make me, dummy. I wanted to. I'd do anything for you. You're my Frankenstein."

"You're my Frankenstein's maker then."

Elise wraps me in a hug, holds me tight. "Actually, wasn't Frankenstein the scientist? Didn't we study that book in English class?"

"Yeah, we did study it, but that doesn't mean I paid attention."

"I'm sure you read the SparkNotes online."

"As always," I say with a slight smile. Elise knows I'm hardly a model student. I haven't had the time, and my family hasn't pressured me when it comes to classes, grades, or school reports. All my pressure comes from my father and has to do with fire and art, not classic literature or trigonometry. My mom used to care. She used to sit down with me every night to work on spelling and vocabulary, on multiplication tables and long division, praising, always praising, when the grades came home.

Now she's sick, and she's stopped caring. I've stopped trying so hard. Now I try for one thing, and one thing only—to get out of town.

"Well, as I recall, Frankenstein was the doctor. Dr. Frankenstein," Elise says.

"I guess you're Dr. Frankenstein then. I'm the monster."

"You're my monster and I love you."

"I love you."

"Now, show me what you can do."

The beach is empty. I stand, clench my fists, then open them, unleashing a gorgeous torrent of flames. Elise laughs wildly as I extinguish the fresh, beautiful, and wholly new fire.

"Daddy will love it," I say sarcastically.

Elise narrows her eyes, shakes her head. "You should give him a taste of his own medicine someday, Ar."

"Yeah, I should but I won't."

I'm stronger than my father. My fire is far more powerful and potent than his ever was, and now his fire has faded, time suctioning it away as time does.

Elise grasps my hand in hers and we return to her car. She shakes her head at me as she backs out of the spot and turns onto the road. "Someday, we won't have to do this, right?"

"Yeah. When they stop expecting me to make fire. When I'm in my midtwenties." I touch Elise's arm so she's looking at me. "It's never run out of me this fast, Elise. Never."

She squeezes my hand gently and doesn't let go. "Don't worry. I'll always help you get it back."

"But what if you're not here?"

"We'll find a way," she says, then we return to the mainland, where I take her out for cherry ice cream. I order a lemon sherbet for myself. In a cup, rather than a cone. Even so, it melts quickly.

Soon, we're joined by Elise's boyfriend, Kyle. He shows up in his tricked-out truck, tires jacked up high, the rims glistening and shiny.

"Babe, I missed you today," he says to Elise, and wraps her in his arms. Big and broad with close-cropped hair, he leans in to kiss her, and she kisses him back. I briefly wonder what it would be like to kiss like that, with abandon. Then I look away and tap on my phone, calling up a photo I found the other night, when I was looking at some snapshots of performers in the New York Leagues. One of the girls on the team has been posting pictures of herself with a new boy. A beautiful boy with dark hair and dark, brooding eyes. There's a distance in those eyes, like he has secrets too.

Secrets he keeps from her.

Maybe I could join the Leagues and find a boy like this. A boy like me.

I trace his face with my fingers, imagining what it would be like to be with someone who knew my secrets, who knew my half-baked heart and didn't mind.

Elise and Kyle stop kissing. "But I'm right here now," she says with a smile that's just for him.

They're so into each other it makes my chest hurt. It makes me feel hollow all over again because I don't know how she does it. I don't know how she gives so much, how she can be so into him, and do so much for me at the same time. It's as if Elise has this endless reserve inside her and she can keep tap-tap-tapping into it.

"C'mon, lovebirds. We need to get to practice," I say as I jam my phone into my pocket.

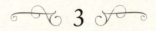

3

The Aria Opportunity

Every inch of me is wet with my own sweat. You could wring me out and there would still be more. There will always be more, because my body temperature is higher than average all the time.

But my fire is back, and that makes me happy, because it will make Daddy happy, and when Daddy's happy I am safe.

My fire is too intense though, as it always is after a renewal, until I can escape to the canals and let some loose. I spray a fireball at the flame-resistant concrete wall, specially built next to the park's bull pen. Our little arena is also home to hopeful ballplayers trying to eke out runs and hits and strikeouts for their Triple-A team, even though baseball, like most other professional sports, is dying.

The flames escape from my fingertips, then race toward the wall like a kamikaze fighter pilot. I swear I see the wall shake from the impact.

"Damn, you have some serious power today," Nava says.

She's perched on the metal bench. She wears a white T-shirt and pink basketball shorts. Her legs are all muscle, corded and sturdy. Her wild curls flare out from under the brim of her ball cap, a baby-blue mesh thing.

"Too much," I say under my breath as I throw another explosive fireball.

This is how it goes. When my fire fades, I lose control. When I replenish my fire, I have far too much. I am an unnatural balance, swaying one way or the other. Tonight I'll go to the canals to restore the precarious balance of me.

"Why don't we try just a tiny little flicker? You can work on your starlight," Nava says gently.

I bet Nava never saw these problems in her native Israel years ago. Her mother was a top-tier fire artist for years, performing into her early twenties. Nava is nineteen and she's fire too, but she suffers from too much stage fright to perform herself, and she's told me that's one of the reasons she likes working with me—I don't have any stage fright. Her family moved here, and she's the fire coach for all the farm-league teams in southern Florida, traveling from ballpark to ballpark to guide the fire girls and boys she trains. Her mother coaches the rookies at a facility in Miami, where all the teams in the M.E. Leagues start training, even though the M.E. Leagues are headquartered in the former Middle East. There are other elemental arts leagues in the United States and around the world, but the one run by the M.E. is the largest and most prestigious. Those who are good enough to be recruited to the M.E. Leagues are then sent to the biggest cities in the United States, to Chicago, Los Angeles, New York, and some even perform abroad. I have posters on my walls of some of the M.E. Leagues performers. They have stage names like Flame Rider and Night Wind.

I bring my fingertips together as if I'm snapping. When I release my clenched hand, I unleash a huge spray of angry orange flames.

I turn to Nava, embarrassed. I hate that it's not night. I hate that I have to be here at practice hours after a renewal. "I'm sorry."

"No, you're tired. You're exhausted. This is your body's way of saying you need to rest. We'll try again tomorrow."

I nod, then my stomach twists as I ask the next thing. "If my dad asks, can you tell him I did fine?"

"You always do fine in my book. So, yes. I will tell Mr. Kilandros so."

All the tension fades away for a moment. "Thanks."

She tips her forehead to the stands. "But he's been watching you."

———

He is here, picking me up from practice. He paces the hallway outside the locker rooms, his footsteps echoing in the hollow space.

"You were magnificent just then, Aria," my father says, beaming. Praise first.

He reaches for me, grips me in an embrace. I stand stiffly as he wraps his arms around me. "How did you feel out there today?"

Powerful. Dangerous. Safe. I feel safe when I am coated in the flames I make.

"Fine."

He releases his hold and turns serious. "Excellent. Because I've got some good news."

"What sort of good news?" I don't crack a smile, I don't light up. There is only one kind of good news I'd want from my Dad—the news that he's commandeered a rocket to Pluto and won't be seen for 248 years.

"I'll tell you," he says, then pauses, careful with his words. "But we need to talk about last night first. I heard you had some control issues."

He wasn't at last night's show. He had to work late. But word travels fast in our town.

"I didn't have any control issues," I say. A boxer dodging blows, I'm always darting and bobbing, attempting new tactics to avoid a hit. They rarely work, so I start walking again, the entrance to the lockers in my crosshairs.

He cocks his head to the side as if thoughtfully considering my rebuttal. "Funny. That's not what I heard."

"I need to change," I say. I'd like to get out of this scratchy black leotard, slide on my shorts and flip-flops, and count down the minutes until everyone falls asleep.

"You lost control," he says, following me.

"No. I didn't. I was trying out a new trick."

"I don't think so, Aria."

"I was," I insist. He is so hard to fool, but if I can convince him that I meant to do it, maybe I can avoid *his* fire.

"I'm sure it was beautiful, then," he says, going along with me. Fine.

"So glad you think that." I push my body against the swinging door, nearly forgetting he has good news to share.

"By the way, I'm hearing rumors that some of the scouts are starting to track you."

Everything stops. The door stops. Time stops. I stop. Scouts are diamonds, scouts are the lottery, scouts are the way to everything I've ever wanted.

I turn around, looking squarely at the man who raised me, the man who in his own mad way made fire erupt from my hands. "From where?" I ask cautiously, hoping he'll say not just any league, but the M.E. Leagues. That's the big time, as high as you can possibly go as an elemental artist. That's catching a comet and riding it so far away from here.

"Various places," he says, and it's clear he's going to hold this one for a bit longer, hold on to his control.

"When are they coming?" I ask, as hope worms through me. This is the moment I've been waiting for since I walked through the swamps more than three years ago to find the legend who taught me how to steal fire from the sky.

"I don't really know. I don't even know *if* they're coming. All I know is you need to be ready. And you weren't ready. So I will help you tonight."

A silent scream tears through me.

But I remind myself it used to be worse; it used to be all the time. I tell myself I've gotten stronger, better, more powerful over the years, that I can take the heat, that I can handle it.

As my dad drives me home, I picture the M.E. Leagues, and all the photos I've seen of their teams. I latch onto the images of the young, the beautiful, the talented who make the earth shake and the air scream with their hands. There's a girl on the New York team named Mariska, an earth artist, and I've seen videos of her shows, both the official clips the Leagues released and cell-phone captured shots. She can turn the ground into a roller coaster, and the audiences screech in delight. She's a star, and rumor has it, she's making serious bank. Oh, what I could do with serious bank. I could escape with everyone but my father.

I'd like to be Mariska for so many reasons.

Not least of which is she's the one posting pictures of the beautiful boy. When I look up their photos again that night on my cell phone, I find a new one. The boy is wearing a button-down shirt. He always wears button-down shirts, even though he looks to be my age. I wonder why he dresses up. I wonder what they do in New York City when they're not performing.

I grab a purple pen from my bag, and I draw the Empire State Building on my body. A promise to myself. Someday I will join them. Someday I will be far away from here. I draw it somewhere no one else can see.

On my hip bone.

Then I drop the phone on my bed and take what's coming to me.

———

His way doesn't work. His way never worked. But soon, soon, nights like this won't be needed. That's what I tell myself as I leave the garage, pushing open the door with a clumsy combination of elbow and thumb, my hands hurting in a way they never do when the fire comes from within, and I walk back inside my dark and muggy house and head straight for the freezer.

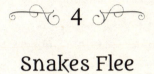

4

Snakes Flee

We don't have air-conditioning. This is ordinarily a very bad thing in southern Florida. But tonight, it's a very good thing, seeing as the windows in our one-story house are always open, which expedites the occasional nighttime excursion after a renewal.

My chest burns again, like it did at the ballpark when my fire rattled a concrete wall. After every renewal, my body roars with too much heat and propulsion. I have to skim some off the top so I don't set the world on fire.

I slide open the screen on my bedroom window and lower a pair of black rubber boots to the ground. My hands are colder now; I've cooled them with ice for the last hour.

Before I can leave, I conduct a safety check. My mother— she is curled up in a ball in her papasan chair in the TV room. Coffee-table-high stacks of newspapers surround her. Each day, she reads the paper cover to cover, circling articles, making notes on the newsprint, and looking up the rare word she doesn't know in a purple, tattered paperback dictionary that's tucked, oddly, between her knees like a pillow. This is where she spends her days and her nights. The navy-blue cushion on the rattan chair must have a Mom-sized indent now, but I rarely see the cushion without its tiny inhabitant.

They are fused together.

A mosquito buzzes past her, flickers near her nose. She twitches but doesn't wake. Her hands are curled up under her cheek, her teal-colored nails visible in the dark. She used to paint my nails when I was younger. She made a big production of it, pulling out a wooden footstool, plunking herself on it like a manicurist in a salon, and painting my nails in patterns of peach and aqua, lavender and mint, every now and then in bright purple and cherry red if I could convince her.

"Purple is my favorite color," I'd beg as I held out my hands, as if I were a sophisticated little lady getting all dolled up for a fancy occasion, even though all we were doing was running errands. We'd put on little wedge sandals and pretty summer dresses for a trip to the bank, the drugstore, the park.

Then she'd do hers, and I'd watch as she carefully, artfully applied the polish, all while whispering to me how she liked to accessorize even for an errand. "I just think you should look your best whenever you leave the house. Besides," she'd whisper, "you never know when you might run into a granter."

My eyes widened. "A granter! Have you ever seen one?"

She'd shake her head and smile. "Nope. And I've no need to. Because all my wishes have come true. I have everything I could ever want."

Now, she never leaves the house, and I never do my nails,

because I don't want to draw any more attention to my scarred hands.

But my mom still paints her nails, though it's probably just a way to pass the time in that chair that's become her burrow. There's a small wet spot near her fingertips. Her fingers leak now and then at night, when she's in the deepest stages of sleep. She was a water artist years ago, before the Leagues began. She never performed in a formalized system, just in the odd tent of a fortune-teller or mystic. Or in most cases, as the party enter-tainment at some pink-shirted, white-jacketed, and overly sun-tanned rich Floridian's swank home with a lavish outdoor pool. I'm told she could make the most beautiful, majestic waves roll off her body and swirl around her.

I find a hand towel on the floor, stained from years of use, and tuck it gently under her fingers. She won't like waking up to a wet spot in her home.

Maybe she does need a granter now. I bet she has a whole new set of wishes. Or really, one wish. To be well again.

My brother, Xavier, is snoring on the nearby plaid couch, an apron still tied around his waist. He didn't even make it to his bedroom. His hair is slicked with grease, the side effect of being a short-order cook. I wish he were awake. I wish he could come with me tonight, but no one can. Besides, I've grown accustomed to being without him after he spent the last four years behind bars for arson.

I tiptoe down the hall and press an ear against my father's door. I hear no sound, no movement. Still, I turn the handle slowly and open the door just the slightest crack. When I see my father lying still, eyes closed, chest rising up and down, I release my breath silently. I look at him for a second; these are his finest moments. When he's sleeping. This is how he should look all the time, never waking, never ever.

My chest tightens; I suck in a hard breath, and hold my hands behind my back so I don't accidentally set my house to flames.

I retreat back to my own room, the one I share with Jana, who's five years younger than I am—twelve. Jana's the reason I need to impress the scout. Because if I succeed in the Leagues, then my dad might back off her. I know he's itching to draw out her powers like he did to me. See, Jana hasn't come into her power yet, if she even has one. Only time will tell; powers don't usually surface until around age thirteen.

Usually.

I was a "late bloomer," as they called me. But I was actually the freak; I was proof that enough desperation could make you upend genetics.

Scientists have been studying elemental arts for years, in a quest to understand why some have gifts but most do not. They started their research with a young boy in Egypt named Rami. He'd been born into a fire-eating family many years ago, and one day he wowed crowds in the streets of Cairo with an unplanned trick more spectacular than merely swallowing fire. He had expelled a huge breath and an accompanying plume, when twin jets of flames burst from his hands too.

From his hands.

A boy who could make fire. A boy who could control fire. He was so much more than a fire-eater.

But the scientists couldn't find a new gene in him, or in any of the others they studied. Their conclusion was that many fire-eaters had some sort of undetectable genetic difference, and that's why they can play with fire. For Rami, his body had been built to accommodate fire, to make it, to create it, to control it.

Soon there were stories of other young teens who could create fountains of water with their hands, who could walk through air. Who could craft and control the elements.

All the bizarre sideshow acts who'd been relegated to circus tents and carnival cages came out of the woodwork.

I can hold my breath underwater for five minutes.

I can levitate.

I can make it rain.

They were the precursors. The freaks before we knew that freak powers could be harnessed, channeled, trained, and turned into something beautiful. Something people would pay to see.

Since there is no litmus test, no pinprick at birth or blood test later on to determine whose DNA has been imprinted with elemental abilities, it is a waiting game to see if powers surface. Most elemental artists come into their powers around age thirteen, but there are usually hints beforehand. The accidental flicker from their fiery fingers or the kid who swims like a fish at a young age. Later, with training and many-hours-a-day workouts and drills, those abilities can be harnessed into something more for those who are good enough. The high school athlete gifted enough to go pro.

Parents with such powers are much more likely to have children with elemental gifts.

Unless a girl born of fire and water has no choice but to find her power another way.

Jana is sound asleep. The clutching in my heart is tighter and hotter, and it wants to burn me alive from the inside out. That's the Faustian bargain I struck when I got my fire in the first place. I bring fire in to save me, but the fire is slowly killing me.

I climb out the window. I slide the screen back in place, grab the pair of black rubber boots, and slip through the tangled grass and fallen palm leaves in our yard.

A pair of headlights sweep the street. I tense but duck quietly behind a bush. I peer through the branches as a sedan rolls by, the telltale sirens on the roof quiet for now. The cop could be driving through or heading home. I'm not doing something illegal, but I'd rather not be spotted. I wait until the street is quiet again, as if the silence itself is its own soundtrack of emptiness.

Then I creep, catlike, through neighbors' patchy yards, crisscrossing cars jacked up on cinder blocks in driveways, winding along wilting acacia bushes and past ceramic flamingo statues, including one with a missing wing. A drop of sweat beads down my back under my black cotton tank top.

I grip my hands together behind my back, the pressure keeping my flames inside me for now.

A bullfrog sits in a driveway a few blocks down. His skin is slick and his chin pulses in and out. When I near him, he scampers away. Animals don't like me, especially cold-blooded ones.

I turn onto the path between two worn-out, weathered homes beaten down by sun and rain and heat. I wedge past leather ferns, then the crunchy Bermuda grass slopes downward as the canal comes into view a few feet away. My heart speeds more, a rhythm that would alarm any doctor monitoring me, the kind of pace that can only be soothed by one thing. It's like a hole is about to sear through me, and I hate the way this feels. I stop walking, take off my flip-flops, and slide on the black boots.

The waist-deep saltwater canals that run behind the homes here are quiet. They're not wide enough for motorboats; they're merely thoroughfares curling out to the bay. I wade past the gnarled mangroves and stand up to my belly in murky water. The water ripples nearby as a giant snake scurries from me. A boa constrictor, I think. Probably someone's onetime pet that escaped. Our canals are rife with boas and Burmese pythons that were once kept in cages.

The snake flees down the water, submerging his body, and he's out of sight.

I'm alone.

I dip my hands in the water and let the fire fly. From my heart, through my veins, all the way out through my fingertips. The water lights up with an orange glow. I glance around, and fear pounds in my ear. I plunge my hands deeper to try to hide the light.

I set off more flames, like I'm letting loose what ails me, what has sickened my insides. I drop down to my knees, the water up to my neck, my hands as far from the surface as possible, extinguishing each flame underwater. And like this, in the brackish canals littered with beer cans and cast-aside exotic pets, the seconds spread. They pool into minutes as all this extra fire pours out of me.

This is the fire in me. Wild and ravaging. Devouring.

Then my heart is no longer racing away, and the tightness subsides, and I can breathe without burning my throat. I crawl out of the canal and flop onto the prickly grass, spent and exhausted, like I have just heaved up a bruised and battered wild thing, a half soul with a an amputated life.

I'd like to say I feel better, like I've just cleaned out the house. And I do feel better, technically speaking. But I don't feel any less disgusting now that my fire stores are normal. Now that I can manage them.

I drag myself off the grass and wipe a hand across my slick forehead, covered in sweat. I'm wet and muddy and I wash myself off with a nearby hose left in a front yard.

I make it back to my house, unseen, unheard. I leave the boots outside the window. I peel off my shorts, underwear, and tank top. The skyscraper on my hip bone is smudged from the hose and the canals. I touch the messy ink marks, wishing I were there. Then I hop back inside, drop the damp and dirty clothes into a plastic bag, and toss that into the laundry basket inside my closet.

No one else does laundry around here anyway.

———

Most artists show their powers sometime around age thirteen. Not me. I didn't spark. I didn't set the world on fire.

Nor had I exhibited any signs over the years. I was nothing like my brother, who was so clearly a fire artist before he came into his powers. Xavier would play too close to the bonfires at beach parties, would traipse around the grill at barbecues, never once burning a finger, because fire could never hurt him.

I should have been the same, my dad contended. He was certain that he had passed on his powers to me, as he had to Xavier. My father's own fire burned out in his twenties, when most gifts fade. But back in the day he'd been a powerful fire-eater and then a fire artist, performing in a circus for a few years before he met my mom. Before there were Leagues. Before there were opportunities to make serious money. One night he took me into the garage, shut the door to the house, and pressed the button to close the big door.

"Aria, sometimes we need to help the fire come out," he told me as he took a box of matches from his worktable, neat and organized with the tools he needed for his car tinkering. "It won't hurt though, because fire can't hurt you," he said, trying to reassure me.

"What are you going to do, Daddy?"

He clapped a hand on my shoulder and spoke in a gentle voice. "The fire is in you." He pointed at my chest. "It is. It's deep inside you, like it was in me. It's just stuck. And we need to help it come out."

"Why is it stuck?"

He shook his head. He looked sad, maybe even despondent, as if this question was the very thing that had kept him awake at night.

"I don't know, sweetheart. But I swear this won't hurt. Fire never hurt me. And you are fire, like me. I know you're fire. You have to be. We just have to remind your body. Sometimes as parents, we have to do hard things for our kids. We have to do hard things to help them become strong. Like my dad did for me."

He'd never spoken much about my grandfather, but he was a stern man, a cold man. My grandmother had died when my dad was younger. The little bits and pieces I cobbled together over the years led me to believe that my grandfather had changed then—become cruel, devastated by the loss. The few times I'd been to my grandfather's house my dad had flinched, involuntarily, each time he walked past his father, making me think his dad had probably hit him. To help him become stronger, I suppose. As my dad wanted to do for Xavi. But whenever my father spoke of his dad, there was no recrimination in his voice. Only a sort of stoic reverence for his father. As if his own father's hard-line ways were the only way.

My dad never hit me. He had a different solution. He struck the first match and held my right hand tight in his. I squirmed. He held tighter. "This won't hurt."

"But what if it's not stuck? What if I'm nothing?"

His eyes flared with equal parts fear and anger. "It's not possible. You just need help. That's all you need."

He held the match against my palm, and I yelped instantly. I tried to pull my hand away, but he was stronger, and he held on tighter, until the wood stick burned to a nub against my skin. "It won't hurt," he said, louder.

I begged him to stop, through tears and through whimpers, but he shushed me, assuring me that it was fine; it was all fine.

I wondered if that's what his dad said to him when he hit him to keep him in line.

"This is how we have to do it," he said to me. "And you only think it hurts, but it doesn't hurt. Fire never hurts a true fire artist, and you are a true fire artist. This will only make you stronger."

He lied. The fire hurt because I wasn't a true fire artist.

Over the next few nights, he went through an entire box of kitchen matches, then over the weeks that followed, he moved on to candles, then the long metal sticks with cotton swabs at the top for fire-eaters.

He was wrong when he said *this won't hurt*. My hands did hurt. Every second of every day. They were blistered and red, and he covered my palms in salves and ointments and wrapped bandages around them when I went to school. At night he unwrapped them, each night his eyes wilder and more desperate than the last. He wanted another fire child more than anything in the world, since Xavi—locked up then—was no longer performing. He especially wanted the money that a fire child could bring in the Leagues.

In his warped sense of the world, he was doing the right thing. I knew he believed that. I knew the pained looks on his face were real. He wanted to help me. He didn't know any other way.

At night, I would go to bed and hope to find a granter. I'd imagine I'd simply run across one the next day. Maybe in a lamp hidden on an old dusty shelf. Maybe in a bottle washed up on the beach. If I found one, I'd wish for him to stop. I'd wish for fire. I'd wish for everything to be different.

I tried one more time to make him stop. "Daddy, I'm nothing. I didn't get the gene. I'm not anything, okay?"

A deviant tear slid down his stubbled cheek. "Don't talk

that way. You're just a late bloomer. You just need help. Xavi made fire, majestic and beautiful, and you can do the same, and you can join the Leagues and then we can finally get out. Things can finally be easy. Don't you see? With Xavi in . . ." He stopped, shook his head. I'd rarely seen my father cry before, but there he was in tears, telling me I was our only hope, our only way out of our lot in life, he said. After my brother abused his powers, couldn't I just try harder to be a good fire girl? Couldn't I just focus and concentrate and will the fire out of me?

As if this were math. As if this were fractions. I just needed a bit more practice. Except there was no fire in me to ignite. There was no genetic store waiting to be tapped. So I found another way to become fire.

The way that is killing me.

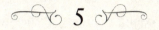

5

Into the Swamp

The first person I told about my scarred hands was Elise.

The second person was the Lady of the Swamp. Though I didn't actually have to tell her. She knew instantly that the scars—the skin of my palms whiter and more rigid than they should be, the backs of my hands marked with pale pink worms of hardened flesh—weren't from fire inside me. She could read the craters and ridges like they were the road map to all my secrets and shame.

I found the Lady because I couldn't take it anymore. My hands were red and tender. I could barely hold on to pencils anymore to do my homework. My hairbrush hurt to use. But as he burned me each night, I grew tougher, stronger, more determined to discover another way to become a fire artist. I started making plans to find the Lady. As the flames carved their way into my hands, I gritted my teeth, tightened my jaw, and ran through the details of how I'd take money from my mom's secret stash on her bookshelves, catch a bus to the Everglades, find an airboat, and track down the Lady of the Swamp. I worked out all the specifics night after night as he set me on fire. One Saturday when he was at work and my mom was in her chair, I waded through the swamp deep into the Everglades, the water like quicksand, because the airboat could go no farther, and even if it could, the Lady of the Swamp didn't let airboats near her home, tucked under canopies of green trees and overgrown with marsh. Her home could be reached only by those crazy enough to brave the alligators and snakes that slunk through her watery front yard.

Or desperate enough.

"You must need something very badly," the Lady said when she saw me trudging through the swamp more than three years ago.

"I do."

"Your hands," she began after taking one piercing look at them.

The Lady knew everything about the elements. It was said she once possessed all the elemental arts—she could cause tremors in the earth, she could weave the wind to do her bidding, she could unleash flames from her hands that towered higher than the tallest buildings, and she could douse them with waves the most daring surfers would trade years off their lives to ride.

All I knew was what Xavi had dug up for me when I'd asked him casually what he knew. He told me that the Lady lived deep in the wetlands with only an alligator as her companion. A snow gator, he was called, because his amphibian skin was ice-cold. The legend was, her snow gator once ate an ice artist, a breed of water artist so rare they're hardly ever seen in the elemental Leagues. It was said too that the Lady won him in some sort of bet with a granter.

When the Lady saw me, she reached out her hand and pulled me from the muck and onto her porch. The gator slept on the other side of her. He didn't even shift his eyes.

"No one has come to find me in many years," the Lady said as she sat back down on the porch swing. She patted the slatted wood, and I sat next to her. She was weathered, with crags and crannies scored into her face, and deep copper eyes that had to have seen everything. "And rarely do girls venture here. How old are you?" she asked me.

"Thirteen."

She raised an eyebrow and cocked her head, waiting for more.

"And six months," I added.

"Ah. I see. Have you been visited by the arts yet?"

I shook my head. "I don't think I ever will be."

"Why are you here then? I'm not a granter. I can't wish the elements for you."

Granters were even harder to find, and you had to have something to barter with if you wanted a wish from one. I had nothing then because I was nothing then. But yet, I'd heard enough around town, and from my brother. When I visited him every weekend, walking past the crisscrossed metal gates of the prison, guards watching nearby, he whispered to me all the stories of the Lady, the stories of granters and the twisted, unsanctioned ways that elemental artists had used, gained, or spent their gifts. Stories he heard from the other abusers of elements who were locked up with him on the other side of the gates.

"The scientists don't know everything, ma'am. Do they?" I said to the Lady.

She shook her head. "Of course not."

"They think you can only be born with fire. Or air or water or earth. But it's just a guess. No one has proved anything about where the arts come from."

"What do you think?"

"I don't think it's just genetic. If it were only about genes, the Leagues wouldn't have laws against stealing the elements," I said, because I knew the hard-and-fast rule of the entire elemental arts circuit—thou shalt not steal. If you were caught stealing the elements, you'd be barred from the Leagues for life, and so would everyone else in your family. A punishment that carried through the ages.

The corner of her lips quirked up. "Smart girl."

"How do you do it? How do you steal fire?"

"Why do you need it?"

I held up my hands. Fire artists always had some burns on their hands until they learned to control their fire. Although true fire artists weren't hurt by their fire, they still had the physical markings. But no one had ever been burned like I was. I told her why my hands were so scarred.

"You need fire for protection, then. From your father."

"Yes." I needed to make my own fire so he would stop setting me aflame. So I could have hands that worked. "I have to know the other ways."

"You do. You do have to know. You have to protect yourself from him, and you have two choices when the fire doesn't come from within," she said. "You can trade for it with a granter, or you can steal it from the sky."

"How do you steal it?"

"There is only one way to steal it. Only one way for you to bring fire into your body so you can make it with your body."

"Please tell me." My voice was a plea, quivering and desperate.

"I will tell you, child," she said, as she reached down to scratch her pet.

My eyes widened as she touched him.

She smiled at me. "You should pet him."

I looked at her nervously.

"Yes. Pet him," she said, and it was the only time she spoke harshly to me.

Later I came to understand that this was the test of my worthiness. Neither granters nor the Lady gave up wishes or knowledge for free. I'd come to her for answers, for a last-ditch hope. I had to show I was brave enough. I had to do what Florida kids are taught to never do. Touch a gator.

"Someday," she continued, "I might need someone to take care of him. When I no longer can."

And that was the exchange. I had to promise to look after her pet when she no longer could. It was an easy term to agree to.

"I'll help. I'll take care of him."

Then I petted the gator. The strange thing was—he wasn't fearsome. I never once thought he'd snap my hand off. The gator opened an eye lazily. There was no malice, no predatory instinct shining in his eyes. I touched the top of his scaly head between those golden brown orbs of eyes. He arched his head against my hand, as a cat would. His skin was rough, like my hand, and he was ice-cold.

The Lady nodded and I put my hand back in my lap, wondering what I'd just shown her.

"Do you know an air artist who'd do anything for you? Someone you'd trust with your life?" she asked.

"Yes."

Then the Lady detailed exactly how to steal fire, like Prometheus did when he stole from the gods. Only I wouldn't be stealing it for all mankind. I'd be stealing it to save myself. She told me in painstaking detail how to catch lightning, how to capture it in a net of air, how to send it careening into my body.

"You must hit the heart. Only the heart."

"Why?" My voice shook.

"Why? You ask why? What if the lightning hit your arm? What if it entered your belly? Or your elbow? Do you think you could make fire from your elbow?" She laughed, but she wasn't laughing at me. "If you want to be transformed into a fire girl, then you have to be transformed. And so does the lightning."

"What does that mean?"

"You can't make beautiful plumes of fire with ordinary lightning. If you were just struck, even in the heart, you'd simply be one of those people who's struck by lightning. Someone whose body runs a few degrees higher. You'd be someone who loses a bit of hearing. Or maybe some peripheral vision. You don't want to be a lightning-strike survivor, Aria. You want to be a fire artist. You want to change your DNA." She tapped my chest, poking her knobby finger against my sternum. "And so the lightning must meet the air first. The air from another elemental artist. The man-made air turns the lightning into a *carrier* of elemental gifts, and when it hits your heart, the fire then becomes yours. A part of you. It becomes everything you want it to be."

Fire that could shield me. Fire that could protect me. Fire that could save me.

"The only thing is, it won't last," the Lady said, creaking back and forth in her swing. My feet swung gently too. "You will be striking a Faustian bargain, my child. You will be Sisyphus pushing the rock up the hill over and over. Your stolen fire will never last. You'll burn out every few months and lose your control. You'll have to get it back, and sometimes the fire you bring into your heart is too much, so you let a little bit loose or else it will smother you. You will do this in the water. You'll have to do this over and over, every year, then a few times a year. And each time, a piece of your heart will become charred. Until eventually it's turned to ash."

My life for my life.

That seemed a fair price to pay.

6

Ice Sister

My mother points to her bookshelves, just a few feet away from her chair. "The one on New York. Can you hand me the one on New York?"

"Do you want to get it?" I ask gently.

She shakes her head; her eyes look like those of a mouse being met by a cat.

I reach for the hardbound book of pictures and hand her the heavy volume—a photographic journey through New York City over the years. The library binding crinkles around the corner. My brother picked this up for her at a bargain basement library sale a few weeks ago. He's at the library a lot for his community service. The three of us have even looked at it together a few times, and it feels good to have all of us back in this house again, even though things aren't the same as they were before.

"Show me your favorite." I crouch down near her shapeless form, which merges with the cushion. She's not fat. She's tiny, she eats very little, and she's simply soft all over, like the air seeped out of her and now she's a raft languishing deflated on the side of a pool. My mother used to be beautiful. There's a framed photo on my dad's nightstand of her standing on a fountain in the middle of an outdoor mall. She looks like she's in mid-dance-step, jaunty and sassy, with a short black-and-white dress whisking around her thighs. She's playful in the picture, her eyes sparkling and teasing, as if she's saying *I can make a fountain too.*

She opens the book and flips slowly through the pages. "Central Park, of course. And the New York Public Library. And Broadway. I bet Broadway is amazing," she says dreamily, then hums a few bars, maybe from a show tune or maybe just a made-up number in her head. *Someday, we'll see a Broadway show,* she used to tell me. *We'll go to a musical, all decked out to the nines, nails done, and best shoes on, tickets we saved up for for months in our hands.* "But this is my favorite," she says as she turns another few pages and shows me a picture of Grand Central Station.

It's swarming with people fanning out in all directions. I wonder if she's trying to tell me something—that she longs to be around people again, that she craves escape too. I want to tell her that New York would be perfect. Maybe we'd even run into the beautiful boy.

I hear the sound of the shower from the lone bathroom down the hall. My father is in there. My mother closes the book. "We could go there someday, Mom," I whisper. "I'm getting stronger every day. Maybe I'll be recruited and we can take a trip to New York."

Something flashes in her eyes for the faintest of moments—hope?

I continue, keeping my voice low. "They have the best doctors there, you know. In New York. We could find someone to treat you."

My mom's never been to New York. She's from Nebraska, grew up right in the heartland, in a tiny little town, nothing but wheat and corn and red, rusty pickup trucks. Then she just up and got the hell out of town. That's how she told the story of her exodus, the first girl in her family to go to college, to a university in Miami.

"Nebraska is an icebox. Don't let that middle-of-the-country thing fool you," she said when I was in second grade. She tapped the map of the United States that was tacked to our hallway wall and crouched down to my height. "It's no place for a water girl. In the winters, the cold smacks your face and bites your skin. Everything is frozen. The horizon is gray as far as you can see."

The way she tells the story, you'd think she'd packed a few swimsuits into a bandanna, wrapped that around a stick, and hitched all the way to the Sunshine State.

"The day after graduation, I walked out the door and turned my back on Nebraska. I had a destination, and I had some determination, so I trekked right across the country and then down south as the ocean called out to me. I needed to be near waves, and warm water, and seas I could dive into year-round," she said, sweeping her index finger along the mapped edge of Florida's coastline, as if I needed the reminder that we lived on a big toe surrounded by blue. But I watched her hands, mesmerized by the way she could weave both water and words, how every move of her body, every ordinary gesture, even her hand trailing along a laminated map, was a ballet.

Now she's camped out on a papasan chair and hasn't felt the sun on her skin in years, stricken by some mystery ailment that's handcuffed her to the house and turned her into a shell of the woman she once was. She doesn't even talk the same.

"They do, Mom. The doctors in New York, they'll be able to figure out what's wrong," I say, trying desperately to plant the seed of escape in her. Maybe we can do more than visit New York. Maybe a doctor can heal her, and then she can protect Jana from our dad. Or better yet, she can leave him, and be the mom she used to be. She can take care of Jana.

She waves a hand, like she's swatting away an errant bug. "Don't worry about me."

"But don't you want to? They have medicine for panic disorders. There are things you can take, you know. I've researched it. I've looked it up."

Her eyes harden, as they do whenever I name it. The thing that pins her down. "Aria, can you go fetch me my newspaper? I want to read the latest on how the Lookouts stopped that tropical storm brewing in the Caribbean," she says.

The Lookouts are the teams of elemental artists who help fight forest fires and turn hurricanes into tropical storms. Elemental artists can't control Mother Nature, but they can help quell her when she slouches toward disaster. The Lookouts are the reason neither Florida nor any other state has been battered by anything greater than a category 1 or 2 storm in the last several years. The reason why brush fires in Los Angeles last for hours now instead of days.

"Yes, Mom. I'll get you the paper."

I open the front door, where I'm greeted by a blast of morning heat. I walk to the end of the driveway, grab the newspaper, and bring it to my mom.

"Thank you, my love," she says, then kisses me on the cheek and opens the paper, closing the conversation.

When I return to my room, I kneel by my bed and pull out an orange crate that holds my fashion magazines. I don't read them for tips on what to wear. I like to draw on the models instead. I give them tails and longer noses or cartoon eyes and extra hands. Nothing fancy, nothing that would make comic book artists quake in their boots. But they're mine. They're my graffiti, and I like to keep them, to look at them when I need a laugh. They've served their purpose many times, after many returns from the garage, when all I could do was use my wrists to flip through pages of my mustachioed models waggling cigars from their pouty lips and quipping cartoon-bubbled sayings— "Get your fish and chips here" and other ridiculous things.

Inside one of the magazines is a worn-out sheet of paper I've kept there for more than three years. It's full of dates, including the one I marked on it two nights ago. The night I lost my fire. The night I regained my fire. The night my fire started to eat me alive.

Again.

———

"What if hair could feel?"

"What if?"

"Do you think my hair can feel your hands?" Jana asks me

as I weave another section of her rabbit-soft brown hair into a French braid. She's folding a flyer from last night's show into a makeshift fan.

"Well, I hope you can feel my hands, dork."

"No. I mean *really* feel. Like details. Like your—"

"Shhh . . ."

"Why?" She finishes the fan, then waves it in front of her face to cool off. It's hot and then some in our house; but proximity to me makes her toastier.

"Don't."

"But I can. I can feel the ridges a bit—"

"Anyway," I say, cutting her off, "what are you going to do today?"

She shrugs. "There's nothing *to* do. I hate summer vacation."

"Words you rarely hear from a twelve-year-old."

"Well, it's boring when you're twelve and don't have a phone or a car, and your mom won't drive you anywhere and your sister is gone all the time."

"It's not as if I love all-day practices either when school's out. Anyway, what's Mindy doing?"

"I don't know."

"Well, call her," I say. Mindy is Kyle's little sister.

"It's too early. She's never up this early."

"Text her. Use my phone. In my pocket."

I loop another strand of hair as Jana reaches into my pocket. Her hand is cold and it tickles. I wriggle a bit. She laughs, then sends a message.

"I'll call you when she writes back, okay?"

"What if you're on fire?" Jana teases.

"Then I guess you'll never know what Mindy wants to do today, silly," I say as I wrap the end of the braid in a tight rubber band. "There. Beautiful."

Jana leans back into me, and I wrap my arms around her. "Do you want to go pool hopping tonight?"

She turns her face to me and grins. "You'll go with me?"

"Sure. I think the Markins are out of town for a few weeks. We can sneak into their yard."

Jana beams. "I love pool hopping with you."

"I know. Because you're a fish."

"Maybe I should just go to the beach today."

I tense. "Okay, but don't tell Dad."

"Why?"

I lower my voice. "Because he'll ask a million questions. You know he will. He'll want to know if you turned into a dolphin or something."

"Maybe I am a dolphin," Jana says, and flashes me a smile, her teeth white and bright and perfectly straight.

"You might be. But don't tell him. Promise me, okay?" I whisper, tightening my arms around her, gripping her as if I can protect her this way. With her promise. With a hope. With a wish.

"I promise," she tells me.

"Time to go," my father barks from the driveway.

I jump up. "I'll draw a dolphin on your arm later if you're nice to Mom today. I'll even give him sideburns," I say as I give Jana a kiss on the forehead, then grab my bag as she tells me *no sideburns ever*. I rush out, shouting good-bye to my mom, who's working the crossword puzzle now. Xavier is still snoring, lying on his stomach, with one arm dangling off the side of the couch. The back of his hand glares at me, marked with a dark *X*, etched like a tattoo.

I slide into the front seat of my dad's car, a 1970 Pontiac GTO he restored a few years ago with parts that had come into the junkyard he runs. He also had one of his car cronies lay a pair of flame decals on the sides. They're hideous.

"Did you sleep well last night?" He twists his gaze behind him as he backs out of the driveway.

"Like a baby."

"Do you feel rested today?"

"Totally."

"I told Nava you need to work on control exercises."

"What a surprise."

"You do. I want pristine control, Aria."

"I'm sure."

"Don't be sarcastic with me."

"I wasn't being sarcastic. I meant it. I'm sure you want pristine control. I have no doubt you want perfect, rigorous, pristine, impeccable control. And you'll get it. So don't worry."

"I don't worry. You are the most talented fire artist there is."

I am, and I like to think it's because I train so hard. I work harder than anyone, but maybe that's just to make up for my crime. Maybe I can never make up for it. Maybe I'm only good because I'm not natural.

Silence fills the car for a few minutes, but at least the air is cool inside these four doors. When my dad fixed up this car, he fixed the AC in it too. I take a pen from the front of my backpack and draw a stick figure blowing up TNT on my thigh.

"Don't do that," my dad says.

I ignore him, bending my head lower to ink out a cartoon explosion. Thighs are wonderful inventions with their dual purpose. They propel us quickly if we work them, and they also provide magnificent, omnipresent canvases.

"Why do you do that?"

I say nothing. This—silence, the occasional snark—is all I have to fight back. To show him that he hasn't broken me.

He relents. "Someone's coming in today to pick through our stock of Fords. Should be a good day. We have a lot of those," he says in an offhand way. As if I care about his love of cars. "Fords."

"That's great."

"I'm betting we'll clear a thousand."

"Fabulous."

"Wouldn't it be, though?" He turns toward me at the red light.

I try not to look at him. "Yes. Money's awesome."

If I'm recruited into the Leagues, I plan to save every last dime and use it to steal again. To steal my mom and my sister and my brother away from my dad.

7

Secrets and Shortstops

I walk through the doors of the training facility. The air-conditioning grinds louder as I pass through. It's heat sensitive, so the AC's working harder, sensing the rise in temperature. I head for the old bullpen, where I practice.

Nava is thrilled with my precision and my stunningly beautiful flames.

"Beauty is always rewarded," Nava says after my flames soar higher than they ever have, curling into lush tails, like a peacock's fan spread open.

"That seems like some sort of wise old adage that is supposed to mean something but really doesn't," I say, teasing her, feeling light and fun again now that I'm back in control.

"What? You don't like my adages? How about *You will obtain your goal if you maintain the course?*"

"Now you're just a fortune cookie, Nava. I thought you didn't even like Chinese food."

She puts a hand on her heart in mock indignation. "Not

like Chinese food? All my people love Chinese food. Of course I love it."

"Do they have Chinese food in Israel?"

"No. We had to go pluck all our food straight from the fields. We had to yank carrots from the ground and shoot arrows into rabbits if we wanted to eat."

"Oh, ha-ha."

"Well, you asked a silly question, so you got a silly answer," she says as we continue to work through my moves out in the bullpen. "But yeah, of course we had convenience stores and Chinese restaurants in Tel Aviv. But I hear it's all changed since then."

"You mean since the Middle East became the M.E.?"

Nava nods. "Since the treaty, yes. I mean, there are still convenience stores and Chinese food. But everything else changed and for the better, of course. When I talk to my cousins who are still there, they tell me how wonderful it is to walk the streets and not fear getting shot or bombed."

"Do you ever want to go back?"

"I'm a Florida girl now. Florida's been good to me. Besides, Florida will be good to you too, Aria."

"Yuck. I can't stand Florida," I say, but unlike Nava I've never even been anyplace else.

"I hope you might like Miami," she says in this coy, flirty voice. And I turn to her, my eyes wide.

"What do you mean, Nava?"

Her voice has a playful glint to it. "Just that Miami, if it works out, might be a nice place for you to spend a few months."

I spin toward her, my veins filling with hope. "Am I going to Miami? Do the M.E. Leagues want me?"

She holds up her slender hands and laughs. "I don't know. But what I do know is this: I took a phone call this afternoon from a certain scout from the M.E. Leagues who's had his eye on our team and a few of our artists in particular."

"And?" I feel like I may rocket to the moon with excitement, that I might very well learn I have wings and can fly.

"And it's a good thing your control is better because he'll be here on Friday."

I give Nava a massive hug, grinning. She pats my back, and I can tell she's smiling too, and I'm so deliriously happy that a tear slides down my cheek.

Nava pulls back, mistaking it as worry. "You'll be fine. Don't worry. You're ready."

I nod, collecting myself. I so rarely let emotions show. I return to my usual stoicism. "Does my dad know yet?"

Nava shakes her head. "I'll call him later and tell him. I wanted you to know first."

I have a secret. Sure, it has an expiration date in a few hours. But it feels so good.

I turn back to the concrete wall, thinking of my dad, of all the ways he's hurt me. I throw a massive fireball that spins on its path to the concrete. For the briefest of seconds, I swear my fire has the faint outlines of a pair of eyes. Then it hits the wall and disappears. Maybe I imagined it.

—◦—

Elise and I walk through the weight room on the way in from the field. The room is filled with grunts and the clangs of iron bars going up and down, as well as with glares from the ball-players. The shortstop is the only one who doesn't stare us down. Instead, he manages the tiniest of smiles, and it makes his blue eyes crinkle in a cute and kind of sexy way. I'm not even sure what his name is, but I'm glad he's on the team.

Elise cups her hands over my ear. "Listen. I heard from some of my friends in the M.E. Leagues. The scout wants something big. Something special."

"Like what? Like the legendary fire twin?" I suggest, though I'm joking because the fire twin is a trick that hasn't been seen in several years.

"Well, if you could do that, then yes. If you want to get out of town, you need to wow him."

"So what should I do that's epic? The spinning-wheel trick? The starlight? I don't know if I have time to develop a new trick."

"Can you combine two? Like marry the arc that you do with starlight?"

"I don't know. I mean, yeah. But is that enough?" I ask, and my voice sounds like a squeak, tripping on my own desperation.

"Talk to Nava. I'll make some calls. We'll come up with something. Maybe ask Xavi?"

I scoff. "Yeah, he knows all the right tricks. But what about you?"

Elise laughs drily, a quick laugh. "You know I don't stand a chance with a scout. Plus, my parents want me in the Lookouts, not the Leagues."

"I know," I say. I've known this for years. Her parents always saw the Wonder team as a feeding ground for the Lookouts. But Elise and I are more than a team. I can't survive without her. Elise is a year older than I am, but we've been best friends for years, and nearly inseparable throughout high school. The good thing is, since she's going to college in Miami, we can still meet up for renewals if I'm recruited.

We leave the weight room, stares following us.

"Go Mud Dogs," Elise shouts, pumping a fist as the door swings shut. Then a shrug. "They already hate us."

"Not all of them."

"Well, the nonhaters are nice. Especially the shortstop."

"He's definitely a babe."

"You should go for it."

"Ha," I say because I don't do that. I don't "go for it" when it comes to boys. Going for it could lead to getting it, and then where would I be? Stuck with someone who'd want to know me, who I'd want to tell all my secrets to. I don't want to share my secrets because I don't trust anyone but Elise. So I don't get too close to boys. They belong in photos on my phone.

Not closer. Never closer.

—

My father holds his index finger to his lips when I walk inside that night. He tips his forehead to the chair. My mom is sleeping.

"She just fell asleep," he whispers, his voice like a pillow when he talks of her. He says this as if it's some wondrous mystery that my mother is sleeping. My mother is the queen of sleeping. Yet everything about her somehow enchants him. He tends to her, brushes her hair, runs the bath for her. Sometimes it seems as if he'd do anything for her. To keep her. The coddling, the kid gloves he wears with her are such a contrast to how he is with me.

"Okay," I say in a whatever kind of tone and head to the kitchen for a glass of water.

He rises from the couch and follows me, padding quietly.

"Aren't you excited for the scout?"

I shrug as I run the tap and drink some water. I am excited, but I will never let on in front of him.

"This is what we've been working for, Aria. This is what all our hard work has been leading to."

I tense, holding my hands behind my back. I clutch my fingers, linking them together, as if that will keep my hands safe.

"Are you ready for Friday?"

"Totally." I won't let him know the scout wants a big trick. If I tell him that, he'll burn me again, as if his matches might elicit something new and magnificent from my hands.

"You need to be amazing on Friday. And I know you can be. You can. And then we can get air-conditioning, and we can get a new chair . . ."

He looks at my mom sadly, but with so much regret and love in his eyes that he seems like a different person. His voice slips and he covers his eyes. If he were a real father, I'd comfort him. I'd tell him I want Mom to be okay too. But I don't want to get her a new chair. I want to get her a new life, and I want him out of mine. I soften, but not for him. For Mom, for Jana, for Xavi.

The Leagues are my path to their freedom. "It's okay, Daddy. I'll be great. I promise."

He hugs me, and I pretend to stumble on an unseen pebble so he can't hold on. I step away from him, doing my best to appear flustered by my clumsiness.

8

A New Trick

I lie awake as I walk myself through each trick, each move, and the amount of fire I must trigger—from the tiniest flicks for starlight to the all-encompassing flames of the fireworks finale. Maybe Elise is right. Maybe I can combine them somehow. Big and small? Power and precision?

Jana is asleep in the bed next to mine. She didn't want to go pool hopping tonight. Said she was too tired.

I get up, walk to her bed, and kneel near her sleeping body. She's deep in slumber, and her face looks so soft. I wonder if she's dreaming of dolphins or friends or buried treasure. Or maybe another time and another place. Or another life, as I do.

I take her hand in mine. It's cold. I tense, but when I place my other hand on her chest, I'm reassured with her breathing. So why is her hand so cold? It's broiling outside even at this hour. It's the middle of the night and the sky is still weeping muggy heat. But her hand is icy, like it was this morning when she reached for my phone.

Could Jana be an ice artist?

I flash back to what I've read about the rare breed of water artists who don't just weave waves and command streams. They are a strain who create not only water but ice. It'd be a great party trick to make those swan ice sculptures you see at brunches. But the talent is much more than a party trick. It's an uncommon gift among only a handful of water artists. The power to freeze your own water.

I shake Jana, wake her up.

"Wha?" she mutters in a muffled voice. Her eyes flutter open, then close again.

"Jana," I say in a firm whisper. "Jana."

She shifts. "What?"

"Jana, why are your hands so cold?"

"Huh?"

She flips to her other side, trying to pull herself back into dreams.

"Jana, is Dad doing something to your hands?" Dipping them in ice? Trying to freeze her?

"No," she says, and shifts back to the other side. "No," she adds.

"Okay," I say, and slip back to my bed, under my own covers. But when I peer over at Jana she's not asleep anymore. She's staring up at the ceiling.

————

Xavier wakes me at five thirty and tells me we are going to ride together. Xavier hates mornings. If he's awake at this hour, it means he wants to talk. I change into work-out clothes, and pull on fingerless bike gloves so my palms won't dig into the handlebars.

We ride hard through the blue light of the fading moon. The headlight on my bike glares on the concrete, and I pedal faster, keeping pace with my brother, who must have worked out during the four years he spent locked up. He's in shape like a whip, lean and taut. His hands wrap around the slim handlebars of his old road bike.

Those X marks on his hands stare at me as we speed through the dawn, along the frontage road, underneath the freeway, far past the edges of Wonder.

I was drawn to his marks the first time I saw them, the first time I visited him behind bars. He told me they branded him the second he walked through the doors of the penitentiary, even though he was a juvenile, just seventeen when he was locked up. But his crime warranted the punishment of an adult, so that's what he was given.

Four years and permanent marks.

Arson will do that to you.

The first time I saw him, I gawked at the black Xs. A sign he used his powers for a crime.

"Your hands," I said, pointing.

"As if a little mark can stop me," he whispered darkly. "Tell me about life on the outside. Have you set the world on fire yet too?"

I hadn't had my own hands set on fire yet.

"No," I said. "I don't think I'm anything. I don't think I'm like you or Dad."

Xavier had been a beautiful fire artist. He had woven flames as if he were conducting an orchestra. He'd been on the Wonder team since he was thirteen, the earliest a fire artist had ever performed in the southern farm circuit. I went to all his shows, sat in the front row, and followed him around like the proverbial puppy dog.

But Xavier liked fire too much. He'd disappear after shows sometimes, and when he returned home a few hours later, he'd rap on my door and tell me what he'd done, like a confession, but guilt-free. "I lit a fireball in a tree. Watched it flame up for a few minutes."

"Then what?"

"Put it out, of course."

Next it was garbage cans, then a few Dumpsters. Each time, he'd put out his own flames. He didn't want to get caught. But maybe he did. I don't know. All I know is he became careless. Or angry. Or proud. Because he started setting cars on fire. Cars he'd find in empty lots late at night. Cars parked along the beach after midnight. He'd set them aflame, watch them burn, and then douse his own fire, leaving behind the charred remains.

I'm not entirely sure what drove him to my dad's junkyard one night. Maybe he had a beef with dear old Dad too.

When he returned, he woke me up, told me the story of how he watched the cars burn, how he presided over them, inhaling the smell of the burning tires, noxious and thick, and the scent of the seat belts smoking. How he watched as a dented, faded red door slowly peeled away from a Mustang.

Dad's favorite model.

Then he extinguished the flames.

My dad was the first to see the destruction, and he crafted

a cover-up for his boss and for the fire department. He claimed a lit cigarette had wreaked the havoc, even though he didn't smoke. But he needed to protect his son, his first hope for fame, for money, for glory. Besides, it was a junkyard, a wayward land for broken-down parts, smashed-up pieces, and really, a cigarette being flicked there could have done that kind of damage. It was plausible enough.

When our dad yelled at Xavier for what he'd done, my brother just said, "What do you expect? You gave me your fire. You made me this way!"

Xavier laid waste to many more cars in our town. Late at night, like some sort of avenging ghost rider, he'd pace down the streets, flick his wrist, and watch Fords and Buicks and Cadillacs ignite.

He was arrested quickly for the car bombings.

Xavier Kilandros wasn't just a fire artist. It was as if the fire in him had twisted too far, forked in on itself, and made him destructive.

Then again, that may be what fire powers do to us. That may be another part no one understands. That behind our hardened skin, we are driven mad by our so-called gifts.

Xavier has been out of prison for one month now. Sometimes, I wonder if my dad would have set my hands aflame if Xavi hadn't been locked up. If Xavi had continued performing and rising to the top of the Leagues. If my dad had another fire artist, a true and pure one, to focus his energy on. But then, maybe my dad was programmed—in his own sick way by his father—to hurt his kids.

I don't blame my brother for anything. I'm just happy that he's home.

He takes a sharp right and guides us onto a long stretch of empty road, only a few houses on each side. The homes thin out more, and we pass an orange grove, then a field. Soon he turns on a hard-packed dirt road, and I grip my handlebars tighter because the wheels of this bike weren't made for roads like this. I'm looking down, and I barely notice where we are.

The abandoned mental asylum in nearby Winter Springs.

"Why are you taking me here?"

"I'll show you why."

We pedal up the road that leads to what was once a serene and tranquil setting for those who'd lost their minds. A sprawling mansion that a Florida couple donated to the state for a mental institution, in memory of their daughter who'd suffered from schizophrenia—the Elizabeth Jane Hansen Center for Respite and Care. It was like a stately southern plantation, but now its big wide steps are cracked and crumbling. The once-white home has turned gray and dirty, like an unwashed back windshield begging *wash me* in fingerprint. The grounds are overgrown with grass, unkempt and wild. The massive front doors have fallen off their hinges, and they hang open, lifeless. A Florida sugar maple tree's untrimmed branches poke into a broken window on the second floor, as if the tree had been grabbing blindly for what lay beyond.

Xavier and I walk through the broken-down doors. Inside, the mansion is dead silent and still as glass.

I wrap a hand around Xavier's arm, and he ushers me up

the stairs, the walls lined with old portraits hanging limply at sad angles. I peek into one of the patient rooms on the second floor. A basin has fallen on its side, with brittle bits of porcelain trailing from its bowl. Another room contains medical equipment, an old gurney, withered over the years, and a series of bizarre contraptions with straps and buckles that must have been for restraint.

"That's where they housed the especially crazy ones," Xavier says as if he can hear my thoughts.

Xavier leads me into a larger room that must have once been the baths. We're surrounded by the shells of old tubs and the carcasses of showers and sinks, with dust and dirt under our feet. I cough. He lets go of me and turns in a full circle, his arms spread out. "This is where I will make fire again."

I half want to smack him. "You're crazy. And you're a jerk for taking me here for that reason."

"I'm serious, Ar. There's a bunch of us who are forbidden from making elemental arts, but we're going to do it here. I visited this place after work the other night and it's perfect. Off the grid, you know. No one ever comes here, but we'll have our own shows here. A new kind of show."

"Like a rave? Some underground theater spectacle?"

He nods enthusiastically and his eyes have the glint of an inventor.

"Why would anyone come here though? Why would they see a show here when there are shows in less creepy places?"

"Because we don't make the same magic anymore."

"What do you make?" I ask with a sick curiosity. Maybe he

has a trick to teach me that will get me out of town. Anticipation balloons in my lungs.

"Watch," he says, and takes a few steps back.

He holds out his hands, the gorgeous way he used to when he stood in the same park where I'll perform for the scout. He spreads them like a magician. As if they're steely knives, he slashes his arms through the air, releasing plumes of fire. I watch, mesmerized, as the flames race to the ceiling high above us, then he calls them back down before they burn a thing. But on their descent, I notice something amiss about his flames. They're taking shape, they're curving and curling, and when he relights them, they are more defined.

They are forming his mirror image.

He made a fire twin.

He made the legendary trick that hasn't been seen in years. One that's whispered of, talked about in hushed tones. One that's supposedly incredibly hard to execute.

I am frozen. Speechless. I point at him, barely able to comprehend what he's made.

A flaming, shadowy replica of himself. Tall and sinewy like Xavier. Shimmering next to him. Mirroring him. Arms moving as Xavier's arms move. Lips curving into a grin as Xavi's do. A burning carbon copy of my brother the arsonist.

"You. You're making . . ." But that's all I can say.

"Cool, huh?"

His face is lit up like a child's. So is his twin's. It's creepy but completely mesmerizing. He steps toward me. His duplicate steps too. I back away, but I can't look elsewhere. I can't stop staring, not as he raises a hand and beckons me closer to him. As they both do. I shake my head, but then I'm following his twin's lead. Inching nearer.

His twin's fire is quiet. There's no crackling or hissing from its flames, and there's a part of me that's tempted to stick my own hand through the shadowy copy of my brother. But then the fire starts to fade, quickly flaming out.

The twin is gone.

He looks at me with expectant eyes. "You like?"

"I'm horrified and amazed at the same time. How did you do that?"

"I learned."

"But how? No one has done one in years. You didn't make that when you were in the Leagues," I say, as if I can point out the unimaginable in what he's pulled off—old, dark elemental magic.

"Aria, we can do anything with our gifts if we focus, if we train them."

"Did you learn this in prison?"

"Yes," he says, his tone light, as if this is all in a day's work for him.

"How, though?" I ask, and I want to clutch his shoulders, demand an answer for the incredible feat he's pulled off. "How on earth do you do that? Did it take years? Did you work on this the whole time you were in there?"

He shakes his head. "Didn't take me long."

"Then why doesn't everyone make a fire twin? The Leagues have been dying for someone to make a fire twin since the last time a fire artist pulled it off a few years ago."

"I have a theory on why I learned it quickly. Because when they make you stop, like in prison, I think the fire, or the water, or the air, or the earth—it builds up in you." He grabs at his own chest for emphasis. "It builds inside you, and it's like it's all bubbling under the surface, and when you can't let it out, it starts to turn into this. Some of us did this in our cells at night when the guards weren't looking."

I know a little something about fire building inside me. Would my fire turn to a duplicate me if I didn't drown the extra in the canals?

"And you're going to perform like that?"

"Yeah. I can make beasts too. Lizards, snakes, and all sorts of horned creatures," he says. Those aren't as rare—but audiences don't tend to care for my snakes very much. Though some audiences might. "I think there's a certain segment of society that would be pretty game to see the other side of the gifts."

I grab his arm as a new worry punches my chest. "Xavi, I don't want you to perform here. You might be tempted again."

"To burn more cars?" he asks with a raised eyebrow.

"Yeah," I say as if the answer is obvious. Because it is. "And I don't want you to be tempted. I don't want you to be sent away. I want you to be safe."

"I won't let it get out of control again," he says, his voice reassuring, but only because I want to be reassured, I want to believe. Because we're the same. We've both broken laws, we've both abused the elements, and the only difference between the two criminals standing in this abandoned insane asylum right now is who's been caught.

And because we're both outlaws, I ask him the next

question, knowing he'll say yes. "I need to know how you do it. Can you teach me?"

"You want to know?" he says in a rough voice that's part protective and part willing. He's the older brother looking out for me, but he's also the guy who can't resist the dark side.

"Yes," I say firmly. This is my ticket out of here.

"You really want to know how?" Xavier asks again.

"Yes."

He takes a step closer, places his palms on my shoulders. The muscles on his arms are corded and strong. "Ar, I can tell you, but you won't like it."

"It can't be any worse than anything else," I say, thinking of the smell of my own skin burning in the garage a few nights ago.

"It can be."

"Tell me. Please tell me."

"Ar, you want to know why they don't teach you how to do this? Why no one in the Leagues or the circuit or anywhere is teaching this?"

Xavier is a chemistry professor, in a darkened classroom, teaching his morbidly curious student how to mix elements in a most unnatural way. Making sure the student is ready, making sure the pupil can handle the underbelly of the lesson.

I am ready. "Why?"

"Because they don't know how. Because they don't want to even contemplate how. Because of where it comes from. To make the fire bend into the dark shape of yourself, you have to go to a dark place. This type of fire art comes from your fear, from your pain, and most of all from your anger. It comes from every dark thought you've ever had. Your fire twin is like the manifestation of all your darkness. Why do you think I learned how to do this while locked up? Why do you think I learned to do this with the other guys? Because we all have that stored inside us."

Like a gasoline station. Tap into it and you've got the fuel you need. Anger? Yeah, I've got gallons and gallons of that. I've got tankers full.

"How hard is it to do though? Is it like a quadruple flip in gymnastics or a quad jump in skating or something?"

"Yeah. It's hard. But you and me, we've always been the best. We can do the hardest tricks. But the other reason why it's hard and why artists don't want to do it? It messes with your mind. When you go to a dark place, it makes you a dark person."

I'm already that person.

"I want to try," I tell him. I flash back to the other day at practice. The faint outline of a pair of eyes I saw when I threw that last fireball at the concrete wall. Thinking of my dad. "I know I can do this."

Two hours later—two hours of picturing my father and all the ways I've daydreamed about using my powers on him— I've managed a crude outline of arms, legs, the beginnings of my face in fiery form. It does my bidding. It moves with me.

This trick could be my ticket to saving everyone.

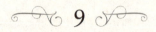

9

Stage Name

The park is a constant hum, loud and buzzing and beating. The whole crowd is expecting something to happen tonight, even though scouts don't make announcements before the crowd. They run under the radar, they dress like the rest of us. We haven't had an M.E. Leagues scout visit our team in more than a year. The last time a scout appeared, he was gone the second the show ended. He was impressed with exactly no one.

Tonight the metal bleachers are overflowing, and for the first time this summer, we have a standing-room-only crowd. I recognize many of them—other guys from the junkyard, friends of mine from school, my history teacher, the track coach, Elise's parents, the woman who sells the old library books at the discount bins on the lawn outside the library, Nava and her parents, the pretty girls from school who rarely come near me, whether because of my fire, my brother, or both. Even Short-stop is here, and he's so damn cute there in the second row. But I don't let a boy distract me as I sweep my eyes over the rest of the crowd. Jana's in the front row, next to our dad, and he keeps trying to hold her hand, and she keeps pulling her hand away. Her hair is still slicked back and wet; he made her spend the whole day at the local pool doing laps.

I wish Xavi and my mom were here. But they're not, so I keep my focus on the rest of the team, on Elise as she harnesses a long swath of wind she's created, turning herself in and out of it like a gymnast. Then Corinne, the water girl, who must be terribly nervous tonight because her fountains are smaller, slighter, and less powerful than usual. Then Angel, who moved here from Orlando and who can make the earth shake and shimmy. He's tall and wispy, and he barely speaks during team meetings. You'd think a boy with the powers of the earth might like making tremors and cracks, but instead he's like Ferdinand the bull in that children's story that I read to Jana many times over when she was younger. Angel likes to make flowers, growing lilies and roses and daisies that he gives to the ladies in the first row. They giggle and sniff the flowers, and if Angel doesn't make it all the way to the top, I don't know who will.

Then it's my turn, and I should be nervous. I should be terrified, and somewhere inside me, I am. But there's a bigger force at play in my body. A razor-sharp desire to leave home. No one ever told me that needing to escape is stronger than love, greater than fear. I figured that out on my own, and I channeled it into my fire.

I take my place on the now-and-again pitcher's mound. I begin releasing flames. Streams of fire are reflected in the eyes of the crowd, brilliant streaks that I weave and thread against the dark of the night. Then a circle of flames, like a coil running around my body. Next is an arc of fireworks, a willow tree canopy of sparks around me. I see my father in the crowds, his eyes wild and alive with some sick hope.

A dark place.

I flash on the garage, the matches, the bandages my hands used to be wrapped in. The wicks of fire that torched my palms the other night. Something flares deep inside me, it collides with the memory of Xavi this morning, with his words, with the trick I practiced. My twin this morning was clunky. But can I pull it off now? As I stare at my father I know it's in me.

After I finish the last trick in the playbook, I go for a coda. Unexpected, unscripted. Something I've only managed to do in an abandoned insane asylum.

One more raising of the arms, high and tight. One more strike of fire into the night. I will the fire to split off, to replicate.

The fire obeys, and I create a crude, rudimentary, shimmery shadow of myself.

I bow, and the girl made of flames bows too.

Then I snap my fingers and she disappears in the night.

The crowd goes wilder than any crowd has ever gone.

If my brother could see me now, I'm sure he'd be thrilled at the wicked grin on my face.

——— • ———

A reporter is the first to find me in the dugout. She thrusts a microphone in my face and asks me how I made the twin. "We've heard stories of fire twins, but no one's seen one in years. Not since a fire artist in London made one. How did you do it?"

I don't know what to say. I've never been interviewed before.

I picture my brother and I think about what he would say. He'd be cool and witty.

"It's just a little something I thought the audience might like," I say, hoping my answer is vague enough.

"Have you been working on it for a long time?"

"I've definitely been working on it," I say.

"But this was the first time you've done it in a show?"

I nod.

"Will we see more of your twin, Aria?"

"I hope so," I say, then I head to the locker room.

"What happened to her hands?"

The question comes from the scout. His skin is brown, his hair is black, and his words are accented with his Arab roots. He speaks English flawlessly, and he has other matters on his mind besides my fiery copy.

He holds my hands in his, my palms up. I don't like having my hands touched. It makes me feel exposed.

I press my lips together and wait. The question is not for me. It's for my father, who stands next to me in the coach's office. Nava is seated in a chair. I feel like a calf at market, the buyer asking the farmer if I've been fed and kept properly. Poking my haunches, prodding my belly to see if I'd be a good cut of meat.

"It happens," my father says coolly, casually.

The scout raises an eyebrow. His name is Imran, he told us. And he's been on the circuit since the Leagues began, years ago.

"Not like this," Imran says, shaking his head.

My father holds up his own hands. His palms are craggy and ragged too. But not like mine. No one has palms as far gone as mine. "It happens with fire artists. It happened to me."

"Yes, I know," Imran says, his voice clipped. He is commanding. He is the one in charge here. "But I have never in all my years seen someone so young with so many scars, so many burns."

"Aria played with fire a lot when she was younger," my father says in an empty voice.

My stomach lurches and I want to lunge at him, to throttle him, to grab his neck and strangle the last bit of life from him.

The scout turns to me; the corner of his lips curls up like there's a private joke that might make him laugh. "Is that so?"

I rearrange my features, return the mask of steel to my face. "Yes. I've always loved fire. It took me a while to control it."

"You have precision control now," he remarks.

If only he saw me a few days back, when my fire was scurrying away from me . . .

Imran runs his hands across my palms, touching the grooves. How much will this calf command?

"Still . . . ," he says, and his voice trails off. It's unclear what his silence means—that he doesn't believe me? Or that I'm not good enough? Didn't he see what I did tonight? Isn't that more than enough? His eyes shift to my father. "*How* did she play with fire when she was younger?"

"Lighting matches, playing with burners. I couldn't keep her away from it. Starting little fires in the backyard. Setting bottles on fire. Firecrackers too."

He lies with such abandon it makes me want to cry, and I rarely cry. I hate crying, I hate weakness, I hate that he makes me weak.

Imran considers the answer, as if he's measuring whether there's any truth to it.

"Perhaps that is good. We want all our players to have passion." Then he turns back to me. "Passion is one of the five tools of the best elemental artists in the world. Do you know the others?"

The five tools have been drilled into me since I could walk, since I could breathe. Xavier had four of them. I have all of them most of the time.

"Beauty, power, passion, presence, and control."

"Yes. You have all of them. You are a five-tool artist. You are rare."

I have goose bumps for a moment, and it feels good to be praised by this man.

But more than good, it feels like hope. Like a map with a treasure in the middle, and I can find it and never let go of the gem.

A gem that I've earned. Because even though my fire was born of a lie and bred from a crime, fire has become who I am now. My fire feels real, as true and native as if I'd been born with it, because it's necessary. Because fire saved me, and fire will save the rest of my family.

"If you were to join the circuit, you would need a stage name. Have you thought about one?"

I have thought about stage names before. Entertained them,

considered them. Names like Nitro or Flame Thrower are passé, not to mention taken by other artists in the Leagues. But I know my stage name. Because I know who I am.

"The Girl Prometheus."

Now he raises both eyebrows and his face splits into a full-on grin. Nava laughs lightly, nodding, though she has no idea why the name is so fitting. She likes it because it's bold. Because I'm the performer she could never be. Fearless in her eyes.

No one thinks it's the truth.

Why would they?

Everything about me is a lie.

Except my new name.

"The Girl Prometheus," Imran repeats. "A fire stealer. It is a perfect stage name," he says, and extends his hand. I try to suppress a smile because I've been taught to keep it cool, to be stoic, to stomach all my emotions. But I'm grinning, I'm bursting. This is everything I've ever wanted. "We'll start you in Miami next week. Welcome to the M.E. Leagues, the Girl Prometheus."

10

A Wish for Peace

My dad has finished drawing a bath for my mother, and I'm getting ready for lunch with Imran and my father to review the details of my contract with the Leagues.

"Wear the pink dress with the scalloped neckline," my mother whispers before she closes the bathroom door and locks herself into her potpourri of lavender and steam. "The one I got you for your birthday."

I head into my room and stare at the open closet. I'm not wearing the pink dress. It's babyish and has a lacy hemline. I've never worn anything remotely like it.

"Isn't it just so feminine and delicate? It'll look beautiful on you," my mom said when I feigned liking it. "Feminine" and "delicate"—that might have been the first time anyone had used those words to describe me. I am motorcycle leather, I am ripped jeans, I am white and black tank tops. I am boots and sunglasses, flip-flops and cutoffs.

The dress is still on the hanger in my closet.

Jana's on her bed, reading one of my magazines. I yank on the pink frock. I glance at myself in the mirror. I look like a doll.

"This dress is hideous," I whisper to Jana.

She nods her assent. "It's totally disgusting."

I tug it off and pull on a denim skirt and a black T-shirt, then sink down on the bed next to my sister. "Oh, Jana, what am I gonna do?"

"Take me with you."

I pull back to look at her. "Really? You want to get away from here?"

"Uh, yeah. Who doesn't?"

"What happened at the pool yesterday?"

She gives me a curious look, like my question doesn't compute.

"Did Dad try to . . . ?" But my voice trails off. Because I'm not even sure what to say or ask. "Did he make you stay under the water or something?"

She shrugs. "He just timed me. To see how long I could hold my breath."

"How long can you hold your breath?"

"A long time," she says with a slight smile. "Do you think I'll be a water artist?"

"Jana, you're going to be anything you want to be." I give her a kiss on the forehead. "I promise."

I step back into the hall and head out with my father.

We drive to the only fancy restaurant around, a steak and lobster joint one town over. It's a darkened place with burgundy booths and chocolate-brown carpets and the air of money.

Thick, heavy menus; waiters and waitresses with white dress shirts and black ties; linen napkins.

"Shrimp cocktail?" Imran suggests after we sit down.

My father nods, and I follow suit. Imran calls the waiter over and orders. I like the sound of his voice, the smooth caress of words like "another" and "shrimp" and "please" flowing from his tongue like warm honey, thanks to his accent. He's older than I am by a few years. He has high cheekbones and lush black hair. Something about him reminds me of my beautiful boy. Maybe it's the hair, or the cut of his jaw. Or maybe it's that he seems kind, as I imagine my beautiful boy to be.

The shrimp arrives and it's delicious. We never eat like this at home. At our house, it's rice and beans and pasta Jana makes because my dad decided cooking meals is her task. As the youngest and the only one without a job, she must have dinner on the table when my father returns home, smelly and greasy, from the junkyard.

He orders a steak and I opt for a garden salad, even though I really want the roast chicken and mashed potatoes. But I have a feeling Imran wants to know I have control over what goes in my body, that I will stay trim and tight. Imran asks for water for all of us, then hands the menus to the waiter.

His brown eyes land on me. He clasps his hands together. "Aria, have you ever been to the M.E.?"

"No, sir," I say. I haven't been anywhere. I haven't been on a plane. I've never left Florida.

A light laugh, then he tells me I can call him Imran.

"Yes, sir."

He shakes his head, bemused.

"It is the most beautiful land in all the world," he begins, telling me of the mosques and temples, of the desertscapes, and the mountains, and most of all how the towns and cities there have all changed. The M.E. used to be a land of disparate countries, torn apart by wars with the United States, with Israel, with each other. There once was a time when you could say, wryly, "What do you pray for?" and people would answer, "For peace in the Middle East." Unrest could be traced back thousands upon thousands of years; this was biblical territory, after all.

But after multiple oil crises and myriad occupations, a miraculous thing happened. The fighting stopped. The wars ended. Not overnight. Not with a snap of the fingers. But over several years, it was as if all the bad will there had unwound, drained itself out, and been replaced by peace and prosperity for all.

A treaty was signed, a manifesto of goodwill.

It's long been rumored that this harvest of peace came about through the region's current leaders. That deals were made with granters, that wishes poured forth like wine. Of course, the M.E. is home to the very first legends of granters. Long ago they were called genies or jinni and were said to be kept in bottles, or lamps, or rings. Once upon a time, storytellers spun tales of magic woven by genies across a thousand Arabian nights.

The genies in those tales never granted peace though. They never granted anything but the most personal wishes of those asking. Money, knowledge, power. I don't know that granters could bring peace to a land, but maybe there's some special clause for wishing for something altruistic, wishing for the thing all your citizens have wanted for years. Or maybe the stakes were simply higher than usual. Every wish comes with a price. Pay now or pay later.

I wonder if the M.E. is rife with granters. If you find them in caves laid with riches; caverns encrusted with rubies and emeralds and golden goblets, or inside dusty, tarnished lamps in the marketplace, tucked into carts, next to baskets of dates and figs. But then again, granters aren't really found in lamps or bottles. Xavier once told me they're found behind doors and hidden in tunnels. I suppose they could be anywhere.

But whether through granters or good fortune, the M.E. is now a land where freedoms of all kinds are embraced and wealth has spread out to nearly all citizens. The M.E. also operates the most talented elemental arts teams around the world, including in the United States. The M.E. Leagues here in the United States have the best stadiums, the most devoted fans, the highest payrolls, with teams in Chicago, New York, Los Angeles all part of the system, and the recruited artists start their training in Miami.

"I am lucky to call it home," Imran continues. "There is no better place in all the world to live, to be young, to perform than the M.E., especially since the treaty."

"Well, yeah. It's the top of everything," I say, because every elemental artist who performs dreams of being called up to the M.E. Leagues.

"That is also why it's so important that the Leagues be pure," Imran says.

I freeze. This is the moment when I've been found out. Someone saw us, Elise and me, on the beach a few days ago. Or someone's been watching us for years. Maybe some other elemental artist, waiting for his or her big break, needing to snatch mine away from me, figuring it's unearned. Figuring I'm a fraud.

Which I am.

"We have the strictest rules of any of the Leagues and we're tightening them even more," Imran continues.

I gird myself to show nothing. To register no reaction to what he's saying. I don't want him to read me, to be able to tell I'm a thief. But inside, I'm twisted and turned, and terrified of what my father will do to me if he knows I've stolen fire. I begin plotting an escape route, first from the restaurant, then from this town. I'll spend my life on the lam. I'll be a runaway. Xavier would help me, shuttle me from safe town to safe town, protecting me, protecting Elise.

"You see," Imran continues, "there have been accusations of granter use."

"Granter use?" my father asks, and there's the strangest sound in his voice. It's higher and it wavers for a moment.

Imran nods. "We've been looking into it and have found no evidence in any of our teams, but we have to maintain the highest standards of purity. We have to make sure our talent does not use granters."

"In what way?" my father asks.

"In any way. But especially not to enhance their powers. To wish for more powers. To buy their powers in the first place."

I breathe again. I'm safe.

"Has that happened?"

"The possibility always exists, and so we are implementing

new safeguards to ensure all elemental artists are clean," Imran continues.

"How can you do that?" my father asks, and that same note of worry repeats in his voice. I sneak a look at my father, his jaw tense. Why is he so worried about granters? Granter use can't be monitored.

"We have ways," Imran says, giving my father the barest courtesy of an answer, then moving on. "And of course, we will expect Aria to uphold our fine standards for purity. I trust you will," he says to me.

"Yes, sir."

"Good. I have so much faith in you," Imran says to me. "In fact, I spoke to my superiors last night. I told them what I had seen in you. I told them of your great potential. I showed the videos I made of the show. They were particularly impressed with your fire twin, as you can imagine," he says to me, capping the sentence with a flourish at "twin." "It's the sort of spectacle that can bring down the house. That audiences will talk about for weeks. Can your twin do more than bow? Can it last longer than a few seconds?"

"I'm not sure," I say quietly. "I just started working on it."

Imran doesn't blink; he doesn't flinch. His confidence is electric. "We will train that talent then," he adds, though I wonder if the Leagues *can* train that talent. If they even know how. "We have the best talent and we have the best trainers. And so we want to move you up quickly. We have tutors and schooling on-site, so you can finish your senior year of high school while training and performing. Should you choose to accept our offer, and we very much hope you will, we have decided we are going to skip Miami and send you straight to New York next week."

All my borrowed time drains in a second, in the shimmery outline of my replica.

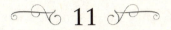

11

Last Night

I study the number of days in between my renewals, but the numbers don't add up. There's no obvious pattern, no way to predict when my fire will wane.

I crouch by my bed in the late afternoon and stare at the numbers again on my sheet of paper, wishing they'd reveal a secret, tell me the only number I need to know—when I'll start to fade. But even if I know when I'll ebb, how are Elise and I going to engineer a rendezvous for a lightning strike? Miami would have worked, since she'll be in college nearby. But now I'm going more than a thousand miles away, and we can't drive an hour and meet in the middle. Will I have to secretly jet back to Florida? Will she fly to New York? I can't picture us chasing lightning in Central Park for all the millions in Manhattan to see. Call me crazy.

A horrid thought lands in my head: What if Elise dies? Oh God, I can't even go there for so many reasons.

An idea flashes before me. What if we reignite my fire well

before it runs out? What if we got on a schedule? I study the numbers once more, then the training schedule Imran gave me. In sixty days I'll have my first break from training. That's late August, right before Elise goes to school. We'll meet up then. I have to be highly strategic now about everything. I'll schedule renewals with Elise, and I'll make sure my brother keeps a close watch on Jana. I hate leaving her, but it's the only way I can help her in the long run.

I text him, telling him I have to see him even though he's working an all-day shift. I leave the house, hopping on my bike to head to the burger stand by the beach where he works. The sun bakes me as I ride, turning my already tanned skin even darker. My tank is drenched with sweat when I reach the bike rack and lock up my wheels.

I walk to the screen door.

French fries snap in hot oil.

Xavier gives the metal basket a quick shake, then dumps the sizzling and greasy fries on a metal tray to cool them off.

"Be right back," he tells his coworker. He steps into the alley behind the shack. We're next to a Dumpster. It smells like all the fried food in the world and like the sea too.

"What's up? You okay?"

"Xavi, when I'm gone I need you to do something, okay?"

"Name it."

"I need you to look out for Jana. I need you to keep her safe. Keep her away from Dad. Don't let him hurt her."

"How would he hurt her?"

I never told Xavi what our father did to me. I trust my

brother with my life, but I'm terrified of what he'd do to our dad if he knew about the nights in the garage. Xavier is locked and loaded. He'd fire without a warning shot, and he'd burn my father alive. If Xavi did that, my brother would be locked up forever. I can't condemn my brother by laying at his feet a temptation that he could not resist.

So I don't reveal. I tease it out.

"I worry that he'll think she's ice and he'll do anything to bring it out of her, okay?"

I press a palm against his chest, flattening my hand against my brother's flimsy T-shirt, so the scars can be felt through the fabric. Like everyone else, he thinks they are fire-art scars.

"You have to protect Jana. Promise me. Promise me. Promise me," I repeat the plea, until my voice hitches. But he's already said yes.

He says it again.

"I promise," he says, and I have to believe him, even as the guilt over leaving Jana gnaws at me.

I hold on to that guilt as I unlock my bike. I can never let go of my self-loathing, to the possibility of my father taking Jana to the ocean, of him pushing her head underwater and my not being there to prevent it. I think of him dipping her hands in buckets of ice. I don't stop the reel in my mind as I ride to the empty practice field, head out to the bullpen, and let flames fly from my hands to form my mirror image.

I raise my hands high in the air. She follows suit. I bend down to the ground. She does the same.

I look at my fiery copy, then stalk toward it. She stalks back, marching right up to me. I freeze. What would happen if I kept walking through my twin? Would her fire hurt me? I snap my fingers, like I did earlier.

She's gone.

I should be happy that I did it again.

Instead, I am exhausted and entirely twisted up inside.

———

The Mud Dogs shortstop finds me as I walk through the echoey concrete hallway after my last practice before I leave. "Hear you're getting out of town," he says. Though I've admired his body, the muscles of his arms, and the trimness of his waist from afar, this is the first time we've spoken. I'm not even sure of his name. Jake, maybe? John?

"Yeah."

He stops walking, and I do the same, out of courtesy. He shakes his head. "Do you have any idea how . . ." But then his voice trails off. *How lucky you are? How much I want a ticket to the show too?* Pick any option to end the sentence, and they all add up to envy. I have what they all want, and yet I can't help but think I will spend the rest of my life holding my breath, waiting for the moment—the phone call, the summons, the knock on the door—that I've been caught.

"Yeah. I do," I say, and nod. "I hear you're a great short-stop," I add, even though I've heard nothing of the sort. But this fabrication can't hurt.

"Yeah?" He raises an eyebrow, and the corner of his lips quirk up in that tiny smile I've seen now and then. Suddenly my opinion matters. Suddenly what I've heard means something.

"Totally."

He holds out his hand, fingers curled in tightly, so we can bump fists. I oblige. "Hey, can I have some of your luck?"

"What do you mean?" I ask cautiously.

"Let me rub your head or your hands or something. You're legend now. Not just because you're leaving, but because of that trick."

I don't know what to say about that, so I lean toward the superstitious ballplayer, tipping my forehead. He places his palm against my hair and rubs. It feels nice, like I'm a cat and he's stroking my fur.

"Good luck, fire girl," he says, and walks away.

"Hey!" I call out before he reaches the door. I never go for it with guys. But I won't see him again. "There's a group of us getting together before I go. Let me know if you want to join us."

"That'd be awesome."

I hand him my cell phone so he can enter his number. He keys it in, then hands back the phone. "It's under 'Shortstop.' Just in case you forget my name."

I never remembered it in the first place.

———

Elise and I do doughnuts in her brown hatchback on my last night in Wonder. We turn in tight circles, easily outpacing Kyle in his truck. The tires squeal as Elise takes the car on yet another orbit around the empty mall parking lot. The black asphalt is all ours tonight. Just Elise, and Kyle, and the mall security guard who knows Kyle and so won't say a word about the kids blasting tunes and burning rubber at the back of a mall that's got nearly as many stores going out of business as staying in business.

Elise hollers loudly as we make our final circle, then slams on the brakes. I bounce forward a bit, but my seat belt keeps me in place.

She turns off the ignition and looks at me, a half-sad, half-happy, all-wistful look. Kyle's stopped his truck too and has the door open, but he's a gentleman and when he sees ladies talking, he knows not to interrupt.

"I'll see you in August. It'll be fine."

"Right," I say, nodding. "August. We'll do it in August."

Elise reaches her hand to my hair, petting me. "Don't worry, babe. It's an unbreakable date."

I nod and give her a hug, hoping against hope that I've got enough battery life in me to last till then.

"I'll miss you," I say. "And not just because of the . . . *you know*."

"I know," Elise says.

"You'll miss our doughnuts most, right?" I tease.

"And the soda, and chips, and pretzels too."

I pat my belly. "I'm going to be on one of those Hollywood lettuce-only diets now. I'm sure they watch every calorie that goes into your body."

"I bet they have calorie monitors implanted under your skin."

"Barbara, we have a code nine on the girl from Wonder. She just consumed a Snickers."

Elise laughs and elbows me. "Dummy, you're going to break

your lettuce-only diet for a Snickers? Get something good like an ice-cream sundae."

I salute her. "Now, this is the real reason I'll miss you. That kind of sage advice."

"You know it."

Then we open our car doors, and Kyle is waiting for his girl. He wraps her in his arms and lays a kiss on her right in front of me, like he always has, like he always will. She's lucky. She can go to college, she can control her future, she can be near Kyle, since he's stationed here.

"Kyle," I say, turning to him. His sister, Mindy, is Jana's best friend. "Look out for my sister, okay?"

"Sure, of course," he says, his innate sense of duty kicking in, even though he doesn't know details.

"Let me know if she seems, I don't know, strange. Or stranger than usual."

Elise steps in. "We will. Promise."

I see a pair of headlights coming toward me. The car they belong to pulls into the next parking spot, and the driver cuts the engine. Shortstop joins us, and the four of us sit on the hood of Elise's hatchback, drinking sodas and eating chips and chatting about Wonder, and baseball, and fire, and that *epic twin* I made. Then Elise and Kyle make themselves scarce, and Shortstop sits on the curb with me.

"Thanks for inviting me," he says.

"No problem. I figured you needed a good head rub." I offer myself again.

He smiles and takes me up on it, rubbing my hair with the

palm of his hand. Then the rubbing becomes less playful, more flirty. "I'm glad you texted me," he says in a low voice.

I don't say *me too*. I don't say I'm glad he showed up. I don't say anything. Because there is nothing to say. Instead, I grab the neck of his T-shirt and pull him against me, fumbling toward closeness, lurching into a connection. I wrap my arms around his back and kiss him hard and hungry. He responds instantly, a bruising and frenzied kiss, even though I don't know his name and probably never will. And maybe, because of that, because this is my last night in my hometown, because I am a fraud and a fake and I haven't any real luck to pass on, or maybe just because I'm tired of being the only one without someone, I pretend. I pretend he's the boyfriend I've never had, the love I'm leaving behind. And with that, I imagine I'm telling him with my lips that crush against his that I've longed to escape into him. I try to tell him with my hands tangled up in his hair that every day I'm afraid, and that's the reason I can't love him, because I don't know how to love. I try to tell him with the way I press my body against his that I can't fall in love, that I'm defective and my heart is scarred and ugly, and it's better off like this.

They're all better off without me.

———

Later that night, I take Jana pool hopping.

"Last time," Jana whispers, tapping my arm. We tiptoe across the crunchy grass in the yard.

"It'll be the best time," I tell her.

The Markins live several blocks away on a much nicer street. But their fence is easily scalable, and we're already over it.

I open the screen door that lets us into their pool area—screened in as nearly all Florida pools are, unlocked as theirs often is. I pull off my T-shirt and shorts, stripping down to a bathing suit, and Jana does the same.

"Now, what did I teach you?" I ask.

"Silence is golden when you're pool hopping," she says with a sly smile; then she dives in and swims the length to the shallow end. I meet her there, walking down the steps into the pool.

"Not. Very. Quiet."

She raises her eyebrows and shrugs playfully. "What can I say? The water brings it out in me."

"You're trouble," I say, then I splash her.

"Hey! Who's being noisy now?" She splashes back.

"The whole neighborhood can hear us now. You know what that means?"

"It means I need to dunk you," she says, and then drops a palm on the top of my head and pushes me under. I pop back up a few feet away.

She's smiling, droplets glistening on her face. She is in her element. Playing in the water.

"Race me," I say, and we take off underwater, dolphin-like bullets shooting along the length of the pool.

It is no contest. She reaches the deep end well before me.

"Tie," I declare when I rise up.

"You wish."

"Do over?"

"I'll even give you a three-stroke head start," she says, and I love how much fun she has in the water.

"Deal," I say, taking off.

But once more, as I expected, as I wanted, she beats me.

"I'm going to miss this," I tell her, shrugging off the teasing and the joking.

"Me too."

"I want the water to always be fun for you."

"Yeah. Same here."

"I'll be back soon. I promise. You know that, right?"

"I do know that. I'll be waiting."

We swim more, and Jana shows me her forward somersaults, and how she can swim along the bottom, and do handstands too, and then in the middle of the night, we finally get out of the water.

The next day I leave Florida.

12

New York Minute

Some guy in front of me wears basketball shorts, black high-tops, and a T-shirt the size of a tent. It billows when a truck screeches by. The guy talks loudly into his phone. Everyone talks loudly into their phones. He stops at Eleventh Avenue, glances down the street, tosses his fast-food bag on the sidewalk, and walks across—no, *struts*—hitting the other side just as the traffic comes rocketing down.

I pick up the greasy white bag, crumple it up, and wing it on top of an overflowing garbage can on the corner, because litter sucks.

I cross another block and head to Chelsea Piers, which used to be some sort of sports recreation center, with bowling and golf and even an ice rink a few years back. But now it's been bought by the Leagues to train all its New York performers.

My first show is in three weeks, and I'm not even remotely ready. I've been the worst kind of awful since I arrived, like I'm an awkward, gangly freshman in a school full of cool kids.

Some of them aren't too fond of me either, including Mariska. She's the first in her family to make it to the Leagues, and she followed all the rules and worked her way up. I thought we'd be friends. Or at least, cordial teammates. But instead, I'm the girl who got a free pass out of training camp, thanks to a twin I can't replicate properly, and so no one likes me much, and I texted Elise last night to tell her.

I text her again: I still suck.

She writes back: No you don't. Keep practicing! You can do it!

I'm a block away from Chelsea Piers when I see him.

For the first time.

The beautiful boy from the photos.

My heart stops, and some primal instinct tells me to run so he never knows I've admired his face. But I don't run. I stare.

At Mariska's boy. The one she poses with, arm draped over his shoulder, like she owns him. He's flesh and body now, walking toward me, and he's more beautiful in person, even from a distance. Mariska's with him, and she keeps reaching for his hand. He keeps taking his hand away. Why won't her boyfriend let her hold his hand?

I duck into the doorway of a hardware store that makes keys. I flatten myself against the concrete wall, but then lean out so I can see them. Strange. She's turned the other way, heading back to Chelsea Piers, and he's no longer with her. But as I scan the block, I see an arm beneath a sidewalk grate, pulling the grate back in place. On that arm is a dark-blue shirt.

Then the grate is in place, and the boy is . . . underneath the sidewalk?

I shake my head, as if I'm seeing things. Maybe this is what happens when you make fire twins—madness.

I start walking again but slow down as I reach the grate he disappeared into. I peer through the slats, looking for a well-dressed boy. I see nothing but darkness, and when I crouch down and try to listen, all I hear is a hollow sound.

I leave and tell myself he must have stepped into a nearby store or coffee shop. When I yank open the heavy blue doors to Chelsea Piers, I head straight for the locker room, where I drop my bag inside my locker.

"You better start showing up early."

I turn my head to Mariska. "Yeah?"

She nods, stares intensely at me with her dark eyes. "You need to work harder here. They expect you to pull off those tricks," she says, but her words don't feel like friendly encouragement. More like admonishment.

"Okay," I say, because I don't know if she's giving me useful advice or not.

A black-haired girl shakes her head at me. Claudia. She's a water artist and Mariska's best friend. "Everyone wants to see your twin," Claudia adds. "Did you leave it back home in Florida?"

I look away, a red tint creeping into my cheeks.

"Well?"

"I'm working on it," I mutter.

Mariska stomps over to me, parks her hands on her hips. "Work *harder*," she says, spitting out the last word. "That's how we're all here. Because we work our butts off." She tries to poke me in the chest, but I pivot away. She yanks her hand back before she can touch me. "You do the same."

"Got it. Message received."

"Or don't," Mariska adds, shifting to an offhand tone. "Because I can handle the big tricks without your help."

I don't fashion a comeback or a sharp retort, because my mouth is dry and I feel so incredibly stupid. I would mock me too. Because my twin is nowhere to be seen. During every practice I've been asked to show my special ability. I've tried to picture my dad, I've tried to draw on all those vast reserves of rage inside me, but the distance must be muting my anger and my talent.

Because I've managed no carbon copy. All I've produced is an arm here, a leg there, half a face. Sometimes a shadowy shimmer of a body that lasts for two seconds.

I leave the locker room and head out to the fields for fire practice. The fire coach is a guy named Mattheus. He shakes his head at me when I make a smoky shadow. I can't get this right. I can't even get close to this trick here in New York. Maybe it was just a Florida thing. I spend the afternoon working on other skills, practicing the timing of our team routines that I'm just learning, the nuances of the fire sprays, the circles of flames, the way we're expected to make them skitter through the night sky with our wires. Mariska watches me the whole time, a smug, satisfied look on her face. I feel so dumb with her eyes on me, like I don't know where my feet are or how to work my hands.

———

94

I call Xavi later that week from my dorm room, launching straight into the most important part. "How's Jana?"

"She's fan-flipping-tastic," he says.

I furrow my brow, though he can't see me. Xavi rarely talks in such exuberant terms. "How so?"

"Just swimming a ton. Hanging with Mindy. Having fun like a kid should do. Don't worry about her, Ar. I promise. I am being the best big brother."

Something in his over-the-top manner worries me. As if he's covering up. "Are you sure? Is Dad doing anything to her?"

"Nope. I swear."

I have no choice but to believe him. "Are you making fire?" I ask.

"I am just fine. Don't worry. Focus on the Leagues. We are all good."

We chat for a while longer, and then say good-bye. I end the call and dial Elise next.

"Do you miss me?" she says the second she answers.

"Like you can't even imagine."

"So what's it like? I can't believe you say you suck."

"It's like heaven and hell at the same time," I say, then tell her about Mariska and my lack of a fire twin. "I've been trying so hard, but I can't do it."

"Do you think the weather there is different or something, and maybe it affects what you make?"

I stretch out on my single bed. "Maybe. I don't know. Maybe I have to be angrier. Maybe I'm only angry when I'm near my dad," I say with a dry laugh.

"I'll send you pictures of him if you need incentive," she offers.

"Ha. No thanks. So we're still getting together in August?"

"I told you. It's unbreakable. There's nothing that can stand in the way of that happening."

I exhale, my shoulders falling, and I realize I've been holding my breath since I left Florida. Of course, I'll probably be holding my breath again until the next renewal. I suppose I am always holding my breath.

"What about boys? Any cute ones?"

"There's one," I say, but then I trail off. Because I haven't even talked to Mariska's boyfriend. I don't even know his name. On top of that, he's taken. "But he's not an option," I quickly add.

"Well, find someone who *is* an option."

Her directive reverberates in my brain later that night as I walk to the common room in the dorm to find some cereal. Music plays from the kitchen, and a faint light is on. I walk inside and see Mariska, Claudia, one of the water boys, and then him.

I stop in the doorway, and it's as if my feet can no longer move. Mariska is painting Claudia's nails, the water boy is flicking through channels on a TV, and the beautiful boy is reading.

He's not even next to Mariska, who's stretched out on the couch with Claudia. He's sitting in an armchair, reading a paperback.

Mariska looks up at me, arching an eyebrow. "Are you coming to join our party? Solo tonight, again?"

It's clear that I'm not welcome. That until I pull my own weight on the team, she'll continue to be cold.

"Just wanted to get some cereal," I say coolly, and I unroot myself from the doorway and head to the cupboard.

"It's always a party in the New York Leagues," Claudia says with a snort. "The more the merrier, you know? You could bring two next time."

I remain impassive. I don't want them to know how much my failure embarrasses me.

"Watch it, Claud, or your nails are going to smear," Mariska says to her friend, and their interest—or disinterest—in me is done.

As I find the cereal box, the boy looks up from the book, meeting my eyes. I've never been this close to him. I've only seen him on my phone, in pictures, and at the end of the block. Now he's mere feet from me, and I'm glad the lights are low because my face is flushed as I take him in. He's more beautiful than in the pictures Mariska posted. His eyes are the purest brown, as if they've been flooded with the richest, deepest color that money could buy. But there's something more to his eyes than the color. They look as if they've not only seen the world but also known it. I feel unsteady because I'm not used to such beautiful boys looking at me.

Beautiful boys who belong to other girls.

I have to find the strength to look away, but whatever discipline I might possess in this regard has seeped away.

"Hi," he says to me, but I can't read him. I can't tell if he's friendly or bored.

"This is Taj," Mariska says, over her shoulder. "He's with me."

"Indeed I am," he says, flashing me a closemouthed grin.

Mariska looks up from Claudia's hand. "But I don't know that I need you anymore."

He springs up from the chair. "So then I can go?"

I have the feeling I'm about to witness a public breakup, so I take my bowl of cereal, say good-bye, and hightail it out of there.

Seconds later, I hear Mariska say, "I'm done."

And then Taj is in the hallway, his book tucked under his arm, walking quickly in my direction. He slows when he sees me. "Hello again."

I tell myself I just met him for the first time. That I haven't been checking him out from afar. "Hi. How's your book?"

"It is excellent, and I'm going to do everything I can to finish it in the next ten minutes," he says, and he seems buoyant with his plan to read.

"Why? Do you turn into a pumpkin in the next ten minutes?"

The corners of his lips curl up. "Perhaps I do."

"What's the book?" I'm surprised that I'm talking to him, but then talking has never been my problem. Letting someone in is.

"*The Hitchhiker's Guide to the Galaxy*," he says, showing me the book. "Highly recommend it. I needed a laugh." Then he tips his forehead to the common room.

"I wonder why," I say, and that earns me another smile. My God, he has beautiful teeth too. Straight and white, and it's scary how everything about him is perfectly put together. His lips look so soft, and for a moment I find myself wondering what it would be like to kiss him.

"Yes. It's a mystery, isn't it?" he says, a playful glint in those deep brown eyes, and suddenly we're in on it together—the Mariska joke.

"So I guess it's over with you guys?"

"Honestly? It never even started," he says, but there's nothing crass or cruel in his tone.

"Oh."

I'm not sure what to say next. I want to tell him I saw his picture online. But even though I don't have a ton of experience with boys, I know not to say that.

Then he exhales heavily. "Sadly, I must go."

"It was nice meeting you, Taj."

"It was nice meeting you too . . . ," he says, then waits expectantly for my name.

"Aria."

He offers a hand to shake, and I gladly take it. Then, as his fingers wrap around mine, I remember the thing I should never forget. My scars. I press my teeth against my lips, embarrassed that he's touched my hands. But his are warm, and there's something electric in his touch, the start of a spark in my belly. As he walks away, down the hall, down the stairwell, and out into the night, I find myself missing him.

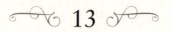

13

Shiny Things

The next few weeks pass in an exhausted blur, full of all-day practices that tire out every particle of my body. When practice ends, I drag myself to the nearby dorm the Leagues use, grab something to eat, call my brother, talk to my sister, and crash. I see my teammates many hours every day, but we are hardly teammates at all. We are competitors vying for the same spot—the *next* spot, the next thing, the next rung on the ladder up, up, up. But I'm still the flailing rookie, the kid they called up too soon.

One afternoon in the locker room as I'm zipping up my worn-down black combat boots—I wear them even when it's hot out because flip-flops in New York City are an invitation for crushed toes and because boots make me feel safe—one of the earth artists speaks to me. I brace myself, prepared for more thinly veiled barbs or aloofness.

Gemma is a "chorus" earth artist, like the backup dancers

to a pop star, an understudy to Mariska. Gemma, along with a waiflike beanpole of a boy named Cameron, crafts mini fault lines and creates tiny flowers to pair up with the bigger quakes and the oak trees that Mariska draws from the ground, like a magician making things appear, then disappear. Our creations are fleeting.

"Hey," she says.

"Hey."

"I hear you're from Florida."

"Yeah. I'm from Florida." I answer cautiously, not sure where she's going, uncertain if we're making conversation or if I'm being set up.

"Me too."

"Oh, yeah?"

She nods. "This tiny little town in the Panhandle no one has ever heard of." She tells me the name of the town, and she's right—I haven't heard of it. I adjust my denim miniskirt and pull my gray tank over the belt buckle of my skirt.

"How psyched were you to get out of Florida? It's the most backward place."

"Totally," I say. I'm not sure how I'd even begin to answer how half of me is happy to be away from home, but the other half is shredded with guilt over leaving my sister, a guilt that's only been eased somewhat by Xavi's updates—Jana's doing fine, he claims.

"Florida is too hot, too full of old people, and too full of scam artists." Gemma runs a hand through her black hair. It's shoulder length, straight, and the color of midnight.

"My mom always said that. The part about scam artists," I add. "She ran into them when she was on the party circuit years ago. She's a water artist. Well, used to be."

"You know, I think it's cool that you skipped Miami. I've seen your moves. You're good. Really good."

"Thank you," I say. She sounds genuine, and it's a sound I could get used to. "So are you."

Gemma waves a hand in the air. She wears several rings, big sparkly ones in various colors—blues, maroons, reds. Costume jewelry that she clearly doesn't wear when she's practicing or performing. "I was in Miami for a few months before I came here, but even then I was counting down the days till I could leave," Gemma says as she places a foot on the bench, then bends over to tighten the laces on her sneakers. She wears deep-pink sparkly sneakers. She's an explosion of color, the color copy of my black-and-white photo.

"Cool shoes," I say. They remind me of Elise.

"Thanks. Yours too." She tips her forehead to my boots. My armor, my shield. Then she extends a hand. "I'm Gemma, but my friends all call me Gem." I already know her name, but I like her friendliness. She waggles her fingers. "Since, well, I like sparkly things. Maybe they should call me Squirrel."

I laugh out loud at that.

"Hey, want to get an iced coffee?" she asks.

"Sure." Then I add, "Squirrel," and now it's her turn to laugh.

We're about to leave when the head coach barks at us. "Team meeting. Now! Back on the field, but don't suit up. Head of scouting and artist development is here."

I glance at Gem, and she shrugs. I walk outside with her to the field into the heat of the late afternoon. Imran stands next to a short, curvy girl who's probably about our age. The girl wears black slacks and a crisp white blouse.

"As you all know, granter testing is going to start," Imran says in his soothing voice. "I've talked with many of you privately, so this should come as no surprise. But just to reiterate, this is the first year we'll be undertaking this process. And we are going to expect you all to check out. This is Raina. She'll help facilitate the testing."

Raina gives a quick nod but says nothing. Her hair is dark and thick, with the kind of loose, effortless curls that everyone wants but no one gets without a salon. She can't be any older than sixteen. She looks as if she never laughs.

"All the teams are going through testing. And I expect all the teams to be clean. Especially the New York team. The others look to New York to set the standard, so you need to do just that. As you know, if anyone is found to be using, you'll be banned from the Leagues forever and ever and then some." Imran pauses and flashes his reassuring smile. I don't think the man has ever raised his voice. I don't think he has to. Even when he issues orders, he sounds like he's giving praise. "So do as Raina says."

Another crisp nod from Raina, and then we're dismissed for good this time.

As Gem and I make our way out of Chelsea Piers, I ask her what she thinks Raina will be doing.

"Nothing," Gem says with a scoff.

"Why do you say that?"

"Because how could they possibly know?"

"I don't know. How could they?"

"They can't. That's the point. You can't test for granter use. It's not like getting a wish leaves some sort of mark. It's not like there are trace amounts of leftover wish dust in your pee."

"So you think it's all a ruse?"

She nods her head. "Totally."

"But Imran made such a big deal about it when he recruited me. Why would he do that?"

"They don't *want* us using granters. But they can't *stop* someone from using a granter. Besides, everyone in Miami was talking about granters all the time, and how you find one. It's virtually impossible," she says as we walk to the coffee shop.

"How is it impossible? What do they say?"

"That's all I know. But it's not like finding a genie in a bottle. Everyone says it's more . . ." Her voice trails off.

"More what? Complicated?"

"Not complicated in the sense of a scavenger hunt or riddle complicated. But more like you have to be ready for it," she says as we reach the coffee shop and order our iced coffees.

"Hmm," I say because there's not much else to say. Imran made it clear I needed to be clean, and so I will be clean. Besides, Elise is my granter for all intents and purposes. As long as she's in my life, I'd never need a granter.

After coffee Gem takes me to her favorite shop in the East Village for rings. The store's exterior is black, and the windows are full of leather bracelets and silver necklaces as well as tattoo designs.

"When I get out of the Leagues, I'm going to come back

here and get a tattoo," Gem says, pointing toward the back of the shop where a bleached blonde with a nose ring is sitting stoically as the tattoo artist inks a design along her arm.

"What are you going to get?"

Gem shrugs. "I don't know. Something pretty. Flowers maybe, since, you know, I do like flowers."

I nod. We can't have tattoos in the Leagues. Our arms are often exposed in the shows and the unmarked skin is part of the uniform.

"Maybe I'll even be a gardener when I'm too old to perform," Gem muses as she taps her fingers absently against a glass case, checking out the costume jewelry underneath it.

"Ha. You'd be the best ever and put everyone out of business."

Gem laughs. "True. So true. But my *made* flowers never last."

"Doesn't matter. You'd be the flower magician, and everyone would come to your store to see you make roses and lilies."

"Boring," Gem says.

"What's boring?"

"Those flowers. I like daisies. Those crazy Gerber daisies, you know? They're in every color. Purple, pink, blue, peach. Perfect for me, don't you think?" Gem says as she models a silvery ring with a gleaming aqua sunburst in the middle. I'm not sure if she means the ring or the rainbow of daisies, but my answer's the same either way.

"Yes," I say as she roots around in her purse for cash. She finds some bills. She plunks them down on the counter and smiles at the clerk. The clerk hands Gem some change, and she thanks him.

"You're cute. Do you want to go out sometime?"

He smiles, blushes, and says yes. Then they exchange numbers.

I'm all grins and awe as we leave. "How did you do that?" I ask her with the same sort of admiration that nonelemental artists probably feel when they see us make fire or air. Still, asking a guy out seems about the equivalent.

She shoots me a look like I'm crazy. "You saw it. There was no voodoo. Just a simple ask."

"I'm impressed."

She shrugs happily and admires her ring. "This ring is awesome."

"Have you talked to him before? Do you know him?" I press on, wanting to know how she can be so gutsy to ask out a guy she doesn't even know. Kissing a boy on my last night in town is one thing, but laying it out there—*you're cute, do you want to go out?*—is entirely another.

"No. But now I can get to know him," she says, and the smile on her face is so natural, so normal that I bet Gem never had to keep the kind of secrets I keep.

———

A few days later, my phone buzzes with a text from Elise.

Mindy invited Jana to the mall today. J said couldn't go. Said she had to spend the day at swim practice. She'll come over later though for dinner.

My spine stiffens. I write back, pressing hard against the dial pad.

See if her hands are cold.

Really?

106

Yes.

After practice that evening Elise replies.

Hands are warm. Said she was tired from swimming all day. She went home.

I call Jana at home. She doesn't answer. No one answers. I finally reach her the next day.

"Are you okay?"

"Yeah. Why wouldn't I be?"

"You didn't answer last night."

"I fell asleep."

"Is Dad working you too hard in the water?"

"No. I just—"

But she's cut off by the sound of my father. "We need to go."

"High tide is soon," she whispers to me. "He wants me to become stronger by swimming against the tide."

Swim away from him. Swim across the ocean, I want to say.

14

Looking Out

By the time the first show rolls around a few weeks later, the legend of the fire twin has been scratched from the lineup. I've been relegated to the "chorus," where I back up the better elemental artists.

We perform in Intrepid Arena, which was built several years ago in the middle of the green fields of Central Park for the New York Yankees but has become better known as the home for the Coeur de la Nature show, the name for our troupe. The Yankees still play here, but only in the mornings now, and the ground crews have to slap up sliding walls over most of the seats because the team only generates a fraction of the crowds that they did back when spectators used to watch big boys smash balls.

A slice of the ground has been left exposed, a canvas of dirt and grass for the earth artists to paint on. On each side of our stage is a glittering black curtain that shimmers in the breeze, with silver—real silver—streaked into it to make the arena appear as some ethereal night. The stage itself is set like New York City, with backdrops of tall buildings, glowing streetlamps, and luminous building stoops after a rain.

There is no starlight in New York City. There is too much light pollution. But tonight, it's my task to make starlight. It's one of the hardest tricks I've had to master in the last year because it requires pinpoint precision and patience. Tonight I craft the tiniest little flickers, scatter them above me, and keep them stoked because my starlight becomes the backdrop for Mariska as she makes the ground in Central Park rumble, the earth under the audience shifting and tilting.

After the show, I call Elise to tell her about my first performance in the M.E. Leagues. We chat as I walk back to the dorm, and a construction crew jackhammers a section of concrete on Broadway. "It's always like this here," I say, laughing over the noise. "Even at night. How's home?"

"Boring without you."

"Ha. I find that hard to believe. Kyle is probably thrilled to have you all to himself."

"Yeah, but doing doughnuts in the parking lot was more fun with you."

"I bet other things in the parking lot are more fun with him."

She laughs, then her laughter fizzles out. "So listen, I have something to tell you," she says.

No good news has ever begun with those words. But I barely have time to brace myself because she continues. "I've been recruited too."

"Are they sending you here too? Because that would be perfect." I let myself feel hope for a second.

"No."

"Where then?"

"The Lookouts want me."

"The Lookouts? But what about college?"

"My dad wants me to postpone it for a year. My dad thinks it's good experience. A real honor, he says. Like this honest, noble thing you can do. He said it'll look great on my résumé."

"But, do you want to?"

"I'm not talented in the way you are, Aria. But I can use these talents in other ways. To help with the storms. To lessen the impact," she explains, but she barely has to because the Lookouts are the perfect fit for Elise. They're the altruistic elemental artists. They don't use their gifts for fame and glory. They use them to make the world safer. They *give*. Like Elise does.

"Right. Of course. You'll be amazing."

But there's a heaviness in the phone lines, a cracking pause, and I have a feeling everything in my life is about to rattle out of order, two sides of a fault line slipping far away.

"The thing is, Ar," she continues. "They're sending me to sea next week. With the Coast Guard. I'll be working on a boat for the next few months. I'll be on storm duty in the Atlantic."

"A boat?" I repeat as if it doesn't compute, because it doesn't. I'm finally settling in, I can finally see freedom, and so this just can't be happening.

"Yeah, we train out at sea, in the middle of the ocean. We're stationed there too so we can fight the hurricanes."

"A boat," I say, the words like tar in my mouth.

"I'm so sorry, Aria. I feel terrible. But we can still try to meet up in August. I'll see if I can get leave, okay?"

I want nothing more than for her to tell me she's pranking me. But that isn't her style. The Lookouts is her style. I just wish I didn't feel as if the sidewalk is crumbling under me.

"No, it's okay," I manage to say, even though my carefully planned life is slipping away. "Don't worry about me."

"But what are we going to do?"

"I'll figure something out," I say through tight lips, my insides hollow.

"You will?"

"Sure. There are always other ways."

That's what the Lady said. You can be born with fire. You can steal it. Or you can bargain for it.

With a granter.

I weigh the odds. On the one hand, stealing fire can bring life punishments.

But I've been stealing fire since I was thirteen and I haven't been caught. All I have to do is maintain my track record. After I end the call with Elise, I dial my brother and we make small talk for a minute or two. Then I slide into the important stuff.

"How's Jana?"

"She kicked my sorry butt in Monopoly tonight," Xavi says with an appreciative tone in his voice.

"That's because I had Boardwalk," Jana shouts in the background.

"You're really playing Monopoly?"

"Yeah. I told you I'd look out for her. She spent the day at the pool with Dad, and now she's with me."

I cringe inside, picturing her daily water workouts with Dad. But at least for tonight she is safe. "So, I have to ask you a question," I say, and I bet he can smell the lie coming, but I also doubt he'll care.

"Hit me."

"The Leagues are crazy intense about granter use and say they're doing some new testing this year. Everyone here is kinda freaking out, and some say you can test for granters, and some say you can't, and no one knows. You know some guys who used them, right? Is there a way to test?"

"You using a granter, Ar?" Xavi asks me, but he doesn't sound like he's judging; more like he's impressed.

"No," I say, forcing a laugh. "I'm just curious."

"Here's what I know. All the guys who were caught got caught because of what they wished for and what they did. But there's no way to test for granter use. That's the craziest thing I've ever heard."

Good.

Because I have no more choices. When I run out of fire in a month or so, they'll know I stole my fire in the first place. I've come to the end of a rope knotted by all the untenable choices I've already been forced to make.

The choice now is clear.

Somewhere in this city of millions there's got to be a granter who'll bargain with me.

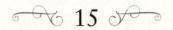

15

Thoughts and Actions

They're found in tunnels, they're found behind doors.

Xavier's earlier words about granters clang around in my head a few nights later as I walk along the edge of the park after our performance. There's an apartment building across the street with double brass doors and a doorman. Maybe the doorman is holding the door open for a granter.

Maybe that's why Gem said granters are virtually impossible to find. There are tunnels everywhere. Doors everywhere. There could be granters everywhere.

But that doesn't matter. I have to find one. If I have to open every door in New York City, I will. I've been hunting for the last few days, inspecting every last one. But I've found no door marked "G," no tunnel that leads to the lair of a wish giver.

I trek across town, continuing my hunt. An hour later, I'm on the East Side, and I walk past a subway stop. Maybe there's a granter down in the tracks. I'd claw my way through the dirt and grime to uncover a granter. I'd race in front of a train to track one down.

After I hunt through the subway station, I walk south toward the Chrysler Building, wishing I'd never stolen fire in the first place. If I'd been tougher and stronger, I wouldn't be wandering through Manhattan now in a frenzied state of *wanting*. I wish I'd never become a fire girl, because now I can't be anything but a fire girl. I need too much, more than I needed back then.

Now I *am* desperate. Consumed by a desperate wish for a granter.

My boots are heavy against the sidewalk grate. Where do these things even lead to? What's under these stupid grates that women are afraid of getting their heels caught in? I flash back on the boy descending below the grate when I first saw him. But all I can picture is a cesspool of grime and dirt, of cigarettes squashed and stubbed out, of flimsy white plastic bags from the drugstore floating in dankness, of a wet dirty muck oozing underground. Then I picture a door in the grate, and suddenly I stop.

Because it's not my imagination.

There is a door.

The grate has become a door, and I see a pair of hands pushing from underneath the grate, lifting the iron hatched bars above the sidewalk.

Then a loud clanging *thunk* as the grate hits the concrete.

There's a boy stepping out of the sidewalk vault. A boy with strong cheekbones and dark hair, wearing pressed pants and a white button-down shirt that looks freshly laundered and black shiny shoes. He hoists himself up onto the sidewalk, and I look around, out of instinct, to see if anyone else notices. The crowds have thinned, and the people far on the other side of the street don't seem to care. It's just me and the Chrysler Building and this boy.

The beautiful boy.

16

Bound

Taj readjusts the grate, positioning it back over the vault so the sidewalk is safe for others.

He wipes one hand against the other.

"Do you need help?" I ask, each word coming out as if I've never said them before, because I'm not sure what to say or do.

"No, I'm totally fine. But I have a feeling you might need help, Aria." He gestures to the long stretch of sidewalk in front of us, the ribbon of concrete that lies between us and the tip of Manhattan island. "Ah, but isn't it freeing to be able to go for an evening stroll?"

There's envy in his words.

I'm not sure I should go for a walk with him, seeing as he's emerged—though unscathed—from a grate. But in some weird way I feel as if I know him, even though we only talked that one time in the hall. Besides, he's not the picture of a boy who'd be scrapping around underground. He's the picture of the boys in fashion magazines, the ones with sculpted bones, smooth skin, and smoldering eyes, who wear clothes as if the clothes should be lucky to be so close to their flesh. Boys who have that enigmatic sense of where they're from—they don't tell; they're just not from here.

"Sure."

We walk, and he lifts his face to the night sky as if he's soaking in the stars. He takes a deep breath, and when we reach the light at Forty-Second Street, we both stop, waiting for our signal to cross. He shifts his head from side to side like he's working out the kinks in his neck. "Ah, no one ever tells you that all that time in between gives you one sore neck. It's been a while."

"Been a while?"

"Yes. It's been a while since I've been summoned. Well, a few weeks to be precise. You were looking for a granter, weren't you?" He can read my mind. "It's okay. You can say yes. I've never been wrong before. It's just kind of . . . one of those things. That's how it works with us. You really want us, truly need us, we appear."

"You're a granter? Mariska was using a granter?" My jaw hangs open. Mariska is so straitlaced, so by the book. She's constantly harping on about the need to work harder. I can't believe she'd use a granter.

Taj shakes his head. "I don't grant and tell."

"Like doctor-patient privilege?"

He shrugs evasively but says nothing.

"You weren't her boyfriend? You were hanging around because she was using you?"

"I love how you just cut straight to the chase. But I'm afraid there's nothing I can say about the past. So let's focus on now."

"Okay," I say unevenly, because I don't even know how to process all this information flying at me—the beautiful boy in her pictures is a granter. But then the brilliant truth lands in my lap, bright and shiny. Mariska was using a granter and she's still in the Leagues. Ergo, both Gem and Xavi are right. You can't test for granter use.

My luck is changing.

"So you just appear? Like that?" I snap my fingers. The light changes and we cross.

"Did you think we were found in bottles or something?" he asks as if I'm a little kid who believes in fairy tales.

"I wasn't sure," I answer quietly.

"Because that whole genie-in-a-bottle thing is a total myth. I don't know where that came from."

"I'm pretty sure it came from *1001 Arabian Nights*."

"Ah, but perhaps all those stories are myths too? The genie and the merchant, the genie and the fisherman, Aladdin and his wonderful lamp? Perhaps the jinni in those stories are all fables too," he says, and we're circling each other's words. Suddenly I'm not so sure it's a bright idea to be jousting with a granter, especially one who seems so ready to call me out on the slightest inaccuracy. After all, I don't really know *1001 Arabian Nights* that well. "Now you see them, now you don't."

He snaps his fingers and is gone. Like that. Nothing left behind. Here one second, gone the next. My heart speeds wildly, bangs its tiny fists in my chest. I didn't want him to go, and I have this impulse to hunt for him like a crazed woman who has lost a diamond ring. Because I need him. *I need him.*

And of course, that's why he appeared. He appeared because

my wish for him was so deep, so potent, so full of raw desire. That's all it took for him to appear—monstrous need.

They're *virtually impossible* to find. Unless you absolutely must have one. Maybe I can return him to me with that same canyon of need. I close my eyes and make a wish he'll show up again.

When I open my eyes I'm still alone on this stretch of Lexington Avenue, and he's neither behind me nor in front of me; neither perched in a doorway nor hiding around the corner. Then I spot him. He's across the street, leaning against the streetlight on the corner. He waves at me, a "gotcha" sort of wave.

I cross Lexington. "So you don't live in a lamp, and you can just come and go as you please?"

He narrows his eyes and purses his lips. They look soft. "I wouldn't say I can come and go as I please. But the lamp thing"—he waves a hand to dismiss the idea—"ancient history. Would it make you feel better if I told you that not everyone who wants a granter can have one? That you've got to be desperate enough to find one?"

Desperate. That sounds about right. Even so, something doesn't compute. "But I didn't find you. I thought granters had to be found," I say. Because even though he's telling me how his kind work, I somehow feel the need to point out—with my extraordinarily limited and thirdhand knowledge of granters— that he might be wrong.

He rolls his eyes, then speaks slowly, as if he doesn't expect me to get it. "We are found. We are found in the wanting, and blah-blah-blah."

I look him over, this tall, dark, and handsome boy walking

119

next to me. This magazine model boy, who was found below a grate. This is crazy. This is a freaky dream I should wake myself from. But I've had lightning pierce my heart, I've made fire from my hands, I've touched an ice-cold gator. I've been stripped free of the capacity for shock.

That doesn't mean I'm not doubtful. "So let's say you're not just an apparition and that everyone can see you, does that mean nobody cares that you just disappeared and reappeared across the street?"

"Welcome to New York City. Where no one pays attention to anyone else, especially those living in the sidewalk tunnels."

Taj tips his forehead west. We begin walking across town.

"Where are we going?"

"Much as I simply adore the foundations of New York City's finest architecture, I find I'm rather partial to the open spaces. I get a bit tired of being underground all the time."

Underground and tunnels. Xavi wasn't wrong with the big picture.

"So we're going where then?" I ask again.

"How does Bryant Park sound to you?"

And so the Girl Prometheus and the granter boy walk a few blocks to Bryant Park in the middle of Manhattan. There's an ice-cream stand in the park.

"Do you like ice cream?" he asks. "Because I'm really hungry and I could definitely go for one."

"Of course I like ice cream."

"What flavor?"

"Cherry."

Taj asks for a cherry cone for me, and the man behind the

stand hands one to me. Then Taj requests a coconut-chocolate popsicle with those crunchy bits on the outside. He takes a bite. "That is one fine ice-cream cone. Bite? They're calorie-free, you know," he says.

"Really?"

He shrugs. "No. But you could wish for that."

"That seems like a waste of a wish."

"I've yet to meet a wish that isn't a waste," he says. His pure brown eyes are shadowed right now, hidden behind things unsaid.

"What do you mean?"

"Nothing," he says dismissively. "Don't wish for calorie-free ice cream. Don't wish for anything yet. Just have a bite."

He's trying to sound cool, but I can hear the tiniest flick of need.

"If I eat this, does it count as some weird wish in a way? Like the you-get-three-wishes-thing and I used one of my wishes without realizing it? Did I just give up a wish?"

He scoffs. "Three wishes? You wish. It's *one* wish. One wish at a very high price. Like your life, your soul, your heart, your livelihood, your family. Besides, I'm not some kind of jackass granter who could be tricked into giving up three wishes."

"What's a jackass granter?"

"Do you have a boyfriend?"

"Where did that question come from?"

"I'm giving you an example of a jackass granter. Play along with me, Aria. Do you have a boyfriend?"

I think of Shortstop, whose name I don't know, and the long bruising kiss we shared my last night in Wonder. "No."

Taj raises an eyebrow. "Good. Now let's say, just for the sake of argument, that you did. And let's say he wasn't quite as handsome as you wished."

I laugh again. "Then why would he be my boyfriend?"

"Ah! See. You only go for the hot ones, don't you? What about his heart? Don't you care about his heart?"

"We're talking about a hypothetical boyfriend I don't have who isn't terribly hot and you want to know why I don't care about his heart?" I toss back, and I finally feel as if I landed a jab. But why does he feel like an opponent? Shouldn't we be on the same side? My side.

He's moving though, swimming like a shark, never stopping. "So you meet a jackass granter and you wish for your boyfriend to be totally smoking hot. Then a jackass granter—"

"Would make him literally on fire," I supply.

Taj nods. "And with jackass granters, the payment is a tad different because the wish itself is often the payment."

"Ironic, though, that you chose smoking hot. Because, you know, I could make him smoking on my own." I waggle my hands.

"Ah, you're a fire girl. As I suspected."

"Wait. You don't know everything about me already?"

"I'm not a mind reader. Just a good listener." He taps the side of his head.

"So you're not a jackass granter then. What kind are you? What other kind of granters are there?"

"Jackass. Benevolent. Ghoul. Infernal. Sea," he says so quickly with barely any space between the words. "And then there's just one more kind. Want to guess what I am?"

"Sure. I'm good in competitions. For starters, I'm pretty sure benevolent doesn't apply to you."

"Oh, you don't think I'm nice?"

"I wouldn't say so, but niceness isn't the trait I lead with either, so I don't see that as a problem. Somehow I doubt you're infernal, because that would imply you're the devil."

"Let's hope I'm not infernal. I'd look awful with horns, don't you think?"

"Are you a ghoul?"

"No, they're creepy. I'm not creepy. Do I remotely seem creepy? I mean, look at this face," he says, and flashes me a huge faux smile.

"Sea granter seems doubtful, since we're on land. So you're obviously the other kind. The *one more kind*. What kind is that?"

"I would be the simplest, the most boring, the standard, average, ordinary granter, who grants the greatest of wishes for the greatest of prices. No more, no less. Otherwise known as a mastered granter."

He punctuates those words, and it's clear that his lot is defined solely by the wisher. "You don't have free will?"

"No. No free will whatsoever. So I hope, Aria, you'll forgive me for asking you not to wish just yet. It's the only way I can have a taste of free will at all."

"What do you mean?"

"I guess I'd just like to play master and granter for a few days. Would you oblige me? Would you mind terribly if you waited to wish just a few nights?"

The realization hits me hard—he must have been hanging

out with Mariska as long as he could simply so he could be free for a bit. Waiting hardly seems like much to ask, especially when he is so trapped and when I don't know yet how to pay for my wish. Maybe with myself somehow? Some kind of trade? And I need to be smart and strategic because this wish is how I will save my family. Still, I don't trust easily. "Yes. But tell me, are you a good granter or a bad granter?"

He pauses, then curls his lips into a tantalizing smile. "That depends entirely on the wisher," he says. "Speaking of, I'm required to let you know that there are three preliminary conditions and exceptions to wishing. Because love is a powerful force in its own right, and often transcends the rules of wishing, you need to know that I can't make someone fall in love with you, I can't bring someone back from the dead, and I can't grant you more wishes."

"Seems pretty standard."

"Oh, yes, yes. Standard. We're so standard, aren't we? And you're an expert now in the rules of wishing and the granting of wishing?"

"No," I say in a tough voice, giving it right back to him. "It's just common sense. Some things are."

He doesn't have an answer for that, so I enjoy a small twinge of victory before I ask another question, "And what if I don't wish at all? What if I decide in a few days to just not wish?"

"Then you don't."

"And you just go away?"

He places a hand on his chest. "Would that make you sad? If I went away?"

I feel unmoored again. I can't tell if he is teasing me or asking seriously. I stick to the logistics. "Is that what would happen if I didn't wish in a few days? You'd just go away?"

"If you release me, oh, Master, then I'd be gone."

"So you're really saying that if I don't make my one wish now, tonight, that I can still make it tomorrow, or the next night, or the next?"

"Absolutely. One hundred percent. You have time. As long as you need a wish, I will be your granter and I will be at your service," he says in a serious tone. He takes a small burnished bronze genie's lamp from his pocket. It's miniature and fits in his palm. "Think of this like a phone. You rub it, and I'll get the message in a lamp I keep with me. Here. Try it."

I laugh. "You just said granters don't live in lamps."

He laughs too. "I know. It's sort of an inside joke. And now you're on the inside." He hands me the small lamp and then disappears again.

I don't waste any time. I rub the lamp once. He reappears. "See. You're my master."

I hate the sound of being his master. "Is there any other way to find you? Like, maybe we could just pick a time and a place?"

"That would work too," he says with a small laugh.

"Tomorrow night then?" I suggest, and we settle on the details. "Taj, I don't wish to release you for now."

"Thank you, Master."

"You don't have to call me Master."

"What if I wish to?"

He raises an eyebrow. Now he's teasing.

"Then I wouldn't wish," I say, crossing my arms. I can play at his game.

His lips quirk up in satisfaction.

I lean forward, take a bite of the coconut-chocolate concoction, savoring the taste on my tongue. Taj leans toward me and without asking he takes a bite from my cone. He raises his eyebrows appreciatively.

"It's good ice cream," he says.

"Yes. It's very good ice cream."

"So will you tell me if you are a good wisher or a bad wisher?"

I don't answer because, really, isn't it obvious? All wishers are bad. Instead I suggest we walk around the edge of the park. He says yes, but I suspect he is not capable of saying no to his new master.

17

Shooting Star

I run into Gem in the dorm showers. She's dressed in shorts and a black T-shirt with a red sequined heart on it. She's brushing her teeth at the sinks. She tips her forehead at me, then takes her toothbrush out of her mouth. "Granter testing started today," she says with a mouth full of toothpaste.

I feel as if the towel wrapped around me is sheer, as if Gem can see through me to know that I haven't wished but that I want to. I half want to tell her. I hate being so alone.

"You better grab a coffee after you shower," she adds, giving me some sort of tip I don't quite get.

"Coffee? Why?" I hang the towel on a hook, step into the shower, and pull the curtain closed. "Is coffee necessary to making it through testing?"

"Hell, yeah!" Gem says. "They did mine a little while ago. It's the dullest thing you'll ever experience."

"Really?"

"Yep."

"What's it like?"

Gem explains and I laugh. "Who would have thought," I say. No wonder I'll need caffeine to make it through testing—I'll need it to stay awake.

I finish my shower, head to my room, and pull on some clothes. Raina comes knocking a few minutes later, her bored and careless eyes barely giving me a once-over.

"Name?" Raina holds a clipboard and a pencil, checking off boxes as she goes.

"Aria Avina Kilandros."

"Date of birth?"

I give her the date.

"Place of birth?"

"Wonder, Florida."

"When did you come into your powers?"

"Around thirteen." *Like everyone else*.

"Your parents were . . . ?"

"Water and fire."

"You're registered."

"Yes. Of course."

"I mean you're registered here." Raina stabs the paper on her clipboard. "You're being registered as clean."

"Excuse me?"

Raina stares at me, her eyes saying *Can you really be this doltish*? Then she speaks ever so slowly. "You. Are. Registered. As. Clean. Of. Granters."

"I am?"

That was all name, rank, and serial number. If the Leagues were truly trying to root out granter use, you'd figure they'd stage a more sophisticated show. But maybe they figure a simple show is enough to keep us in line. That if they can't truly test, the appearance of a quick procedure is all we need to stay straight.

I head to practice, checking my phone on the walk from the dorm to Chelsea Piers. There's an e-mail from Elise.

Yo-ho-ho and a bottle of rum. It's a pirate's life for me out here in the South Pacific.

Just kidding! I'm not in the South Pacific. I'm somewhere in the great God-knows-where of the Atlantic Ocean. This sucker is massive! You ever seen it? ;) Well, don't go google it because it'll make your stomach spin it's so freaking BIG. Like, I-can't-even-see-both-ends-of-the-ocean-at-the-same-time big. Anyway, I'm actually in the Caribbean, and the ship's Internet connection is so slow it's taken me 14 hours and 22 minutes to write this e-mail. I kid you not.

But I'm learning a lot and working hard, and the Lookouts are amazing. The top ones have already held back what would have been Hurricane Danya, had it gotten bigger. Yup, thanks to my new coworkers, Danya was just a mere pup of a tropical storm down here, just a little piddling of rainwater.

Well, enough from me. Are you okay? Are you managing? What are you going to do? I'd call you, but all we have are satellite phones, and they're crazy expensive to use.

I keep thinking of ways to come see you. I'm doing

everything I can to angle for some sort of leave for a day
or two. I promise. I'll keep working it. I don't know if I can
get to New York, but I might be able to pull off Florida
sometime in August.

Xoxox.

Elise

I write back as I walk into Chelsea Piers.

I think I've got it all figured out. Love you much. Your
favorite Frankenstein's monster.

———

I am giddy as I board the subway at Times Square. I am posi-
tively bouncing as the train scoots south a few stops. I am ecstatic
as I disembark at Twenty-Third Street and head to the nearby
Flatiron Building, where Taj and I decided to meet. I have the
miniature lamp in my pocket just in case.

The angular building comes to a point on a triangular block
at Fifth Avenue and Broadway, an anchor for the neighborhood, this oddly molded bit of architecture. The Flatiron Building also happens to be surrounded by sidewalk grates, by vaults
and pits under them, labyrinthine tunnels that lie beneath the
city and once housed coal, Taj said.

I have never felt so free before. Well, not since the first time
Elise stabbed me in the chest with lightning. And even then I'm
not sure it was freedom I felt so much as relief. As I wait for the
light to change, I wonder if the two feelings are that different—
freedom and relief. Maybe they're one and the same. I don't

have my freedom yet. But when I get it, I'll no longer have to set my heart to flames.

That's the real freedom.

I won't be living on borrowed time. I'll be whole again.

Maybe that's why I'm beaming when I cross the street. Like clockwork, Taj appears, pushing up the top of the grate and poking out his head. He holds up the grate with one hand. The iron grate must be insanely heavy. I can't see all of him, but he looks sharp again, sleek again, this time in a navy-blue-checked button-down, the cuffs rolled up twice. He motions with his free hand for me to come down.

He must be joking.

I reach the grate and kneel.

"Are you going to come out? People are going to start to notice the guy under the grate."

"I thought maybe you could come to my place tonight," he says playfully.

"I'm not that kind of a girl."

"Come on. Come on down. What are you afraid of?"

"Um, crawling underground beneath New York City. I think that's sort of a normal fear."

"Aria, Aria, Aria. Do you want to wish to not be afraid?"

I hold back a sigh. He's a bit vexing. "No."

"Then just come down for a minute. I have candy," he says, as if he's luring a child. "Or did your mom tell you not to take candy from strangers?"

"I don't eat candy. I have to watch what I eat in the Leagues."

"You ate ice cream."

"I know, but that was an exception."

"So make another exception. Come on. How many times are you going to see where a granter lives in New York City? I promise you won't get hurt. And I'll hold your hand so you won't be afraid."

I have no choice but to say yes. I need him more than he needs me. Ironic, given that he's a mastered granter, and I'm the one who feels toyed with like a puppet. But maybe this sort of cat-and-mouse play is the only way he can experience free will.

Free will. Don't we all want that?

"Fine, but then we're coming back up."

"I promise," he says, and pushes the grate even higher. He offers me his hand. I take it, and his skin is warm and soft. I hold on tight as I lower myself into his world, dark and dingy, under the streets of New York.

My heart rate spikes because there's very little natural light in here, only slivers through the grate. All my instincts start building inside me, like heat rising to the surface, and I want to set this place on fire, to illuminate it so I can see. I'm about to open my palms and ignite when Taj grips my hand tighter. The impulse is snuffed out by the pressure of his skin against mine as he leads me through a twisty and pitch-black maze. Dust fills my lungs, and I faintly smell coal. Somewhere in the back of my mind, I know I should be freaked out to be skulking underground with a virtual stranger. But another part of me likes how warm his hand is. It's such a simple pleasure to hold someone's hand. A pleasure I so rarely enjoy—to have someone take my hand and not cringe at my scars. He didn't the first time he met me; he's not freaking out now.

A train roars by on the other side of this tunnel's wall, so close I could touch it if there were no wall. My teeth rattle, my bones shake. Then the train passes.

We curve around another claustrophobic corner, and I vaguely remember learning in history class about the catacombs of Paris and Rome, and I'm picturing crumbling skulls and ossified bones greeting me around the next bend.

Soon we near the end of the cramped, cave-like path. Taj reaches forward in the darkness, as if he is opening a door. Light spills in and the door takes shape, high and arched and heavy as it opens into a gorgeous and quiet and beautiful space.

A library under the sidewalks of New York.

18

The Way It Is

The wood floors are dark. Maybe oak, but I don't know types of wood, or types of furniture, or which century this or that armoire or crystal goblet or chandelier is from. All I know is this looks like the New York Public Library, the famous one. Shelves upon shelves of books from floor to ceiling fill one long wall, so long I can barely see where it extends. There's even a rolling ladder to reach the books on the highest shelves. A massive desk squats nearby on an intricately woven rug that looks like it probably costs more than my entire dilapidated home in Wonder. On the desk is a lamp with a pull-down chain to turn on the bulb. A book is open on the desk. A dark-blue couch is pressed against the wall opposite the bookshelves, and a coffee table rests in front of the couch, but there's nothing on the coffee table. No newspapers, no mugs, no evidence of living.

The only thing on the coffee table is a genie's lamp. Burnished copper, with etched markings in a foreign alphabet. I step closer and point to it. "I thought you didn't live in a lamp."

"I don't live in a lamp."

"Why do you have this then? Is this like your phone that you were talking about?"

He shakes his head. "Not this one."

"Then what is this one?"

"You know the queen of England?"

"Not personally."

"Right. Well, neither do I. Know her personally, that is. Though I know many other heads of state, but that's a conversation for another time. Point being, she's a figurehead." He gestures carelessly to the lamp. "And that's a figurehead."

"Like an anachronism," I say, and he taps his index finger to his nose. "Can I look around?"

"Of course. That's why I wanted you to come here," he says, and smiles at me. It's not the faux full-face grin he gave me last night. It's a sweet one, a cute one, like a boy gives a girl when he wants to play her the song he wrote or give her the comic he drew. It's almost enough to make me feel as if I'm special, and I'm being shown something few see. But then I remind myself that this is his job. Good-looking or not, he probably wants all wishers to feel welcome. I run my hands along the spines of the books; some are clothbound, some leather, some just standard hardbacks.

"Did Mariska come here?"

He laughs.

"Did she?" I ask again.

"I never invited her."

"Why did you invite me?"

He pauses as if considering his words. "You're more interesting."

I laugh. Raise an eyebrow. "Well, thanks. I do what I can." I circle around to his desk. "What were you reading?"

"*The Great Gatsby*. Started it last night after I met you. Haven't read a thing in a few weeks."

"Since *The Hitchhiker's Guide*?"

He nods and flashes a smile that's erased as quickly as it arrived. "You remembered. Yes."

"Did I inspire you to read?"

"Something like that," Taj says in a quiet voice that catches my attention. I look up from the desk, and his brown eyes are sad. The barbs of last night are fading, the pointed comments becoming less sharp.

"That's why you asked me not to wish, right? To hold off for a few days?"

He doesn't answer, just nods.

"So you could read?"

"Yes."

"You can't read unless you're bound to me or something?"

He sighs. "I can't do anything unless we're bound. And I like reading, okay?"

I hold up my hands. "I think that's great. It's like a passion of yours."

"You could say that."

"Are all granters like that? I mean, I just think of all those stories of granters. Tales within tales, and stories being able to set you free from debts and stuff."

He shakes his head. "Don't get hung up on the old stories. Just because Scheherazade freed herself night after night with stories doesn't mean—"

"Doesn't mean what?"

"Doesn't mean anything," he says heavily, but I doubt that's what he meant to say.

I shift away from my questions that seem to pierce him. "Well, I'm impressed that you're reading such a fancy book for fun. We were assigned *The Great Gatsby* in English class last year. I just looked up the SparkNotes online," I admit.

"Really? It's so beautiful. You should read it."

"You've read it before?"

"No. I don't reread books. I finished it this morning."

"Fast reader."

"Yes. You never know when you'll lose your place," he says.

"Isn't that what bookmarks are for?"

He doesn't respond. I glance down at the page. The book is open to a line about the green light at the end of the dock. "Hey! I remember that green light from the SparkNotes. It's all about hope, right?"

Taj grins and raises an eyebrow. He seems to have rustled himself out of that temporary mournful state and is now back to teasing again. "Yes. Hope. There you go. No need to read it at all."

"But seriously," I press. "Isn't the green light supposed to represent hopes and dreams? The thing we're all striving for?"

"I think that's fair to say. That's why I like it."

"Because you're striving for something?"

"We all have a green light at the end of the dock, don't we?"

"I suppose."

"You must, Aria. That's why we're talking. Sooner or later, you're going to tell me. You're going to ask for your green light at the end of the dock, aren't you?"

I feel selfish when he says that. Like I shouldn't be asking, shouldn't be wanting, when his very existence in my life is predicated on the possibility of what I might wish. But that's why I'm here. Because of my *need*. Because it is so powerful—my need to stay in the Leagues, to find my way through, to save my family. That is my duty. Jana, my mom, and even Xavier. They are the reason I'm talking to Taj.

"I guess," I admit, though I'm enjoying hanging out with him right now. More than I thought I would. "Do you want me to wish now or something?"

He shakes his head. "No. I mean, not unless you want to. But if you wanted to, I'd have to lay out the conditions. Standard operating proviso, you know. The rules, the regulations, the fine print. The loopholes and all that jazz." He talks in a pseudo lawyerly voice.

I manage a small laugh. "I suppose I don't have to wish this second," I say, because Taj seems as if he could really use a night away from wishing, from his job, from being mastered. "Maybe we could . . ." I'm not sure how to finish the sentence, but Taj's eyes light up.

"Go aboveground?"

"Well, your library is nice. But I kind of like light and air."

"As do I."

"Why did you want to show me where you live then?"

"I don't know that I'd say I live here."

And he's back to his wiggly wordplay. "Where do you live then?"

"When I live, I live here."

His words are chilly. "*When* you live?"

"Ah, you see. We do have lamps, so to speak. Only, unlike the genies of old, we don't live in lamps in between wishers. In between wishers, we cease to live."

I close my eyes for a moment, steady myself by placing a hand against his desk. I open my eyes, but I still feel like I'm swaying, like the room is uneven and hazy. "Do you mean you die after you grant a wish?"

"Not an official death. But we cease to exist when we're not dealing with wishers. It's just nothingness until we're needed, and it's only through a wisher giving us permission to stay that we get to hang around. Like I said, that's why I finished the book last night. You never know when you're no longer going to be needed. Your time can end just like that."

He snaps his fingers.

That must be what happened with Mariska when he left. When he said he needed to finish *The Hitchhiker's Guide to the Galaxy* in ten minutes.

"That's terrible," I say, and my heart—my scarred and bruised heart—feels leaden. It's sad knowing he only comes alive to nod his head and say "Yes, Master, you're a prince, you're rich, you're good-looking, here's a mansion for you."

Stupid people. Stupid wishers.

Stupid me.

"Do you still want me to wait a day or so to wish?" That seems only fair. I can last another day. "So you can be free for a while?"

He smiles. "Only if you want to."

"I feel bad for you. That you just go away."

He reaches for my hand. "Don't, Aria. It doesn't hurt. I'm barely even aware of it. It's not even like sleeping or dreaming. It's just . . . the way it is."

I clasp my fingers around his, keenly aware that we're holding hands for the second time tonight, and it feels natural and necessary.

"Sure, but sometimes *the way it is* sucks. Let's get out of this figurative or figurehead or whatever-it-is lamp of a living room, Taj. Let's get out of here and see New York. Wait, you've probably seen New York many times. How old are you? How long have you been a granter? How many wishers have you had?"

"Eighteen. Since I was almost sixteen. And, *plenty.* To answer your questions. And the other one about New York—I like New York. So let's go."

We leave, and he leads me through the cavernous underground, all the way to a grate. Only it's not the one we came down in. It's in an alley behind a theater on Broadway. As I climb up and out, we're standing under a marquee, lit up in bright shining lights, blaring the name of a show.

19

An Organ of Fire

"Do they all connect? The underground tunnels?"

"Not when you're in them by yourself. When you're with me, yes."

I laugh, not because this is comical but because it's incredible. "So this is part of your magic?"

"I wouldn't call it magic, per se. It's more like knowing the shortcut. When you're with me, you can always take the shortcut underground. Then again, granters in general are kind of shortcuts, aren't they?"

There he goes again. Making some sort of philosophical observation about the role of wish givers. He's right—their purpose is to circumvent.

"But it's kind of like a wish too," he continues. "When we travel through the tunnels, they go the way we want them to, the way we wish. So it's fitting. Do you like theater?" He gestures to the marquee.

"Never been."

"Do you want to see a show right now?"

"Are you going to do that appear-disappear thing to get us in the theater?"

He scoffs at me. "I can, to get myself in. There's just one little problem—I can't take you with me that way. However, there's a thing known as second-acting a show. Ever done it?"

"No, seeing as I just said I've never even seen a show."

We're surrounded by crowds milling about, by theatergoers making phone calls or puffing on cigarettes during intermission. A bell sounds from inside the theater, and the lights in the lobby flash. "Two-minute bell," he says, and places a hand on my back, guiding me inside the theater lobby, then past the refreshment stand, then into the auditorium itself. He stands near the back, scanning the seats. The house isn't full; several back rows are mostly empty. When the lights dim and the curtain rises, he tips his forehead to a nearby aisle, and we snag a pair of seats.

He grins. He had walked in like he owned the place. "Whoever said there was no such thing as a free show? Enjoy the show, Aria."

We've missed the first act, but I don't care because this second act is gorgeous. There's a boat tossed at sea, and crewmen singing about the dangerous waters that heave back and forth. Then a scene on a dock as a beautiful blond woman sings to the moon, a sad, plaintive song. Soon curvy girls with long legs and tap shoes dance around a sea captain as he repairs the ship while crooning a love song. Then the blonde runs out to the stage, and when he sees her, he melts.

She rushes into his arms. He twirls her around, dips her,

and kisses her. Then they come up for air and belt out a final chorus.

The curtain falls and everyone claps. The curtain rises, and soon audience members start to stand and clap as the cast runs back onstage to take their bows. I stand and cheer, and so does Taj. When the show is over, we leave the theater like the rest of the audience, waiting and shuffling, taking our time.

"Did you like the show?" he asks.

"It was amazing. I've never seen anything like it."

He smiles and it's such a natural smile. His brown eyes light up, and I'm reminded of how pure the color is—they're a rich, deep golden brown, a few shades darker than his skin.

"I'm glad," he says, and he seems both happy and genuine.

"My mom has always wanted to see a Broadway show. I'm going to have to tell her all about it, especially since she was a water artist. She would love it."

"What's she like, your mom?"

"She's this smart, sweet, loving, totally vibrant woman. But she doesn't feel well most of the time, so she hardly ever leaves the house," I say, even though that's a distortion of the truth. She never leaves the house.

"Sorry to hear she doesn't feel well. That's a bummer."

"Yeah, it totally is. I can't even tell you the last time she saw sunshine or the ocean. And she loves water. I would love to take her to the ocean and see her swim again."

"She really doesn't leave the house?"

I shake my head. "No. Never, actually," I say, admitting the full truth now. Something shifted between Taj and me in his library tonight. It's as if there's another side on display now.

The prickly, caustic granter he was last night is gone, and he seems like a friend. So I keep talking. "One of the reasons I'm even sticking with the Leagues at all is to raise enough money to help her somehow. To get well again. I need to make enough money so I can get her out of the house and find a great doctor for her."

"You're a good daughter. I hope you can do that, Aria." When we're on the street, he asks me, "What now?"

"I'm kind of hungry, to tell the truth."

"Do you like diner food?"

"I'm from the backwaters of Florida. We went to restaurants once a year. We ate rice and beans for most meals. I like anything."

Soon, we're ordering chocolate milkshakes and French fries, and as we wait Taj asks again how I liked the show. Then he catches himself, remembering that he'd already asked that question. He seems a touch nervous with me right now.

"You know I loved it. Did you like it?" I ask, turning the question around. I don't add that I want to go again, that I want to see more shows, that who knew I'd enjoy a musical so much. But I did enjoy it, so much so that it felt real, as if the boat were truly tossed at sea, as if the crew had actually saved it, as if the captain and his lady did live happily ever after. I believed in it, in the story and the song.

He nods, and then we're both silent for a minute, and it's awkward because it feels like we're on a date—going to the theater, eating out, stumbling on words—but yet we're also in the midst of a business transaction. I'm not sure how to steer things back to business without being a complete jerk.

"So, Aria. Let's get down to business. You want a wish."

Maybe he is a mind reader.

"Yeah. I do."

"And you feel bad for wanting it."

"Of course."

"Tell me what you want."

"Now? Is this how it works? I tell you in a diner?"

"Sure. Or you could wait until I take you to the top of the Empire State Building on my magic carpet and tell me there."

He says it without irony, but I'm sure he's joking, so I manage a laugh. He raises an eyebrow, waiting for me to speak.

"Why do you dress so fancy?" I ask to buy time.

Taj glances down at his clothes, his pressed shirt, his dark slacks, his shiny shoes. "I was raised that the way you dress is a sign of respect for the people you work with, interact with. That's what my parents taught me."

"Where are your parents? Do they know you're a granter? Are they granters too?"

He shakes his head. "Some questions I will not answer. But, yes, they know."

"Do you ever see them?"

"Never. Granters are forbidden from seeing family."

"That's sad. Do you miss them?"

"Terribly. But," he says pointedly, and then stands up and joins me on my side of the booth, sliding in next to me. "We're not going to talk about me now. We're going to talk about you. You should know you're free to wish under certain circumstances. I checked the registry and you've never wished before, which means you get one wish."

"Registry? Like the registry of elemental artists?"

"Something like that. So tell me what you wish for."

I swallow, bite my lip. I'm jangled inside, nerves exposed and antennae up. If I tell him why I need fire, he'll know I stole it. He'll know I did something punishable by the Leagues. "Taj, are you bound by our laws? If you knew something about me, something bad, would you have to turn me in to the Leagues?"

The corners of his lips curl up. "I am bound by you. I am bound by wishers. I am bound by the powers of granting. When I'm in your world, I do my best to pay my bills at restaurants and to cross when the light is green, but no. I'm not obligated, nor do I care much, for the laws that institutions lay down."

"My fire is running out," I whisper.

"Was it never yours to starts with?"

I shake my head, relieved for once to be honest. It feels so amazingly good to admit this, to confess what has twisted me up for so long. "It was never mine."

"I noticed your hands. The first night I met you." I try to shield my hands, to tuck them under my napkin. But he takes my right hand very gently in both of his. He turns my hand over, palm up. He traces my scars, my calluses. "You were burned, weren't you," he asks, as if he can read my hands, as if my palms are telling him a story.

"Yes."

He doesn't let go. He continues to trace lazy circles on my hand. I feel goose bumps on my arms. I look down at his fingers, long and elegant, charting the grotesque grooves in my hand.

He leans into me and whispers, "You stole your fire from

the sky, Aria." There's no judgment in his voice. His tone is completely absent the damnation that stealing elements brings.

I don't answer with words. I answer with movement, with the barest of a nod. I've confessed, and it feels strangely freeing. I open my eyes.

"And you want to be fire naturally now," he continues. "You want me to give you the gift of fire. It is the only way you can keep moving, keep living. Now that you're in the M.E. Leagues, you need it even more. Because powerful people now know what you can do. And if you're found out to have stolen your gift, terrible things will happen, and you will be exiled from the Leagues, and you need the Leagues for your very survival."

I shudder, and it's as if the heat between us has been extinguished, snuffed by the reminder of choices and consequences.

"You promise you won't tell?"

"I told you. I'm bound by the laws of my kind. I don't answer to theirs. I don't care if you stole fire. In fact, I assume you had a completely valid reason." He looks at my hands again. "I don't have to assume, actually. I know you did."

"Do you want to know how I did it?" I'm half-shocked at what I'm saying, but I so badly want him to know all the things I could never tell Jana or my mom or my brother because we were from the same place, the same people, the same rules.

Taj is not.

Here, with Taj, I'm able to let go of the walls and I find that I want to. That I've been wound too tight for far too long by too many secrets.

"Of course," he says with a smile. "I enjoy knowledge more than almost anything else."

"What do you enjoy more than knowledge?"

"Perhaps we'll find out. But for now, tell me how you stole fire."

I begin at the beginning, telling him about my brother, about his crimes, then the garage, the matches, the bandages on my hands, the trek through the swamp, the Lady and her snow gator.

"I've heard of snow gators."

"You have?"

"Yes. I knew of someone who won a snow gator."

"Won?"

"Sort of like in a bet. An exchange."

"They say he became a snow gator because he ate an ice artist."

"Maybe it's the same gator," Taj says.

"Maybe." I continue my story, editing out only Elise's name, as I detail how the lightning enters my body, how my fire sharpens and strengthens, like a climber scaling a mountain peak, then how it unspools, the same climber tumbling down. How my own fire chokes me as it wanes.

"Does it hurt? When the lightning hits?"

I shake my head. "Not really. I mean, it kind of burns. But I'm used to it."

Taj holds up his hand; lets its hover near my chest, as if he can feel my charred heart.

"Do you want to feel my heart? Where the lightning goes in?"

"Very much so."

I take his hand, press his palm against my chest, just above my breasts. My skin is bare; I'm wearing only a tank top. My heart beats against his palm. His hands are so warm, but they're no match for the heat in my heart.

Then the waitress brings our milkshakes and French fries and we let go.

We eat, and I know I want to drag out this wish for another night. Because this is the closest I've ever felt to freedom.

20

An Example Of

Figured it out? Color me intrigued. Did you find another air artist who'll knock you out with lightning? Say it ain't so. Have I been replaced so easily??? But seriously, if you have, that's awesome. Do tell, do tell.

Xoxo, Elise

Are you crazy?? No way would I ever ever ever find another Dr. Frankenstein. You're my one and only. But . . . shhh . . . I found another way . . . you know . . . THAT way . . . *1001 Arabian Nights* way . . . He's beautiful too.

Love, me

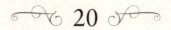

The next morning, I grab my backpack, sling it over my shoulder, and pull my long hair into a high ponytail.

I lock my room, practically bounce down the stairs, and meet Gem outside to head to practice with her. Gem is wearing silver flats today. They are covered in silver sequins. Her black hair is clipped back in a cascade of barrettes with bugs on them—a stylized ladybug, an elongated spider, even an ant.

"Cool hair bling."

"Cool ponytail."

"Right. It's such a talent. My amazing ponytail-making ability," I say drily as we hit the streets. I root around for a pen in the front pocket of my backpack. I find my favorite blue one, the one I jammed in there this morning when I woke up with it in my hand, and shout, "Gotcha, blue pen!"

"Chipper this morning, are we?" Gem raises an eyebrow as we stop at a red light.

"Maybe," I say in the exact kind of tone someone would use if she were starting to like someone and wasn't sure how to tell her friend yet. Instead, I finish off a doodle I started on my thigh last night when I couldn't fall asleep. I kept replaying the moments at the diner, Taj's hand on my chest, how his skin feels—well, *radiant*—against mine. I study the drawing, a kaleidoscope of ink and flesh, and I see patterned swirls and whorls bending and weaving, as if I were looking through a lens to see a psychedelic image. I wasn't in the mood to mark up a too-school-for-cool model or sketch random thought bubbles in a magazine, so I took to my own flesh as a canvas. It's my most elaborate body graffiti ever.

I cap the pen and drop it into my backpack as the light turns green.

Gem points to my leg. "That, my friend, is certifiably awesome."

"Certifiable something, that's for sure."

"I totally want you to do one on me."

"You do?" No one has ever asked me to draw on them before.

"Hell, yeah!"

"I thought you were waiting till you retired from the Leagues."

"For an official tattoo. But you can do a temporary one. Can you do a badass flower? Like maybe a daisy with a scowl on its face?"

I laugh at the image. Gem has a little bit of Angel in her, and a little bit of Ferdinand the bull too. She plays backup for Mariska each night onstage, but what she'd really rather be doing is gardening. Making flowers. Growing sunflowers and pansies and daisies, her favorite.

"Could you make it wink too? Like a real sassy, saucy wink?" Gem demonstrates, scrunching up one side of her face in an exaggerated and ridiculous mangled wink.

"Your wish is my command," I say, then I look away, blushing stupidly at what I just said, and how it returns me to another memory of last night. Telling Taj all those things. I felt safe telling him my secrets, and it's almost as if I'm a little bit lighter now because of it, as if my shoulders have been unkinked after years of knotted muscles. Such a strange feeling, especially since none of my burdens are truly gone.

"So, after practice maybe?"

"Sure. But you have to do it on your leg."

"Duh. Obviously," she says, and bumps me. Thighs are always covered up, and while tattoos are forbidden in general, we can get away with homegrown markings on hidden skin.

I yawn as we pass a truck backing into an alley.

"Out late last night?"

"Actually, I was," I say, and since it felt so freeing to tell Taj the truth, I decide to give Gem a little bit of honesty too. "I think I kind of had a date."

"Think? You *think*? Spill. I want to know everything."

I tell her. Not everything, not even close, because I don't breathe a word about his library or the way the underworld of New York City can shift and move like a secret map when you're with a granter, but I tell her about second-acting a show. I tell her about the diner, about how we held hands, and how we're going to see each other tonight too.

Gem grabs my arm. "What are you going to do tonight?"

I shrug. "I don't actually know. We kind of play it by ear."

"Wait. Is this someone you've been seeing before?"

"Just once. We met the other night."

But it feels like I have known Taj for longer. I'm sure that's what everyone says when they start to fall for someone. But maybe it's a cliché for a reason. Because when it happens to you, it's no longer a cliché. It's the truth. I do feel as if I've known Taj for a long time, and it's because he knows so much more about me than almost anyone.

"Well, what's he like?"

"He's smart and funny and kind of sarcastic, but in this weirdly clever way. And—" I stop before I say the next word, because I worry it might sound cheesy.

"And what?" Gem asks with a rabid smile.

"Soulful. He's sort of soulful."

"And anything else? How does he kiss?"

"I don't know. I don't even know if he wants to," I admit,

because I don't. Sure, I felt a spark when he placed his hand over my heart, but I don't know if he felt the same. Or if he can. Perhaps he was sweet to me simply so he could stay alive a little longer in between wishers. Maybe he is only nice because I'm his master. I must remind myself not to fall for him. I need things from him. And I have to find a way to pay for my wish. But how will I pay? With my life? I might have enjoyed talking to him, but if I get caught up in how free I feel with him, then I'll lose sight of the prize—fire without stealing.

"You should kiss him tonight. Kiss him and report back to me."

"Speaking of kissing reports, how's it going with Henry from the jewelry-tattoo shop?"

A discussion about kisses carries us the rest of the way to the facility, up the stairs, and into the locker room, as if we're floating on a well-drawn waft of something delicious—the morning-after conversation between friends.

I stop abruptly because the TV is on. The TV is never on. Gem and I turn to look at the screen hanging high in a corner. A news anchor with a severe blond bob talks seriously into the camera.

"In Chicago an eighteen-year-old boy was placed on probation from the Leagues for alleged grand larceny today. Reginald Cramer is being held without bail for theft of air powers, according to officials from the Leagues."

A man in a pinstriped suit appears on the screen. His name flashes on the TV, and his title. Winston Cody. Head of Standards and Practices with the M.E. Leagues. "We've been investigating Reginald Cramer for several months now and have amassed a substantial body of evidence that we believe demonstrates his theft of the air element more than three years ago. This is a serious violation of Leagues rules, given that performances in the elemental arts are highly regulated, protected, and pure. If he has, in fact, stolen his powers he will be banned and his family will also receive a lifetime ban from the Leagues."

A reporter asks Mr. Cody a question. "How did Cramer allegedly steal his air powers?"

"The specifics are classified, I'm afraid. But suffice it to say he had an accomplice, and we're fully expecting to apprehend his accomplice at any moment."

The reporter tosses back to the blond-bobbed anchor, who recounts past cases of theft. "The last known case of theft of elemental arts occurred ten years ago, when a teenager in Saudi Arabia was found to have stolen water power. This occurred when the M.E. operated under different rules, and the teenager was promptly executed. In other news . . ."

I want to reach for Gem, to grab her, to tell her how awful this is. But I can't let on that I have anything in common with Reginald Cramer. So when Gem shakes her head and mutters something like *how sad*, I do the same, mimicking, as if I'm just a normal artist who acquired powers the normal way, rather than a thief, the mirror image of this Chicago boy.

The news anchor begins talking about the stock market, but she's cut off, and the piece starts over. It's being played on a loop. The anchor's voice is a rusty saw to me, and I have to get away from it, so I yank on my practice uniform and head to the field.

On the field, we move through our drills, running laps in

the rising morning heat, then sprints, then push-ups, then crunches. We separate according to our powers and begin rehearsing our tricks for the next shows, reviewing the familiar ones, improving the newer ones. As I shoot flames from my hands, I picture them, those who make the rules, those who require registries, those who get to decide who can and can't be powerful, who get to deem the ways we can and can't be successful. Those who don't care if you had to steal just to survive.

Images of them—the rule makers—parade before my eyes. I grit my teeth, clench my jaw, and it's easy, so insanely simple, to craft my fire twin this time.

Mattheus hoots and I'm shocked. I didn't expect to replicate myself. I didn't plan it. But as in Wonder, as in my brother's warped world of underground raves in insane asylums, the fire has fled my body in the shape of me. Instinct kicks in, and I spread my arms over my head. My fire twin imitates me, creating an arc above her that shoots higher than mine, racing, sprinting to the sky. I clasp my hands instantly, and both she and her sparks are snuffed. Mattheus marches over to me, beaming.

"Tonight. Next show. Can you do that again?"

"Yes."

I answer without hesitation because I know now I can do it again. My twin isn't a fluke. I wasn't angry enough before. When I came to New York and moved away from my father, it's as if the distance muted my anger. But the rules and the laws and the stupid, awful reality of my half-baked heart are all too real once again. I don't even know how I'll pay for my wish, but I'll have to figure that out soon, and hell if that doesn't make me mad.

I fire off several more replicas. Several more copies that shoot flames as high and as wide as they can go. Mariska watches me. Her jaw-dropped, google-eyed stare makes it clear she'd never mock me for my work ethic again.

The fire inside me crackles and growls. It burns off corners of who I am, like flames stalking through a forest, ripping off branches and swallowing twigs. I keep going, an artist gone wild, who no longer makes sparks and starlight but fearsome, legendary, wild duplicates.

If my father were here right now, I'd shoot fireballs in his direction. Then I'd roast marshmallows on the flames as he cooked. I'd watch, steely-eyed, as the fire he tried but failed to make in me, the fire I went out and took from the sky, burned him alive.

My image is broken when Mattheus whistles. I notice all the coaches and all the teammates and even a few of the staffers, the woman who processes paychecks, the guys who clean the locker rooms. They've all migrated to the field. To see the Girl Prometheus do the thing she skipped a grade for, to finally after all this time, deliver.

To see her unleash wildfire from her hands. Bending, racing, rising high and hot above us, obedient to only me. Fueled by the desire to not just kill her own father but to also rage against all the rules that have trapped her, that have made her into *this*.

Something I never, ever wanted to be.

Now I am.

Now it's awful, more awful than it ever was.

21

Master and Servant

It's show night, and Intrepid Arena is packed.

Imran is here. Mattheus called him after practice. Imran was in Boston visiting some of his underscouts, who check out the newly gifted and chat up parents about the farm leagues. Mattheus told him to take the next shuttle back, and now Imran is here in Central Park for tonight's performance of Coeur de la Nature. He finds me before the show, plants his hands on my shoulders.

"I knew you'd be a star."

He's beaming, proud of his find. I don't know what to say. My heart feels like coal. My head feels vacant. I am probably narrowing my eyes at him, at this man who gave me every chance I've ever wanted. Only, when I take those chances, I feel parts of me sliced off, making room for darkness, for badness, like my brother warned. I force my mind to my sister. To her sweetness. To her snarky sense of humor. It makes me feel the slightest bit human again. She is worth this. She is worth everything I will ever have to do.

"Thanks."

I walk to the stage, decked out in the slinkiest of black outfits—a sleek, tight thing covering most of my skin, and I give the audience what they want; fireworks and flaming art.

Then I move on to the main attraction, to the special trick the audience has been whispering about since they walked down the aisles, slid into seats, and waited with their programs in hand. They'd heard tonight's show would be special; rumors had started to spread.

At last the girl from Wonder might be wonderful.

I start small with the twin, moving her hands and her arms with mine.

Then I move on to the release, to the flames she shoots high. Her shadowy, shimmery talent elicits gasps and cheers. I even turn in a circle, my twin turning with me. Bending, bowing, almost dancing, though I don't really dance. But then, she has a mind of her own. She steps without me. I startle, look at her, my mouth agape for the briefest of seconds. Then I snap my fingers to turn her off. But as she burns out, one small piece of her flames shears off, racing away from me, and my chest lurches.

I *know* this moment.

I know it too well.

The spark drops quickly down to the ground, landing in a fading fireball at my foot. I stomp it theatrically, raise my arms triumphantly.

I meet Imran's eyes, and he's so immensely satisfied with me. He has no idea what the errant spark means.

Loss of control.

I tell myself it's a misstep. This is the first night with a new trick. It's not an unraveling. It's not the beginning of the end. But I don't know that I believe me.

Later, I sit on the bench in the locker room, my head dropped into my hands.

"Hey, you all right?"

Gem's voice is soft, concerned. I look up at her, wanting to say I feel like soot, I feel blackened, and I'm terrified now too. How is it possible to house so many different feelings in one body? How is there room for all this emptiness, all this fear, all this hate?

I nod. "Just tired, I think."

"You want to walk back together?"

"Actually," I start, but I don't have to finish, because Gem jumps in.

"You're going to see that guy tonight, aren't you?"

I manage a slight smile, and it's partly for Gem and partly for Taj. They seem to be the only things that can counteract the tangled mess of me.

"I think so," I say. "I mean, yes. Yes, I am."

Gem smiles broadly, and I mirror her, and soon she's telling me to go for it, and I tell her I want to, I really want to.

"You can do my daisy tomorrow."

"I promise."

Taj isn't waiting for me outside the Lipstick Building. He's not near any of the grates. I've circled the block three times. I've peeked into all the nearby grates that surround this building shaped like a tube of lipstick. I've whispered his name, I've called his name. I don't want to rub the lamp. Not yet. It seems so . . . demeaning.

I try one more time. "Taj. Are you there?"

"Lost something?"

I look up, startled. An older woman with white hair and a bent-over back looks at me kindly.

"Um, I thought I dropped my phone," I say, improvising. If my phone were named after a boy.

"Oh, dear. These grates are so dangerous. I thought perhaps you'd lost a doggie under the sidewalks. I once did. But then I found him near the park. A nice young man brought him back for me."

Then there's a bleating sound from my back pocket. My ringtone. I grab my phone. Elise is calling.

"Looks like you found it," the lady says with a smile and shuffles off.

"Hey," I say into the phone. "Aren't you out at sea?"

"Yeah, but we're closer to shore now, so I finally got a decent signal. But it won't last long and I have to tell you something."

"Is everything okay?" I ask, as I step away from the grate and walk to the doorway.

"Yeah, obviously. But I kinda think I should be asking you that question. Are you using a granter?" Her voice sounds tense.

"Yes. But what do you have to tell me? Is everything okay?"

"Listen, it's your brother."

I close my eyes and grasp for the nearest thing, the rough edges of a brick building, to steady myself. "What's going on?"

"He's fine, but Kyle said one of his buddies saw Xavi over at the abandoned mental institution and that he was using his fire. You know the place I'm talking about?"

I know it too well. "Yep." I sink down to the sidewalk, crouching. "Is he doing more than lighting up at the abandoned asylum?"

"I'm not sure. Kyle thought he saw him shooting off flames near an old car too. He gave him kind of a warning. Kyle said Xavier was there with a bunch of guys he might have known from his time in prison. They were doing all sorts of stuff, you know?"

"Yeah, I can imagine."

"I know you can't stop him. I know you're not even here and you have a million things on your mind. But maybe you can talk some sense into him. I mean, if he's caught by the authorities, then, well, you know. It's life, for sure."

"I know," I say, my voice heavy. "I just don't think he'll listen to me, though."

"But you should try. And, I'm still working on August. You may not have to—"

Then the line goes dead.

But I have to, I want to say. *I have to.*

From my perch on the sidewalk I dial Xavier. He picks up on the first ring. "You need to stop," I tell him, not bothering with small talk. "They're onto you. The cops are going to find out. You need to stop and you need to stop now before you do something stupid. You need to look out for Jana."

"Stop? Ar, you're crazy. We've already sold like eighty tickets to our first show. We're going to bring in some serious change."

"Don't you get it, Xavi? You have a record. They know who you are. They're keeping an eye on you. They'll be thrilled to send you away forever if you light up another car."

"Aria, I've told you not to worry about me."

"I am worried about you, Xavi. I need you and I love you and I can't have you locked up again. And you have to look out for Jana. So stop this stuff, please? I'm making some money, and next year when I'm eighteen, I won't have to split the paychecks with Dad. And I can give you whatever money you need."

"Aria, I'm not taking money from you."

"Why not?"

"You're my baby sister."

"And Jana is *our* baby sister, so you can't afford to get locked up. Be careful, Xavi. Are you keeping an eye on her like I told you?"

"Yes. I even went with them to the beach on Sunday, okay?"

"The beach?" I say, tensing up because that's the worst place for my dad to take Jana.

"Yeah, the beach. That big expanse of sand that meets the ocean. You familiar with it?"

"Yes, Xavi. But . . ." I let my voice trail off, afraid to say the words out loud.

"But what?"

"Did anything happen?"

"Happen like what?"

I suck in a breath then blurt it out. "Did Dad hurt Jana?"

He scoffs as if the idea is ludicrous. "No! He was swimming with her the whole time. Whole day. It was fabulous. I was even able to fall asleep in the sun."

My heart falls. "Xavi, please be careful. I love you."

"I'll try," he says. "I love you too."

Then we say good-bye, and I stare at the phone for a few seconds, wishing I could unwind the day, tie it up, and tuck it away in a drawer while I rewrite my messed-up, broken family into a normal, happy one. Instead, I try again for Taj. I return to the Lipstick Building, to the grate where I'm supposed to have a kinda, sorta, maybe date.

I exhale when I see a strong hand holding up the grate a few inches. I kneel.

"Hi."

"Hi. Can I come up?"

"Do you need my permission?" I ask.

He nods. "Yes."

"But you didn't the first night."

"That was the first night. And last night, you came down to the library, but I couldn't leave until you okayed it. Because now, I am at your beck and call. You know, that old bond thing between granter and wisher."

Master and servant—the roles don't technically make sense because the granter possesses incredible, monstrous power, yet the wisher claims all the control.

Taj shifts his eyes to the grate he's holding up. His arms must be quite strong, his muscles under those long shirtsleeves sharp and defined. I stare at his arms, at the way the fabric of those crisp shirts he wears stretches across his muscles when he holds up the grate.

The heavy iron grate.

"Of course. Come up," I say, breaking my reverie.

He lifts the grate higher and swings his body up onto the sidewalk, then drops the grate with a heavy clang. He brushes one palm against the other. "Sorry I'm late. I was talking to my mom."

"Your mom? Is she down there?"

"No. But we have other ways to communicate. We try to talk now and then, since granters can't see their family members. But I like talking to her."

"I wish my mom would talk to me," I say wistfully. Then my eyes go wide at the word I just used aloud with a granter. I hold up a hand. "Wait. That wasn't a wish. That wasn't an official wish."

"Don't worry, Aria. You'd have to offer me something first. Don't forget—there's always an exchange."

"What should I offer you?" I ask because I know soon I'll have to pay. Soon I'll need to come up with some kind of currency.

"Do you want to get into this? Into how the exchange works? Whenever you're ready, I'll tell you. That's how it works. You say you're ready, and I am instantly obligated as a mastered granter to review all the rules, provisos, and conditions of wishing and the guidelines you'll have to follow for payment."

There goes his free will again. There go his choices. The more I get to know him, the more I learn he's a lot like me.

He doesn't have a lot of choices. But I still have free will, and so the least I can do is let him have a taste of what it's like to be free for a night. After my evening, I'd rather have a respite for a few hours.

"No. Not now at least. Let's do something else," I suggest, then insecurity rears its head. I don't even know if he likes me. "I mean, if you want to."

"Want to crash another show? Go bowling? Mini golf? Walk in the park? See the rooftop of the Met Life Tower?"

My eyes widen.

"Yes. That one. The last one."

Taj reaches for my hand, and we're not underground, he's not leading me through the tunnels. He's just holding my hand. I slide my fingers into his and meet his eyes. There's a flicker between us, a spark in our touch, and I'm pretty sure it has nothing to do with being granter and wisher and everything to do with being boy and girl alone in the big city at night.

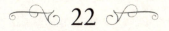

22

Ticking Clock

The Met Life Tower is streaked with gray, but it's not from dirt or soot. It's from a marbling of the stone that forms the building. At night, the building is eerie and shadowy, as if it's shrouded in secrets. As if the building could talk, tell us things it's seen in this city after hours.

Or maybe Taj is the one who could tell me things. He must have seen all the corners of New York. He dips his free hand into a pocket and shows me a key.

"Granter perk?"

"Nope. I did a job for a security guard's sister a while ago."

"And so, naturally, you have a key to the Met Life Tower."

"To many buildings, actually. New York Times Building. The new World Trade Center. Even the Empire State Building."

"Really?"

"Really, indeed. O ye of little faith."

"And you got them all from a security guard?"

Taj shrugs casually. "He had to make a trade. For his sick

sister. He needed to pay up. That's what he had, so that's what he paid with. It works well for me."

Soon we'll have to talk about payment. Soon I'll have to find the currency I can trade with too.

He notices the change in my features. "Don't worry. You'll get to pay me too," he says, making light of this reality. Of the fact that he probably hates being a bank for people like me.

"I don't have much."

"Everyone thinks that, but everyone has something they can part with when they have a great enough need. Does this mean you're ready?"

Yes, I want to say. Yes, because of Xavier now. But I need one more night for me.

"No. Not yet."

"Good. Because I hear it's beautiful on the balcony."

Taj puts a hand on my back, and his fingertips slide across the fabric of my shirt in a way that sends shivers through my skin. I wonder if he knows his touch is doing something to me, making me feel things I've never allowed myself to feel. He steers me around to the side of the building, to what looks like a fire exit. He presses the key into the lock and pulls the door open. We're in a stairwell that extends to the top of the building, as far as I can tell.

I start to walk up the steps.

"We can take the elevator." He nods to the door that must lead to the lobby.

"Oh, I can manage the stairs," I say playfully.

"You think I can't? That's cute. That's really cute."

Up we go, nearly fifty flights of stairs, legs burning, lungs aching, panting as we reach the top floor.

"Didn't realize you'd be getting a workout tonight too, did you? See, I know how to bring it when it comes to F-U-N," he says.

"Next time, let's try the Empire State Building. You might be forgetting this girl works out every day."

"Ooh, show-off," he teases, and now he's just the boy who likes to have fun with a girl. There are so many facets to him, and I want him to know that I have many sides to me too, only I hardly ever show them.

We're near the top of the building now, and he holds the door open for me. I walk out onto the balcony. It circles the peak of the Met Life Tower with a spire above us, a clock right below us. A high fence surrounds the perimeter, and there's a perfect view of Manhattan, the rivers that surround the island, and the towns that lie far beyond. I gaze up at the sky. The stars are barely visible. The city below is a quiet hum of a radio at night.

"It's amazing," I whisper as I wrap my fingers around the railing at the edge of the building.

"It is. It really is," he says, and his tone has the sound of the first time, as if he's drinking in this view for the first time.

I turn to look at him, at his profile, his sharp cheekbones, his dark skin, his hair the color of night. He shifts his gaze to me.

"You've never been up here before, have you?"

He shakes his head.

"What about the other buildings you have the keys to?"

"Never been to them either."

"Because your wisher would have to want to go?" I ask, though it's more a statement, because this is a puzzle I'm putting together.

"You got it."

"Can I ask you something?"

"Of course."

"Do you usually take your other wishers or potential wishers or whatever they're called, whatever we're called," I say, stumbling through my question as my cheeks flame red. "You know, around the city or whatever?"

He doesn't answer right away. Instead, he touches my wrist with his index finger, tracing a line across my skin. His touch is magnetic. I want to feel his fingertips draw road maps all over my arms. I try to concentrate on something else, on the view, on the city, on the phone calls I just had, on my faraway family, but I can't grab hold of them. They are slippery, and they slink away like banished ghosts, forbidden from my here and now.

"No," he says, then runs his finger up my bare arm, across the inside of my elbow. "I never wanted to. Nor did I ever have the opportunity. Most wishers aren't interested in hanging out. They don't want to get to know their granter. They make their wish, they pay, and then they go. Or they don't make their wish, and they leave."

"So what does that make me? Indecisive?" I ask, as his hands reach my hair. I lean into his hands, letting him slide his fingers through the thick strands of my hair. His moves are slow and gentle, as if he savors each touch. I don't have questions about him anymore. They are all vapor; they have all turned to mist. There are only answers, and he's giving them all to me in a way I feel is not a one-way street.

"I don't know. Are you indecisive? Do you want to make a wish right now?"

"Kind of," I whisper.

"What would you wish for?"

His hand reaches the back of my head, his other hand finds my waist, and rests on the edge of my miniskirt. We are so close now, separated by less than inches.

"Hypothetically, of course," he adds.

"Hypothetically," I repeat, my eyes locked on his deep-brown eyes, as if I'm in a trance. "I think I might not have to wish for it. I think it might happen anyway."

He raises an eyebrow in that playful way he has.

"Presumptuous, are you?"

I nod, lick my lips, as he holds me tighter, brings me closer, my hips against his, his hand in my hair. "I want you to kiss me," I say.

"Your want is my command."

His lips brush mine. His kiss is soft and tender, his lips gentle and lingering on mine. It is a slow kiss, a warm kiss, and it's enough to make me melt into his touch. I part my lips and soon we're kissing more deeply. My hands are reaching into his hair, silky and soft. He doesn't have that soapy, woody smell of other boys. He smells like oranges, and he tastes like sunshine. The perfect contrast to the shadows in my body, the dark space between my muscles. The more I kiss him, the more I taste him, the more of him I want. Somehow, we've managed to move even closer, and I feel warmer than I've been before, and freer. I don't bring any baggage, or history, or walls when I'm with him.

I'm the opposite of who I've been, and with him all I want is closeness. All I want is more of this.

Soon we pull apart for air.

"To answer your question, no."

"No what? What question?" I ask.

"Have I kissed my wishers before?"

"I wasn't going to ask that," I say, but my big fat grin gives away my white lie.

He runs a finger across my top lip and I'm about to lean in for another kiss, but then his hands are on my cheeks, cupping my face. "You're the only one I've spent time like this with, Aria."

My face is flushed and my heart is lurching toward him. I don't know how any of this has happened, but yet I know exactly how it's happened too. Because he's the first boy I've ever let into my heart, and I don't want to make a wish, because in so doing I'd be wishing him away.

"I thought about you before I came to New York," I whisper.

His eyebrows knit together in question.

"I saw your picture when I was in Florida. Mariska posted it online. I thought you were . . . beautiful."

"Beautiful," he repeats with a smile.

"You are. I want to draw you."

"Draw me?"

"I make little graffiti drawings. I want to try drawing you."

"I want to watch you do that."

"I want to keep seeing you," I whisper.

He leans his forehead against me. "Me too."

Then he pulls back. "But I have a job to do, and you have a need, and we should talk payment soon."

He's serious again, but this time he's business serious, by-the-book serious.

"Taj, I don't want to talk about that."

"But we have to."

"Why? You said we only had to talk about it when I brought it up. That that was part of being a mastered granter," I say, and the last two words taste bitter. Still, I don't want to go there right now.

A shadow falls across his eyes. The warmth of a few seconds ago starts to dissipate. "Because that's part of being bound. You might be able to do whatever you want, but I can't just run around forever and ever. Sure, you're my master and you can dictate what I do, but we can't play at this until the end of time."

"Why not?" Maybe I should run away. Maybe we could run away. "We could get out of here. Get out of town. We could go. You'd never have to live underground again. You'd never have to stop living again. You could just be, right?"

It occurs to me that it would be far too early in a normal relationship to suggest running away with a boy. But this isn't a normal relationship by any stretch, so I don't feel clingy or needy by asking him. I feel as if I'm taking charge of my own fate.

"Ar, I love the thought. But I can't." He holds his palms out, showing me they're empty, of course. "There's always a ticking clock."

"Why? Do you turn into a pumpkin at midnight for real? Do you expire after seven days with a wisher?"

He shakes his head. "If we ran away, then you'd, for all

intents and purposes, no longer be in such desperate need of a wish. That's how I found you, remember? That's how you found me. I don't come to everyone who needs something. Some people need things in life—a home, good health, escape—but they're not wanting to wish, so we don't appear. But when someone is so hungry for a wish, like you were, that's when I'm called. I could sense your need, your deep, desperate need to wish. That's what summoned me to you. When you stop needing a wish, you'll no longer be my wisher. When someone decides they no longer need a wish, I can't be kept at their beck and call," he explains.

"Is that what happened to Mariska the night I met you? She was done wishing, so you were no longer at her beck and call?"

"Her situation was a bit different," he says evasively.

"So what happens if I don't need a wish, then?"

"I won't be able to come out to see you. I'll cease to exist, whether you wish or not. It's only the condition of your needing something so badly that keeps me with you. When that goes away, I can't stay."

It's as if I've been dreaming, sinking farther away into pretend, into the land of make-believe. Now, I've been harshly awakened. This thing between us is like my fire. Always ticking, always unwinding.

I kick the rooftop, a petulant child.

"I wish there were another way." I walk away for a minute. "That wasn't a real wish," I call out, and I pace toward the other edge of the balcony, thinking, working through scenarios, looking for a loophole. But I find none, because magic makes its own loopholes. It circles back in on itself and twists inward, like those trees whose roots sprout back up to form new branches, but they're all part of the same mother tree, never splintering off to become their own.

I walk back to him. The faint sound of a siren plays far below, cars and life happening many stories away. "How exactly does the payment thing work?" I need information so I can come up with a plan.

"Wishes don't come free."

"That much is loud and clear. How do I pay?"

"*Dearly*. You pay dearly," he says through clenched teeth, as if the words pain him.

"Like how dearly? The key the guy gave you? That hardly seems very high a price."

"It was for him. The keys were his livelihood. He didn't just give me keys. He gave up his job in exchange for the wish. Besides, his sister became well again, so I assume he felt it was worth it."

"Oh. So the keys are sort of symbolic. But that doesn't seem fair for him to give up a job."

"I don't make the rules, Aria. I have no say in them. I only administer them. It's not as if I wanted this job. It's not as if I asked for it. I may have the magic, but I have *no say*," he says, enunciating the last two words carefully.

"So how else do people pay for wishes? With money?"

He shakes his head. "Rarely with money. Some people have paid for wishes with their children."

I stop pacing and stare hard at him. "Their children? You can't be serious."

"Big wishes come at a big price."

"That's awful."

"Some people pay with their hearts. Some offer their souls. Some offer themselves."

"Themselves? Like they give you their bodies?" I ask, and I can't keep the jealousy out of my question.

He senses it and laughs. "No. Not that way, Aria. But I'm glad to know it bothers you."

"Stop," I say. "Don't go all sexy on me again. I want information."

"Sexy? You think I'm sexy?"

"Yes. Anyway, how do they pay with their bodies?"

"Not their bodies," he says, laughing. "Some pay with themselves. They offer themselves in a trade. Then when it's time to collect on the debt, they would trade places with a granter."

"But you're still here. So no one has offered you themselves."

"Correct. But I've seen what other wishers have offered."

"In the registry? Is it like a big book?"

He nods. "Yes. Granters are all in a union. We're regulated. And every wish is recorded in our registry within twenty-four hours of it being granted. That way, wishers can't ever wish again. You get one wish for life, and that's it. It keeps wishers from abusing granters. It prevents granter addiction. That was a big problem many years ago. Wishers kept coming back, or they'd find other granters they hadn't used before, so the union implemented more checks and balances."

"That makes sense," I say in my businesslike tone. "Elemental arts are like that too. We're super regulated. We have to be registered, and then the Leagues have all these crazy rules too about our powers. So that's what you meant when you said I was free to wish, right? Because I wasn't in the registry, right?"

"Exactly. Plus, we all have different districts we work in. Like jurisdictions. But some granters just work for the union, so they're not underground, and they don't really deal with wishers. They just enforce the rules. The career granters love rules. They are crazy about rules. They love setting them up and administering them."

"Is that something a granter aspires to? Working in the union? Is that like a move up? Being a career granter?"

"I guess. In the union or as a career granter working in administration you get to live all the time."

He says it in such a matter-of-fact tone, but the words are another punch in the gut. *Live all the time*.

"You have a jurisdiction. What's yours? All of New York City?"

"I'm Manhattan."

"Manhattan," I say, trying on the word in a new way, as if it's his name.

"That's why we're required to record all wishes in the registry. So if someone went to a granter in another country or state or wherever, they'd know and they could turn them down free and clear."

"Has that happened to you? Has someone summoned you, and you found out they had a past," I say, sketching air quotes, "of wishing?"

"Absolutely." He nods his head in a resolute way. "We're like a drug to some people. One wish is never enough, so they try for more. Or they try to undo the wish, or undo the payment."

"So when do you collect on these payments?"

"Some I've collected on already. Some are coming due soon. It varies. The length of the loan, that is."

I breathe out hard and something clicks. "Right. Because that's what a wish is. A loan right? You always have to pay up somehow?"

"Yes. You do. There is always some sort of price. Even with a jackass granter, the wisher pays literally in the way the wish is made. As for all the others, only a few very savvy wishers have found their way around the payment."

"Like with the snow gator?"

He shakes his head. "I can't tell you, Aria. Granter-wisher privilege."

"Right, but a snow gator? C'mon. That's the legend around him. Won in some sort of bet for knowledge. Did she get to keep him after proving she wouldn't abuse the arts or the knowledge or something?"

Another shake of the head. "You won't get this one out of me," he says.

But where else would a snow gator come from? He *has* to be from a wish, or a payment.

"So some payments are delayed. And some wishers pay off their debt. But do all wishers have to pay up?"

"Oh, they all have to pay. But every deal is different, different conditions, provisos, quid pro quos."

"A deal with the devil," I say.

"Some say that."

"So what would I pay with?"

"I don't know. What would you be willing to give up?"

I have so little to trade. And the thing that makes me valuable—my fire power—is the thing I have to wish for. I can't bargain with my gifts. Do I offer my soul? My heart? My life? Myself? My family? None of those sound vaguely appealing.

I picture the TV screen from this morning. The Chicago boy being hauled away. I think of my mom in her chair, my sister's frozen hands, my dangerous brother, and my father. I wish I could trade him, but he's faulty and flawed and no one would want him.

I press my palm against my forehead.

"This makes my head hurt," I say softly.

"Mine too."

I take a step closer, then lean my head against his chest. I hate these stupid consequences. I hate the way everything has a dark side. I hate my own dark side, how it lashed me today. Most of all, I hate that I wanted to feel every dark thing, to do every dark thing.

I don't feel that way now though. I feel safe, and it's so foreign but so welcome. "I don't want to think about payment right now," I say into his shirt.

He strokes my hair. "So don't. At least for tonight. Do you want to lie down and look at the stars instead?"

"Yes."

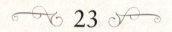

23

Starlight

Taj lies down on the rooftop and I join him. He clasps his hands behind his head. He is lithe and beautiful, witty and trapped. For this moment, though, he is free, as he gazes at the endless night sky.

He reaches for my hand and laces his fingers through mine. Butterflies race through me with the slightest touch. I like this. I run my free hand through his soft hair. "How did you become a granter? You said you've been one since you were almost sixteen. That's not long."

He doesn't answer right away. I wonder what's going through his head, or if he's just drinking in the stars and the sky, soaking in the nighttime, the outdoors, the things he rarely sees.

Then he turns to me, shifts onto his side. "I was payment."

My skin prickles at his words. "Payment? In what way?"

"I was traded. I was the debt. And it came due."

"How do you mean?"

"I haven't told this to anyone before, Aria. No one has ever asked." His voice is low, pinched with nerves.

"It's okay. You can tell me," I say, doing my best to sound brave, as if I can handle whatever he's going to say.

"You've heard rumors about peace in the M.E.?"

"Well, they're true. It is peaceful there."

"Right. But I mean how it came to be peaceful. Do you know what they say? What people say about it?"

"All I know is, they say it had something to do with granters, but no one really knows."

"Well, I know how it happened," he says, punctuating each word like they're thumbtacks. "It came about through the leaders of each country. They made a pact with granters. The leaders worked together and they found nearly a dozen granters, and they made a wish. A wish so big it had never been wished before. A wish so big, so expansive, the granters weren't sure if they could deliver on it. So the granter union and the granters too set terms, and a time frame. Like a loan. To see if they could do it, to see if they could bring peace to a war-torn land. And the leaders made their offerings. They offered their children in exchange."

I am cold all over; my charred heart turns to ice. "They offered their children?"

"That was the payment. That was the deal. That in ten years, if peace still reigned, if the granters had delivered on the wish— delivered peace—then the granters would be freed. In their place, the firstborn children of the leaders would become the next generation of granters."

"Your parents traded you for peace?" I ask, as if saying the question can make it not so, as if expressing my own incredulity can turn this conversation into something that makes logical sense.

"Yes."

"Both of them? Both of them did?"

"Well, it was my father's idea," he says. "My father is in charge of one of the countries in the M.E."

"Your dad is in charge of a whole country?"

If we weren't high up on a rooftop, all of Manhattan might have just heard me. They might have heard me anyway.

"Yes."

"And your mom went along with it?"

"That's sort of how it goes when your dad runs the country."

"That's like my house too. My dad is in charge of everything. But," I say, shaking my head, getting away from my lame little family in a run-down Florida ranch home, "do you talk to your parents? Can you ever see them?"

"I talked to my mom the other night."

"Do you just talk on the phone or something?"

He laughs. "Yes, on the phone. I'm allowed to call her once a month when I'm free."

"Do you ever talk to your dad?"

He shakes his head. "No. Can't say I care to."

"I take it you're not too fond of him."

"I understand why he did it. I do, I really do," Taj says emphatically, as if reminding himself that he's cool with his dad's sacrifice. "But I understand it on a big-picture level. Like, yeah, peace. Peace is good. We all want it. We'd all wish for it. But the price, I don't know. I suppose it could be worse. I'm just a granter. I'm not dead."

"I think that's a terrible thing to do to a child," I say as if I'm the authority on this matter. Then I back down. "I'm sorry. I shouldn't diss your family."

"It's okay. Like I said, sometimes I understand it. And sometimes I hate it. And sometimes I wish I could just tell the story and it would be so entertaining and so compelling that it would free me."

"We'll write you a new story, and somehow the story will free you," I say, even though I know we can't. "I'm sorry about your parents, Taj. And I'm sorry about what happened."

"Thanks. It'd be nice just to be normal, wouldn't it?"

"Totally. Sometimes I just want to be a normal kid. Try to get a normal job. Make pizzas or be a barista. Not this. I don't want fire."

"If you wanted to be free, you could wish your powers gone."

"Ha. That'd cause me even more problems."

"But you could. You could wish to be normal."

"Would you? Wish to be normal if you could?"

"What I would wish for is irrelevant."

"Why? We're just talking."

"It just is."

"But I want to know," I say, pressing the issue as the stars flicker in the sky. "Tell me what you'd wish for, Taj. You'd wish to be free, wouldn't you?"

"This isn't some movie where you get three wishes and you use the last one to free me. Wishers don't use their wishes on me, even though wishing a granter free is the only wish that requires no payment from the wisher. And so, the only thing that can break me out is the only thing that will never happen."

"Why?"

He waits before speaking, touches my face, tracing the edge of my hair.

"Besides a wish, it's love," he says, by way of an answer.

"Love?" I ask, and I'm warm again, craving nearness to him when he talks about love.

"Yet another proviso of granter-hood. The only other way you can be freed is if someone falls in love with you."

"Who would make that rule? I get the whole wish-you-free thing. But how would a rule come to be about love?"

"Because love makes its own rules," he says in an off-hand way.

"What do you mean?"

"Because love can often transcend rules. And that's why the granter union made a rule. There was a time many years ago when wishers were falling into infatuation with granters, and that freed the granter. *Poof!*" He holds his hands out as if he were a magician who made a dove disappear. "Because love was powerful in its own right, and the union needed to control that power the only way it could. By attaching a rule to it. The union couldn't stop love from freeing granters, but they could ensure that only true love did, and that granters weren't slipping out of the system through unregulated infatuations that would then fade quickly away. Now the only kind of love that can free a granter is the kind of crazy, in-love-with-your-whole-heart kind of thing. It erases any payment due from the wisher, and it frees the granter, right then, right there, on the spot. But as you can imagine, that hasn't happened. Infatuation, yes. Lust, yes. Crushes, absolutely. But true and real love?" He shakes his head. "Wishers don't have the time or inclination to fall into a deep and abiding love. Besides, how would I know when it happens? I've never been in love."

"I've never been in love either," I whisper. Then I kiss him, and as we recline high above New York City, hanging out on a rooftop, I picture using my wish on him. I have that power. I could set him free.

But then I'd have a whole new set of problems to deal with.

24

A Gust of Wind

I am bleary-eyed as I stumble into practice the next day. I have my sunglasses on and coffee in my hand, and I'm starting to get used to the beverage and the need for it. We have another show tonight, but our practice is only a few hours today. I didn't sleep much last night. I stared at the ceiling, making checklists of pros and cons of various wishes. I could wish for true fire and then never have to pierce my heart again. That would be the fastest and safest way to ensure I could protect my family. Or I could wish Taj free and save someone who's been enslaved.

If I did that though, could I find a different way to save my sister? What if I ran away from the Leagues and sneaked Jana out in the middle of the night, then trekked with her cross country, far away from anyone who could hurt her?

But I don't have the money yet. That's the problem.

We run through our morning drills, the standard stretches and sprints, then we break out into our packs, air artists in one spot, wind artists in another. I move with the fire artists, and we run through our tailored drills—the fireballs, the plumes of flames, the arc of fireworks high overhead. We all peel off these moves as if they're second nature, because they are.

But at the tail end of practice a fireball skitters away from me. Mattheus grunts, tells me to pay more attention. I nod, like it's just a gaffe. Then my chest tightens hard, like a fist gripping my heart. Another sign that the unwinding is near. Soon I'm going to spit up all my sputtering fire, only this time it's taken me less than two months to come undone, and this time the consequences are far worse.

I manage to fake my way through my fear, like I've faked my way through most of my life. I make it through the final ten minutes without flubbing any more moves, and it's enough to give me a speck of hope that I can pull off tonight's show without any problems.

Gem and I are about to leave and grab something to eat when Raina appears in the locker room, her sculpted arms on display in a sleeveless silk top. I imagine inking her bicep with a cartoon cat stretching its back luxuriously. But the cat's tongue will stick out. It will have forgotten to pull its sandpaper tongue back into its mouth.

Raina says nothing, just walks close to us. Her nose twitches when she passes me. It's as if she's smelling me.

"Let's go get those sandwiches," I say to Gem.

After we eat—I opt for a salad instead of a sandwich, back to my good-girl ways—Gem stretches out her leg across mine. She's wearing shorts, and she points to her muscular thigh. "Now."

I take a pen from my backpack, lean over, and begin drawing a don't-mess-with-me daisy. This daisy scowls. This daisy would wear a leather jacket and light matches on the bottom of her boots. This daisy would toss her desk over in one fell swoop to knock out a bully.

As I color in the petals, Gem presses for details of my date.

"We kissed," I say, grateful to tell her, and then I'm suddenly sharing all details, and I sound like a schoolgirl, not a badass daisy, and definitely not like the fire thief who on her last night in Wonder made out with a guy whose name she didn't know.

"What's his name?"

"Taj."

"Cool name," she says. "Where's he from? It's kind of unusual."

"Not here," I tease.

"Obviously. But where?"

I mention Taj's home country. "His family is from there. But they've been here for a while." A white lie, but it's close enough.

"So does he go to school?"

School. Such a foreign thought. But those of us who haven't graduated yet—like me—will be tutored come fall and go to school a few hours a day.

Thinking about the fall reminds me of other things about the fall. Like where Taj will be. Where I'll be. What will happen to him if I wish for myself. What will happen to Jana if I wish him free.

Because I'm going to have to make my wish soon enough. Sooner than I want.

Hi. It's starting again. I can't wait till August. I'm sorry.

I'm sorry. I would swim to New York right now if I could.
Xoxo, Elise

At the show tonight, I ignite several magnificently tall flames that reach for the sky, that dare to stretch to the stars. I unfurl a series of successively larger canopies of fire that rain over my head, causing gasps and cheers among the thousands here. Then I unveil my twin, my heart and lungs twitching with nerves. What if I lose control of her again? But she behaves, mimicking me as I craft two plumes that howl and hiss and coil around each other. Hers do the same. Then the tip on one of my streaks of fire snaps off. No warning, no shudder in my heart to tip me off. Just a careening, crashing flame that turns into a very ordinary-looking fire when it hits the ground.

I do what I always do.

Improvise.

I fall to my knees and coax the fire back to my hands. Even though I'm fading, I somehow find enough in the reserves to turn the flames back into an arc above me. Then I see my twin. She's started to wander away from me, heading into the audience. Some stare at her in shock, bend away from her.

I close my hands and kill my twin.

They cheer. As if I meant to do that.

I take a bow, and I see Imran is in the front row again, and he doesn't look as happy as he did last night.

———

Gem and I walk to the dressing room in silence. Words are bottled up in my throat. I want to tell her how I feel, to admit that this insufferable fire is choking me from the inside out. That my fire is sick and twisted, but I don't have time to say that, because Imran is waiting for me. I can't read his expression—whether he's upset or concerned.

His arms are crossed and his honeyed voice is bare as he tells me, "Aria, we need to talk."

Gem meets my eyes, tries to ask silently *what's up* and *are you okay?* But there's no way to answer and no way to know. All I can think of is Reginald Cramer, the boy from Chicago who was made an example of by the Leagues. Will they make an example of me too? Or will they shoo me away, shut me up, a hush-hush case they won't want talked about? The thief who slipped into the system.

Leaden and heavy, I follow Imran, a prisoner being escorted to her own trial.

I have feared this moment for so long, and now it's here. I've ridden my chances to the edge, and now I have to pay.

"For starters, Raina has told me you are clean and I am pleased to hear that. I know someone with your abilities might have been tempted to use and to enhance them, especially seeing how powerful your creations are. And we've kept a close eye on you, given your family history."

The last few words are pointed and cutting. It seems unfair to my brother that they're eyeing me suspiciously because of him.

"But that's not why I called you in tonight. I'm afraid I have bad news."

I swallow, a nervous animal backed into a corner. But I steady myself, keeping my feet planted firm, my hands at my side, my head held high. Whatever he says, I'm going to take it. I'm going to take it like I know how to take bad news. I brace myself, ready to hear the words Reginald Cramer heard.

"It's about your brother."

All that steadiness rushes away. I feel blindfolded and turned around. What is he talking about? "What do you mean?"

Imran continues. "There were some new car bombings in Winter Springs. He was caught in the act."

My brother. My wild and careless brother. The brother I looked up to, the brother I loved, the brother who should have protected his two little sisters but in the end couldn't even look out for himself. I picture visiting him in prison again, talking to him through bars. My eyes grow hot and prickly, tears forming behind them. I try to blink them back, but one tear slides down each cheek.

I will miss him like crazy.

I have *always* missed him.

"Ordinarily, I'd give you some time off. I'd even arrange for a flight and let you spend a few days with your parents. But I really think it's best for you if you stay here and focus."

Imran doesn't want me near my brother. He thinks my family is tainted, that they'll rub off on me, on the Girl Prometheus. "Sure," I say, just to say something.

"I know it's hard," he continues. "But we believe in you, Aria. And even in spite of your family history, given all the things that they've done, we want you to stay and we know you can rise above."

"Of course," I say through tight lips that want to quiver, through eyes that want to pour out tears.

Soon he dismisses me, and I check my phone to see that Xavi called and there's a message too telling me he's sorry and he hopes I'll come visit him in prison.

———

My mother answers. I imagine her expelling a withering *oomph* as she reaches for the phone, a plaintive sort of moan to underscore the gigantic effort of making a movement.

"Hello?" Her voice is wavering. I suppose learning your eldest child is going back to prison for the rest of his life would be a little unnerving.

"Hey, Mom. It's me. I just wanted to check in on you. I heard the news."

She gulps and I hear tadpole tears in her throat.

"I'm sorry, Mom." I'm sitting on a stoop, on the steps outside someone's Upper West Side apartment building. The stoop is dark brown and the paint is cracked. The windows on the first floor have green shutters, and are dirty.

"Ohhhh." That's the only sound she makes. A sad and defeated *ohhhh* that loses steam.

"Are you sad?"

It's an obvious question. Of course she is sad. But in my

family, we have to ask the obvious question if we even want to circle the answer.

We talk about Xavier some more, and she cries deeper tears this time, big sobby ones that swim upstream through rivers and fling themselves on shores. I tell her it's okay, that she can cry with me, because I have a feeling she doesn't cry in front of my father.

"I wish I could be there right now. Do you want me to come visit? I can see if I can get away for a weekend or something," I say, even though I know I can't.

"Of course I do, sweetie. But your father's gone for his fishing trip, and I'm sure you'd want to visit when he's in town."

I snort. Hardly. This actually sounds like the perfect time for a visit, if only I could get away. "How long is he gone?"

"For about a week."

"Does he even know about Xavi?"

"Yes."

"And he went away anyway?"

"Well, there's nothing he can do about it, honey."

"Except maybe be there for his son, but that'd be too much to ask," I say, kicking the ground with my boot, wishing it were my father.

"Oh, darling. Don't say that about your father. He loves Xavi."

"Yeah. Well," I say, and suck in a breath. "Are you sure you don't need me? How are you managing on your own?"

"You need to focus on your job now. Don't worry about me. Never worry about me."

"I always worry about you, Mom."

She is small and shapeless. A tiny stain in her papasan chair.

"Hush, that's silly."

"How's Jana?"

"Oh, you know," she says, as if that constitutes an answer.

"No. I don't know. How is she? Her birthday is coming up soon, Mom. Her thirteenth birthday. We're going to know soon if she's something."

"Yes, in a week. Her birthday is in a week," she says, stating the obvious, avoiding the implications.

That's her answer? "Mom, how is she doing? Do you even see her? Is she staying with Mindy a lot, like she's supposed to?"

She must be shifting in her chair, squirming. Tough topics make her uncomfortable, and in this moment I want to lash out at her. She never used to be like this. She always used to talk, to answer, to teach. She taught me to read, to ride a bike, to look both ways when crossing the street. She used to be somebody, she used to be strong. Now she says nothing, does nothing. I want to tell her that right now she's as culpable as my father.

"Mom," I push. "Tell me what's going on."

"She's hardly around, Aria," my mother says, snapping at me, backed into a corner by my insistence.

"Is she staying with Mindy?" I ask again. "Please say that's where she is. Please, please." I don't know how much more I can hate myself for leaving her there. But if I have to, I can surely hunt down more self-loathing. Because this is all my fault.

"She's always at the pool or the beach, and when she comes home she won't talk. She goes to her room and slams the door. So there. I have failed her too. She won't talk to me. She won't tell me a thing. My son is in prison, my youngest won't speak to me, and you're the only one who cares."

A tsunami of tears comes next, waves of self-loathing from my mother, her admission—out of the blue—that she has failed.

I make some soothing sounds, telling her it'll be okay. But it won't be okay; she can't fix my sister, she couldn't help Xavi, and she can't stop my father.

Then my mother surprises me with what she says next. "Jana was leaving for the beach yesterday and I tried to talk to her, I tried to ask her how she was doing. I even got up. I made it to the door, but, Aria, I opened the door—"

"You opened the door?"

I haven't seen her near the door in years.

"Yes, but I couldn't make it past the door. I tried to step outside, but it was as if there was a gust of wind that blew me back inside."

"A gust of wind?" Maybe she's going crazy.

"And then I just felt as if everything had gone dark and black, and I fell down, and when I came to, I dragged myself back to my chair."

What kind of gust of wind would knock her out?

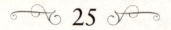

25

Cooling Effect

As my boots pound the sidewalk on the way to a grate on Sixty-Sixth Street, I have to fight this flickering inside me. It's like I have a nervous tic the way my shoulders seize up, but it's because my chest is an accordion, pinching and stretching all the organs inside it. I've never been around so many people when I'm in this state, all raw and exposed, a human body painted on a poster in science class with insides shown and labeled.

"And this, class, is the dangerous part," the teacher would say, her pointer aimed at my drawn and quartered heart.

I keep my head down, my hands laced behind my back, my fingers twisted around each other, so I don't unleash any flames. I want to sneer and bark at anyone who walks past me, to shout at them to get away, to ask why they're out at this hour. But it's New York. It's not Wonder, Florida, where I can wander around in the wee hours without being seen. Besides, it's my newfound darkness that makes me feel so mean.

As I round the corner and turn toward Lincoln Center, to

the grate Taj and I picked to meet at, I breathe out this coiled tension, but it has nowhere to go, so it filters back into me.

I reach the grate and call out to Taj.

He appears right away. I picture him racing through the tunnels, a rock being slung out of a slingshot, called forth by his wisher. He pops up the grate and asks if he can come up.

"Of course," I say, but I don't smile, because I think it's awful that he can't emerge without my permission.

Then he's beside me. "Hi."

"Hi," I say, and feel a little less awful. There's an awkward moment, as if neither one of us knows what's next and whether we're allowed to repeat last night, or whether we return to the way it was before. Then he moves first, leaning into my lips. I close my eyes, and his soft lips are on mine. With each second that ticks by, I can feel my chest loosening, a knot unwinding. My body doesn't feel torqued, and I realize it's because of him.

He leans his forehead against mine and asks the simplest of questions. "How was your day?"

It melts me that he wants to know, and it melts me again that I want to tell him how absolutely awful it was.

"Crummy," I say, stepping back and resting against the concrete wall that hems in Lincoln Center behind us. We're ensconced in a quiet little nook off the street, a semiprivate corner that makes me feel as if we're alone. "Yours?"

"It was good. I read a book."

"What book? Wait. Let me guess. Something fancy," I tease. "*Moby Dick*? *Ulysses*?"

"Mock my taste, why don't you?"

"I just did."

"I read a thriller. Espionage and government secrets and stolen identities across Europe. See, I have a wide range of tastes." He pauses, then the teasing recedes from both of us as he touches my cheek.

I take his hand and put it on my chest. His palm is warm against my skin, and his touch shoots sparks through me. He raises an eyebrow.

"Do you remember when you first put your hand on my chest?"

"Of course."

"I liked it a lot," I say, and I know it comes out shy sounding, and it's not because I'm a shy girl, it's because I've never let myself be vulnerable.

"Me too."

I place my hand over his, closer to me, covering my heart. "But it's more than just that when you touch me. Because a few minutes ago, all I wanted was to set the world on fire. And my chest hurt, like my bones were being squeezed. But when I'm near you, I don't feel that way at all."

I always thought I'd squirm if I ever told a guy I liked him, if I ever truly opened up to someone. But maybe that's because every boy I've ever known has been too much hometown, and home is what I've always wanted to leave.

"When I'm with you, I feel free," I whisper, and now I am vulnerable; now I have let down my guard. Instinct tells me to flee, but I resist.

"I feel that way too, Aria. When I'm with you, I feel free too." The words are heavy because, of course, he's not free. He can't be free unless I set him free. And here I am again, circling the same problem, arriving at the same answer. There are no more nights of waiting one more night to wish. I have to wish tonight. The prospect of losing him pierces me.

"Hey," he starts, shifting the conversation in another direction. "Why was your day so crummy?"

He takes my hand and we walk around the front of Lincoln Center. I feel unmoored again, now that we're not kissing or touching. I have the faintest desire to flick my fingers, to unleash a few sparks, and I know the contact with him has only cooled me momentarily. I am a steaming teakettle that was taken off the burner for a minute, but now it's been re-placed and the dial has been turned back up.

Reprieve doesn't last for long.

We reach the front of Lincoln Center and sit on the marble steps. I tell him about my day, about my brother, about the call with my mom, about what I think is going on with Jana. Taj stops me when I mention what happened with my mom, how she tried to open the door but couldn't.

"What did she say happened?"

"She said it was like a gust of wind. Everything went black and dark."

"Like she couldn't leave the house?" His throat sounds constricted as he asks.

"That's what she said."

"Aria, you told me before that she never leaves, right? That you haven't seen her out of the house in years?"

"Right."

"And now she said she was almost physically stopped by some sort of force before she left?" he asks carefully, taking his time with each word, as if each one is a clue being assembled into a proper order.

"Yes. Why? What is it?"

"Aria," he whispers. "Is your father's name Felix?"

Felix.

I never use his name. I try to never think of his name. It humanizes him. Hearing someone else speak it feels out of joint, a hinge being hung on the wrong-size door.

"Yes. Why?"

"I have to show you something."

"What? What do you have to show me?" I've had far too many surprises today. I don't want another one, especially one that has to do with my father.

"Trust me, please. Can you come with me? To my library?"

Underground we go.

26

Stupid Wishes

The tunnels are the kind of dark where you can't see the outline of your fingers, where you can't tell if the floor is beneath your feet.

We crunch along through the tunnel, its floor formed by hard-packed dirt and dankness, by naked walls under city streets. His hand holds mine so tightly they might as well be fused together, or maybe it's because I'm gripping his fingers so hard, forging them into mine. We turn a sharp corner and I stumble, separating from Taj. I fall on one knee, shooting out a hand to brace myself. As I connect with the floor, I release a small plume. The fire lights up the tunnel, and Taj jumps back, pressing himself against the wall.

"Aria, it's okay." He's trying to calm me, but I can tell he's scared too. Of what I might do. Truth is, so am I. Because I didn't mean to do that. It just happened. I yank the flames back into my hand, consuming them in my body, without any grace or art, just a sheer blunt tug.

I stand. "Sorry," I mutter.

"We're almost there," he says, but I suspect what he means to say is *Get a grip on your fire, girl.*

But I can't. Right now, the fire is becoming stronger than I am, eating me from the inside. I've never been away from Elise on nights like this when I start to lose my fire. I clench my fist and picture my heart in a vise, immovable metal holding its convulsing center in place. The heart can't escape; the heart is held. The heart is calm. We reach the door, and Taj opens it, and I practically spill into his *home*, his library.

I grab him, pull him against me, wrap my arms around his strong frame. He senses what I need right now isn't kissing, though I wouldn't complain if his lips were on mine. What I need is the pressure of his body against mine. Somehow it settles the fire in me.

After a few minutes, my chest isn't sputtering. I can manage for a bit.

"What did you want to show me?"

"It's the book. The registry of wishes."

My jaw drops. "But you said you can't reveal wishes."

"I know." He scrubs a hand across his jaw as if this pains him. "This is completely forbidden. I shouldn't be doing this at all. But you need to see this."

He nods to his desk. The thriller he was reading is off to the side. He pulls open a heavy drawer and takes out a large red book. It's fat and tall—the size of a giant dictionary.

"I'm told this used to be about the weight of a flimsy magazine. But over the years, over the centuries as more wishes get made, the book gets bigger."

"They're all in here?"

He nods, then opens the book, spreading its heavy pages apart at his desk. "With each wish, names are added," he explains.

"But this is just one book. How they do get in every granter's book?"

"Whenever a name is added in one book, it appears—like magic ink—moments later in another's. That's how the registry works. Almost like a shared document that we all have access to. Any update in one book is reflected in the others."

"How many names do you think are in this?"

"A lot."

The book looks like a ledger, with ruler-marked lines and names in dark script. Payment is listed in one column, then whether the account is due, past due, or paid in full, he tells me, and I suspect the Lady must be in here somewhere and listed as *paid in full*. As Taj flips the pages past the *H*s, the *I*s, the *J*s, everything comes into focus.

I stiffen when he lands on the *K*s and begins running his index finger down the names. "They don't always get recorded properly by jackass granters," Taj says, speaking matter-of-factly, as if he's a doctor explaining a simple procedure. "Well, that's not entirely true. They always get recorded, because we have no choice in that. You are compelled to record every wish precisely as it's wished, and it's too powerful a force to resist. But sometimes the jackass granters don't always have the best handwriting."

He turns several more pages, passing the names starting with *Ka*-, then *Ke*-, then the few *Kh*- names in the book. As we come closer to my last name, the pages start swimming, letters levitating and curving toward me. I press my fingers against the bridge of my nose to focus as Taj's index finger lands on a name, scratched out in poor penmanship, like a kindergartner eking out words for the first time.

Felix Kilan——

That's as far as the granter got. The last four letters that form our name—Kilandros—are just one long scratchy line. But it's him. It has to be him. I follow the line, squeezed in between so many other wishes, straining to keep my eyes on the right wish, the right payment.

Then I see it.

I wish for my wife to never leave me as long as we both shall live.

"Oh my God," I say, and I repeat it over and over as I press my hand to my eyes again, as if I can shoo the wish away and the record of it. But I can't, so I force myself to look again, this time to the payment column.

Paid in Full Upon Transaction. Literally!

That's how it's written, with an exclamation point, and I can picture this jackass granter—I'm seeing a Rumpelstiltskin figure, clicking his heels with glee, a tiny little figure, cackling as he entered this wish in the registry. My father got what he wished for all right. A wife fallen ill, a wife saddled with a mystery illness, a wife who literally and figuratively can't leave him because she can barely even leave her chair.

They say be careful what you wish for. They say wishes come with a price. I always knew that in my head. Now I feel it in my heart.

Wishes don't come in bottles, granters don't live in lamps, and you're not given three wishes by benevolent genies who nod their heads, wiggle their noses, and say "*Yes, Master.*" I should be mad at the jackass granter—I glance over at his name. *Shaw*. One name, that's it. But Shaw didn't make the wish. Shaw simply granted it, wholly intact, upon request, before my father could even offer payment. Because that's how jackass granters work, and the wish come true was both wish and payment.

I turn to Taj, anger flaring in my eyes, my body sharpened with a new form of hate for my father. How could he do this to her? "That's why she's confined to her stupid chair and stupid house, because of my stupid, selfish father?"

"It would seem that way."

"So this is how a jackass granter works," I say, taking deep, sharp breaths. "Just like you told me when we first met. They work *literally*, and the payment is often the wish itself."

"Yes. Apparently the wish was carried out with a horrific sort of exactitude."

I shake my head several times, as if I could wish this all away. "He made her this way. It's all his fault."

Taj says nothing. But an idea hits me in the silence. One more way to spend my wish. On my mom. "Can I wish her free? Can I use my wish to wish her free?"

He nods. "You could. But unraveling another granter's wish is complicated. If every wish came undone with another wish, then the fabric of wishing would be compromised. You have to be very precise in the wording if you're unraveling a wish. And wishes can only be undone with another wish by going before the granter union to make your case."

I roll my eyes. "Well, that pretty much screws me over. The Leagues won't let me use a granter, and even if I'm not using one for my powers, they'd probably kick me out anyway."

"They probably would."

Then it hits me. *The wording.*

It's all in the wording. I look back at my father's wish in the book reading every awful word. *I wish for my wife to never leave me as long as we both shall live.*

Maybe that's the loophole right there. *Live.* My mother will be free when my father is dead.

I could kill him. I have the means. I have the weapons. I could burn him to a crisp. I open and close my hands as if I'm practicing, getting ready to light him up.

Then I press my fingers into my palm. A reminder that I won't go there.

I don't set people on fire, so I can't undo my father's awful work, his terrible wish gone awry.

My heart clutches again, like it's gasping for breath. I ball my hands into tighter fists, as if I can contain my fire with sheer will. But the stretching and pulling in my chest becomes too much. I inhale sharply and I let go of a messy jet of flames. Taj's eyes widen, but I grab the fire, letting it retreat into me.

The relief is temporary. I'm a time bomb. The clock in me is ticking perilously close to some kind of destruction. Taj pulls me over to the couch and wraps his arms around me. I breathe in. I breathe out. I've been broiling in the sun, but it's as if I just dipped into cool blue waters for a moment.

The calm before the storm. The quiet before the wish I have to make.

I know he can't hold me forever, but I'm going to do my best to relish these last few moments, before I do something I hate, before I become more like my father and make a wish that will hurt a person I love. My father has molded me in his image, and I've detested it, and him.

But I am more like him than I thought.

I feel Taj's hands on my face, brushing hair from my cheek. An amnesty for another moment.

"I like this," I whisper in a ragged voice, like I'm barely holding on.

"So do I."

"I like you," I continue, more roughness in my throat. I have to get these words out. I have to say this, even as my body rages against me.

"I like you too, Aria."

"There's more though," I say, and now I'm scared in a new way, in a way I've never been afraid before. I'm going to put it out there. He pulls back so he can look at me. His eyes are clear, and kind, and full of everything I never knew I wanted, but everything it turns out I really need.

I practice the words silently first—*I'm in love with you*. The strangest sensation fills me from head to toe. Lightness. I feel as if I could float, as if I weigh nothing. I'm not coiled or tense or looking behind my back. I'm happy, and I'm safe, and I've accomplished safety in the presence of another person, not a towering plume of flames that I made myself.

I say the words again in my head, and I don't feel like I'm

floating anymore. Because now I'm flying, now I'm soaring, and though we're lying very still and quiet on the couch, I'm higher than I was on the rooftop.

Maybe this is how I'm different from my father. He wished out of fear. He has lived his life out of selfish fear. I'm not my father. I'm not my mother. I'm not my brother. I'm more than a thief, I'm more than an artist, I'm more than my lightning-struck heart. I'm myself. And maybe I can have the things I want and the things I need. I can save my sister, I can save myself, and I can save this marvelous boy too.

I sit upright. "I'm ready. I'm ready to wish."

He winces, as if this pains him, then he straightens up too. He takes a small notebook from his pocket. He becomes businesslike, and I get it. We have to discuss the terms.

"Let's go aboveground," I say. Because I want air, I want space, I want room to revel in how much our lives are about to change for the better.

We leave, and this time we take the short route, emerging near the Flatiron Building moments later. He walks me over to Madison Square Park across the street. It's after midnight, it's dark, and we're the only ones here. We stop near a park bench and stand next to it.

"What are you going to wish for, Aria?" he asks in a mechanical voice, because he is all business now, and he has no choice. But this will be one of the last times he has to feel what it's like to be mastered.

"I'm going to wish for you to grant me natural-born fire, fire that doesn't fade every few months, fire that doesn't need lightning to replenish it, fire that I can call on wherever and whenever I need it for the elemental arts. Fire as if I'd been born with it."

"And how do you propose to pay?"

I've thought long and hard about it. I don't have much to offer, but the fact is, it won't matter. I won't have to pay up because he'll be free when my debt comes due. There will be no one to collect, so it'll be as if my loan has been wiped clean.

But even so, to make this work for both of us, I'll have to wish first because I need natural-born fire to stay afloat in my world. I need to bargain for it properly. If he knows my payment offer is as good as crocodile tears, I fear some granter magic may prevent him from agreeing, may clamp down on him and keep him bound to granter rules and regulations. So we'll have to determine terms first, as if we're really going through the whole wish-and-payment officially, even though I know the payment will be erased when I tell him how I feel.

Love, *it erases any payment due from the wisher, and it frees the granter.*

"Myself," I say, my voice bright and certain. "I offer myself. I offer to trade places with you."

He shakes his head. "That's crazy. You don't want to be me."

I reach out to touch his arm. "Trust me. It'll be fine. You said that's how some people pay. With themselves. By taking the place of a granter. That's all I have—myself. That's all I can offer. It has to be good enough. You said it could be. So I offer myself. I offer to trade places with you."

"And when do you propose I collect?"

"You can collect on the payment in one week. That's it!

Seven measly days is all. And you can collect and I'll take your place as a granter."

He scoffs. "Are you insane? If you turn into a granter in a week, why do you need—"

"You know they're fair terms." "I say, cutting him off. You know they're more than fair. Taj, this will be fine. It'll all be fine. You have to trust me. Please tell me you trust me. Please tell me you know that I know what I'm doing."

I pick a week because it won't matter. In a few minutes, I'll have fire and he'll be free and there will be no need to collect. The payment I'm making will be wiped clean.

He presses his lips together, keeping his mouth closed. His jaw is set hard. "The terms are satisfactory," he says through gritted teeth, as he finishes recording them on his notepad, terms that will never be entered into the ledger for all granters to see. Terms that will be erased when I tell him the next thing. I'm practically bouncing, and I want to spill the secret. But I have to keep this wish on the up and up.

"And now, your wish, officially." He gives me a perfunctory little bow, doffing an imaginary hat in deference to his wisher.

Who also happens to be in crazy love with him.

I'm not sure which to say first—that I love him or what I wish—so I speak quickly, getting all the thoughts out in one big breath.

"I wish, as I stand before you, fully and wholly in mad, crazy love with you, Taj," I say, and his eyes widen when they register what I've said, and we're in cahoots now, we're team-mates, we've beaten the system, and he knows it, and he's smiling and so am I as I finish, "for natural-born fire. And just in case, it wasn't clear, I'm in love with you, I'm in love with you, I'm in love with you with my whole entire heart. So there."

He parts his lips, like he's about to say something, and I hope he's going to form the words *I'm in love with you too*, but then some force makes him say what any granter must say after any wish, whether he's about to be freed or not.

"Your wish is my command."

He spreads his arms wide and far, like he's parting the seas. Mist rises from his hands. But the mist isn't cold or wet—it's more like a waft, like twin lines of sweet smoke that have the power to move the earth, to shake the mountains, to deliver the greediest or loneliest or hungriest of wishes. The park is humming, as if there's a low buzz somewhere, a rumble in the smoke. As I watch them radiate from his hands, I can feel the heat in them, the natural-born fire I've wished for, the fire he's giving me. The two lines of smoke wrap around each other and weave their way to me. They meet at my heart, passing like spirits through my skin, then my bones, seeping into my marrow, into my very DNA, leaving their imprint, as if my parents' genes had marked me the right way back when I was formed.

Now I'm being formed anew, reborn, forged by magic more powerful than DNA, stronger than the lightning I stole from the sky.

The wish pours through me, reclaiming my stitched-up parts, restoring my ashen heart. I can feel the wish taking root, cleansing my dark and dangerous insides, transforming them into something good again. My body grows warmer because there is new fire inside me, a healthy fire, a whole fire. It's removing the clutching, the tightening. It's extracting the waxing and the waning and leaving in its place a steady and a strong natural-born fire.

Then Taj closes his hands, and I'm about to run to him, to kiss him and tell him it worked, it totally worked, and now we're here and we're free. Both of us.

But he is gone.

27

Better Luck Next Time

I look around, in case Taj pulled his disappearing act again, in case he's playing with me. Or maybe he's relishing his freedom, boinging and bounding around, a happy dog jumping through snowbanks, carpe diem-ing.

Or maybe when a granter is freed, he returns to his home. Did I send Taj back to the M.E.? Back to his parents? But I want him here with me. I want to rejoice in our freedom. I want to hug him and kiss him, and yeah, I want him to tell me he loves me too. I want to see the twinkle in his eyes that says he knows I pulled it off, and I saved us.

I hunt through the park, look under benches, peer up in trees. I run to the playground to see if some *I'm free* moment came over him, and maybe he's climbing the swings and hooting at the sky. I search through every corner and then do a loop around the city blocks that surround the park.

It occurs to me he might have just up and left. *Thank you, ma'am, I'll be on my way*. But Taj wouldn't run off. He had to be feeling it too. I don't think I was the only one falling. I flash back on that smile when I said I loved him, the way he was about to speak too. The memory reassures me, so I search again.

When I return to the spot where he granted my wish, there's a note tacked up to a park bench, a note that wasn't there before.

I pluck it off the bench. The ivory sheet of paper has been stamped from *The Union of Granters*.

Underneath the spot is a note in pristine cursive script.

Dear Aria—

In the world of granters, we operate according to rules, guidelines, regulations, and a little thing known as the quibble. A quibble, if you will, is a catch. Some might call it a loophole. We also refer to it as "reading the fine print."

Here are a few provisos, loopholes, conditions, etc., etc., you might not be aware of in the granting of wishes, and in the freeing of granters. The condition of freedom via love can only be achieved when the wisher has a whole heart, as in said granter must be loved by someone with his or her whole heart. Perhaps you might love with the entirety of your heart. But alas, our world operates according to the profound power of semantics.

Here comes the quibble. You, Aria, do not have a whole heart. Yours has been charred. The rules are clear when it comes to love, and you simply do not have the proper parts to set a granter free. We'd wish you better luck next time, except there won't be a next time.

   Sincerely,
   The Governing Body of the Union of Granters

I sink down onto the bench, my legs heavy cinder blocks, my head a brick.

You don't get to have it all. You can't beat the system. I am what I have always been. A defective thing, a Frankenstein's monster, and in seven days life as I know it ends.

———

The sun wakes me cruelly. It glares through the open window of my dorm room. I fling an arm over my eyes to block it out.

Then my alarm goes off. Time for practice. Time for work. Time to make beautiful flames.

I should have wished to be normal. That's what I really want. I should have wished to be free of fire and elements and Leagues and expectations. I could be a waitress. Or a cook. I could go to college and learn about *The Great Gatsby*. I could paint houses, I could train for marathons, I could be a tattoo artist. I could do all the things that the ninety-nine-and-more percent of the world that isn't encumbered by elemental powers can do.

But the alarm buzzes again, my reminder that I have chains.

I get out of bed, my heart hurting. Funny, now my heart is healed. Now it's no longer burned. But it hurts way more than it ever did, a long, slow ache for Taj. For what I've done. I banished the one I love, and he's not even living anymore. Or

215

worse, he might even have been summoned to a new wisher, someone who wants horrible things too. But then it aches for me because in seven days I will know his hell.

I pull on shorts, a sports bra, and a tank top. I lace up my sneakers, and there's a knock on my door. "It's Gem."

"Come in."

She opens the door and closes it quickly.

"So, tell me. I want details."

I don't even know where to start. But I'm tired of lying. I'm exhausted from maintaining a facade. I've done nothing but keep lies and secrets my whole life, and now they have unspooled. "It's all a mess."

She quirks up her eyebrows, concerned. "How? What do you mean, sweetie?"

But before I can tell her, there's another knock.

Gem pats my knee, protectively, as if to say, *I'll take care of this.* She opens the door, and it's Raina. What is she doing here now? We're not scheduled for testing or anything.

"Good morning," Raina says, and she's not bored-sounding today. She sounds chipper and pleased. "How are you, Aria?"

"Fine."

"Great. We just have to do a little more testing."

"More testing?"

"Yes," Raina says with a smug smile. "Sometimes we get this crazy notion to do more testing. Now, if you have a moment?"

"Sure."

Raina looks at Gem pointedly, making it clear she should leave.

"I'm fine with her staying," I say.

Raina rolls her dark eyes. "To each her own. How can I quibble with that?"

The hair on my neck stands up. "What did you just say?"

Raina casts me a challenging look. "I said, *How can I argue with that*?"

I shake my head. "No. You said *quibble*."

"And if I did?"

I say nothing, but my senses are now on high alert as she peppers me with questions.

What do I like to do for fun? *There's hardly time for that.*

What are my hobbies? *I like to doodle.*

Who do I hang out with after practice? *Friends.*

I study her the whole time. She's a code, and I'm this close to cracking it.

"And when you hang out with your friends," Raina says, chewing up the last word, "would you say that you do so with your whole heart?"

The room spins wildly with the realization, and I steady myself by holding on to the wall. The floor feels as if it's dropping out from under me as I connect the final pieces. Then everything falls into place, and I know how the Leagues are conducting their granter testing, and I know that granter testing isn't a ruse at all. It's deadly accurate.

Fight or flight kicks in—part of me wants to wrestle tiny little Raina to the ground and contain her, the other part wants to run, run, run. Because Raina is a granter.

Her questions have been dull and uninteresting because they don't matter. The *only* way the Leagues can test for granter use is to check the registry of wishes. Only granters have access to the registry.

That's how the Leagues are rooting out granter use. By painstakingly monitoring who's been entered into the registry of wishes. Her questions never mattered. The way she tests is to look in the ledger.

My mind races quickly, adding up the facts.

Raina must be in the granter union, or she's a career granter.

My name must not be in the registry of wishes yet. That's why she's only toying with me right now. Because she doesn't have enough evidence yet.

She'll know soon, and then Imran will know that I wished for something exceedingly illegal that will get me kicked out of the Leagues.

But wishes are supposed to be confidential, so all I can figure is that the Leagues and the granter union must be in cahoots somehow. Mariska is still here, and I flash back to Taj's words: *her situation is different.* And then how she simply told Taj in the common room that she didn't need him and then he walked away. Of course he walked away—he didn't disappear like he did with me—because she must not have wished. I assumed she did, but that was wrong. She's still here, so she must be clean.

Unlike me.

I steel myself before Raina, my eyes hard, my jaw tight. I won't give an inch. "I do everything with my *whole heart.*"

She nods, uncrosses her legs, and rises. "I'm sure I'll be seeing you again very, very soon. We'll have such family history to discuss."

The floor buckles again as I'm smacked hard with another

wave. *Family history.* That's what Imran was talking about in his office. Not my brother and his crimes. But my father and his wish. That's why Imran kept a close watch on me, to see if I'd use too, like dear old dad. That's why Imran was so worried all along that I'd use—it's in my DNA, thanks to Dad.

"But how?" I whisper in a desperate voice.

Raina laughs drily. "You're not the only one who can make a deal."

Raina leaves.

"What was that all about?" Gem asks.

I turn to my new friend, a friend I'm about to lose. I press my thumb and index finger into my temples, as if I can rub some sense into myself. But that's long gone. I'm past sense, I'm beyond smart choices. I am at the end of all the lines. "I have to go, Gem. I have to skip practice. Can you cover for me? Tell them I'm sick. Tell them I have the flu or something and went to the doctor."

Gem looks nervous. "But they have a team doctor. They'll wonder why you're not there. I mean, of course I'll cover for you. But . . ."

"Can you tell them I went to a friend's house, then? Just tell them I went to a friend's house to lie down, that I needed some quiet or something, I don't know." I hold up my hands. I'm coming up empty.

Gem nods several times. "Of course. Yes, I'll figure something out. But what's going on, Ar? You going to tell me?"

"I don't even know how to start. I don't even think I have time to start. Just that I'm in over my head, Gem, and it's not going to get any easier," I say, but then I figure what do I have to lose now? I've spent so much of the last few years managing secrets, sequestering them and containing them, and where has it gotten me? In worse shape than before. Maybe keeping it all inside isn't the way to go. I tell her, "I used a granter. I wished for better fire. I have reasons. It's the only way I could protect my sister from my father, or so I thought, and I can't go into all the details now. I just need you to trust me that I had to do this. And soon, in a matter of hours probably, the Leagues are going to know. The coach will know, Imran will know. Because Raina is a granter and all granters have access to a registry of wishes, so they are going to be kicking me out of the Leagues. And now I have to get home to my mom to say . . ." I swallow, breathe deep. "To say good-bye."

"Oh, no." Gem's face turns chalky. She gropes for words but can't seem to find any. There really aren't any, I suppose. Then she speaks. "I'm going to miss you so much."

She grabs me and hugs me, and it feels as good as anything can feel right now. "You better stay in touch," she adds, because she figures all that will happen is I'll be kicked out of the Leagues. But I'll be kicked out of life.

"Actually, Gem," I say into her shoulder. "I probably won't ever see you again. I traded myself as payment."

In less than a week my granter will be coming for payment. Coming for me.

28

Command

Ironic.

That's the word that spirals through my head as I board the next flight, as I fumble my way through reading a magazine and doodling meaningless lines and shapes on the flight home.

Ironic, because I was originally planning on coming home right around this time. Rendezvousing with Elise for a little storm-and-beating-heart cocktail. I'd squirreled aside money for this very reason. For a flight back to Florida to restore my bleeding fire. Only now I've cashed out that dough to say good-bye to my mom and my sister, so in seven days I can go take the place of the only boy I've ever loved.

Taj will be free though. At least there's that. Maybe this is how I repay all my debts—to Elise, to the Lady, to the Leagues. By giving up any freedom, and letting someone have it instead. Taj. I take some solace in knowing, come the end of the week, he'll no longer be dying and dying and dying in between wishers.

As I cap my pen and tuck my magazine away, I think of all

the things I want to do and say in the next seven days. My chest tightens as I picture saying good-bye to my mom and my sister, then it's squeezed when I imagine telling my mom the whole truth of all my father did to me and to her. But maybe I won't feel that bad. Maybe telling her is what I should have done all along. It never occurred to me before to tell her what he'd done. What held me back so long? Was it self-preservation at play the whole time?

Maybe I shouldn't have lived that way. Maybe I should have spoken up sooner.

But I will now. I will speak the truth now.

I am like a person dying, who has to say her final good-byes. Who wants to clear the air with everyone before she goes. It will hurt, but it also has to be done.

I step off the plane, walk through the terminal, and check my phone. There's a message from Elise telling me Kyle will pick me up at the airport, and she's pulling every string to return from sea for a few days. Then there's a message from Gem that she thinks they bought her cover-up, but Imran has called too, asking me if everything is okay. I can practically hear each second ticking away as my expiration date draws closer. The only question is what the Leagues will do to me before I trade places with Taj. Or to my sister.

So much for my foolproof plan. So much for the debt that would never come due.

I exit the airport and head for Kyle's car. He's waiting at the curb. The Florida heat is sticky, a wool blanket of wetness. It clings to me, as if I've just wrapped myself in cellophane and sat under a hair dryer.

Kyle opens his door, hurries around to the passenger side, and lets me in.

He doesn't know what I did. But when Elise asked him to pick me up, he said yes without question.

He returns to the driver's seat, gives me a long and friendly hug, and I realize I have missed all the people here who I care about. I thought I hated this place. I thought I wanted more than anything to leave Florida in my wake. But the people are more than the place, and there are enough people here—Jana, Xavi, my mom—who I do love. Even with my half heart.

Kyle drives away from the airport, onto the highway, toward Wonder.

"So . . . ," he begins tentatively. But he's not really waiting for me to tell him more. He assumes I'm here because of what happened to my brother. I don't disabuse him of that notion.

"It sucks," I say, and that's the truth that applies to all situations. The one thing that doesn't suck is that my dad won't be home for another day. He's anchored somewhere in the deep-blue sea, drinking beers and angling for the big one.

We ride in silence most of the way, breaking it only to share small talk about the Coast Guard, because that's about all I can manage, and I'm glad I don't have to fake being happy to be home, though he doesn't know the truth of why I'm sad.

He pulls up to my house and opens the car door for me. "Don't be a stranger while you're here. 'Kay, Ar?"

"I won't."

He leaves and I give my home a once-over. A new coat of paint, an inviting yellow, the kind realtors tell you to paint a house when you're trying to sell it, because yellow homes sell faster, because yellow seems warm and cozy, like this is a home full of love and many happy memories.

I open the door, greeted by the perfectly modulated central air-conditioning we now have, thanks to the money I made that Dad spent, since most of my checks have gone to him. My mom is where I left her, marooned in her chair. She is a little starfish, washed up on the beach. I go to her and hug her, and she lets me.

"Now are you going to let me know what was so important you had to fly down and tell me?"

"Mom," I say, and my voice cracks. Because it's time for her to know.

I start at the beginning, the first time her husband took me to the garage and set my hands on fire. By the time I'm done, I'm pretty sure she's about to pass out from shock. I've drained her, let whatever air was left in her seep out. She is empty, but I have more. I tell her about my father's wish, and she nearly sinks into the floorboards with the realization of why she's confined.

"No," she says over and over, shaking her head. But it's clear she knows I'm telling the truth. It's clear she knows the word *devastated* in a new, fresh way.

———

Soon Jana comes home, and the first thing I do is grab her hands. They're grayish-blue and veiny. She looks like a zombie. "Dad's been freezing your hands, hasn't he?"

She turns away. I grab her arm. She tries to shake me off. But I'm stronger than Jana, and eventually she gives in. "Yes," she says, her eyes hard and dark, the blacks of her pupils threatening to take over her whole iris.

"What else is he doing? Is he forcing you to stay underwater? To hold your breath till you turn blue?"

"Yes."

I slam a fist into the wall. A picture frame rattles. The five of us from so long ago that the sun has bled out the color, and now we're just a sepia-toned half-baked family, a son in prison, two daughters with damaged hands, a shell of a mom, and a monster of a father. I grab the picture from the wall, take it to the garbage, and toss it where it belongs.

I return to my mom in her chair. She is nearly catatonic, but underneath her stillness she is quivering. I want to slap her, to knock her senses back into her. To ask her how she could have let this happen. How she could just play the spectator to her husband's blows. But she was just the collateral damage in the path of the bullet; the bullet of a wish.

"Do you even love him?" She shrinks into herself as I spit out the words. "Do you anymore?"

She is a terrified animal. She doesn't know where to go, what to say, so she just backs up farther, camouflaging herself in the walls of her cage. I kneel, try to be gentler this time. "Do you want to be like this, Mom? Do you? Or do you want to be well? Do you want this stupid wish-curse gone?"

She doesn't say anything for a long moment. The air conditioner hums in the background, cooling the air between us. Then she looks at me. "I want to go out again. I want to swim again. I want to be your mom again."

If I were a knight, I'd unsheath a sword and go slice off the dragon's head. "What are you going to do when he gets home?" I ask.

"I'm going to tell him to never touch the two of you ever again," she says, and for the first time in years she doesn't sound meek or scared. She sounds like herself. As if she's fighting to be the woman she once was even as she's still stuck.

I have to do something to save her from this curse. I have to find another way. I have seven days to do everything I can. I'm not going to let them go to waste. I will solve this problem if it's the last thing I do.

Which it very well may be.

"Mom, do you have the keys to Xavi's old car?"

Jana pipes in. "Kitchen drawer. I'll get them."

"Mom, we'll be back soon. I promise." Then I turn to Jana. "You're coming with me."

———

I haven't driven in ages. I've rarely had the chance or the need. But I manage, slinging an arm across Jana's headrest as I back out of the driveway. The rusty old car sputters as I shift into drive and head down our street to the main drag, then the highway that'll take us to the Everglades.

The trip doesn't take long, but there's enough time to tell Jana where we're going. She doesn't resist and she doesn't freak out, and I take some small bit of pride that she's got a core strength in her, an iron barrier my dad can't touch. I park in a deserted lot by an old dock that used to house a chartered tour company. Some people who live in the Everglades and don't have or rent their own docks will stash their boats here, a risky move, since you're not supposed to park your boat without a permit. But the cops hardly ever clamp down, and since these boat owners aren't exactly running on the right side of the law to start with, I find no moral objection to commandeering one of their vessels for a quick ride.

"C'mon. Get in." I motion for Jana to join me in *The Themis Steed*, a motorboat that's barely big enough for the two of us but will do the job, since the owner was kind enough or drunk enough or stupid enough to leave the keys inside the glove compartment of the boat. This is not uncommon among boat owners.

"You're just taking it?"

"I'll return it. Obviously."

Jana hops in and we power away, driving deeper into the thick reeds and dark reptilian-strewn waters. I know the route. I'd never forget the route. I stop after a few miles and turn off the motor.

I hold out a hand to Jana.

"We have to walk through the water?"

"Yeah."

"But there's probably pythons and boas and eels and so many yucky things," she says.

"Probably, but you're with me, and I'm basically the equivalent of python repellent. They won't come near us. They don't like my heat."

"It's still gross," she says, and she sounds like she might gag, but she's doing it. She's getting out of the boat and stepping into the hot soup of the Everglades. We trudge through the saw-grass marshes, with tangly reeds that try to ensnare our legs and swampy branches that brush our skin, trekking foot by heavy waterlogged foot. The water is thick, and the mangroves are greedy, but we're nearly there, and she's on her porch.

If there's anyone in the whole wide world who knows how to undo a wish it's the Lady. She knows all the ways in and out of things that the rest of us can't see. She has all the knowledge, and she gained it fair and square, along with a snow gator.

"Well, look who's here."

I climb up on the porch, my legs covered in mud and marsh, my sister by my side.

"Let me get you a towel." She shuffles inside and returns with a dingy blue-and-white dish towel. I wipe off my legs, and notice her snow gator waddling from inside her home to the porch.

"He won't hurt you. Either of you," the Lady says, and pats the seat of her swing.

"He won't, Jana. He's nice," I say to my sister as I wipe down my legs, then hand the towel to her. She does the same.

"Sit. And tell me who you've brought. Little sister, I trust?"

"This is Jana," I say.

"Hello," Jana says.

"What's your poison, Jana?"

"Water. Or ice," Jana says.

"You're not sure which?" The Lady raises an eyebrow.

"I think water. He thinks ice."

I grab hold of Jana's wrist and hold up her zombielike hands.

The Lady's eyes narrow, anger flashes in them, and she strokes her gator's head. The gator leans into her hand, like a dog being petted.

Jana and I sit down.

"Determined man, that father of yours," the Lady says with a snort. "Doing the same to your sister."

Jana scoffs.

"Thinks he's got it all figured out. Thinks he can bring out your elements," the Lady adds.

"But that's never how the elements come out," I say, and there's an eagerness in my voice, like I want to prove I'm a good student, that I've learned, that I've listened.

"Never is. Elements don't respond to that kind of human hubris." She looks hard at both of us. "Or that kind of terror."

I glance at my tough little sister, who tries hard to keep it together. But her eyes are wet, a giveaway that keeping it together isn't so easy.

"So what brings you back?" the Lady asks me.

"I need to know how to reverse a wish."

The Lady whistles low and shakes her head. "You wishing when I told you not to?"

"Yes, but I'm going to accept my punishment like a big girl. Only this question is about another wish. It's not for me. It's for my mom."

"Wishes are binding, girl. There's no way to turn one around unless you petition the granter union."

"No other way at all?" I say; then I tell her what my dad wished for so many years ago, and what the wish did to my family. I don't know that my mom could have protected us from him if she'd been healthy. But I know this—she didn't have the chance. He reduced her to a husk of a wife, a shell of a mother.

"Granters are powerful, Aria. As powerful as the elements.

Often more powerful than Mother Nature. More powerful than humans. Look at the peace in the M.E. Only possible because of granters."

My heart leaps into my throat, thinking of Taj's unwitting sacrifice. A tear forms in the corner of my eye—he's one of the reasons why his country is no longer torn apart. But he's one of those who are hurting.

"There has to be a way," I say, pressing on as I return my focus to the Lady. I can't just let my mother spend her days shrinking into a papasan chair. "There's always a way. That's what you taught me. You showed me the way to fire. Another way. How can there be no other way here than to ask the granter union to reconsider?"

"Oh, child. You are fire, through and through. All that passion, all the fury, all that righteous indignation." The Lady chuckles, but she's not laughing at me. "What makes granter magic so strong are the rules. The recording of the wishes. The regulations. The union. The payment system." The Lady links her fingers together to demonstrate that sturdiness. "That makes the bonds of the wishes stronger."

I bang my fist on the arm of the swing. I look at Jana and see the years unfolding in front of her. I couldn't shield her from my dad, and I can't protect her from her future, not when I'm about to vaporize in a matter of days.

"So, what are we supposed to do?"

"Aria, if the world were fair and just, there'd be a spell, a magic potion to undo this," she says, then she lowers her voice to a whisper, even though no one is around. "Wishes can come undone when the wish has been fulfilled or when the wish no longer applies. If you wished to be purple on September 3 only, then the wish would apply to that day. Your father's wish would come undone when the conditions of the wish no longer exist."

"I can't do that. I want to. But I can't."

The Lady nods several times. "I understand. Now, pet my gator and tell me all about how my fire recipe worked out for you."

The Lady leans back into the swing. I bend down, and touch the gator's head. Jana gives me a look as if I'm crazy. The gator's skin is tough and leathery, but he leans into my hand as if I've just come home from work and he wants me to rub his chin.

"See that?" the Lady says, looking at her swamp pet. "You take care of him, you treat him right, he'll take care of you when you need him to. He's no ordinary gator."

"I will take care of him," I say as I look at the Lady. I want her to know that I'd never forget my debt to her. That I always intend to make good on it. "I promised."

"I know you will, but that's not what I mean," she says, and we pet him together. She doesn't say more. She doesn't tell me what she means, so I don't ask. Jana watches me, shifting her eyes from me to the gator and back again, and it registers for her that she can touch him too.

"It's okay," I say to my little sister, the girl I'm not able to save. "He won't hurt you."

The gator lifts his massive snout high in the air, waiting for a tickle. Jana obliges, one intrepid finger stroking his chin.

29

Wish, Officially

My father still hasn't returned when Imran calls the next morning.

"Aria," Imran says, rocks in his voice. "I'm disappointed."

He says it like a father who just discovered his daughter cheated on a math test, or worse. Who fibbed her whole way through high school, eyeing the papers of other students, plagiarizing their ideas and thoughts.

I sink down to the floor of my bedroom. Every part of my body feels heavy, my arms and legs like sandbags. My wish is now official.

My imagination hunts for Taj in the underground tunnels of New York City, but I know he's very likely nonexistent. He's a cipher until the next reckless, bankrupt fool needs something he can't get on his own. Or until he's freed in six more days, when I replace him.

"You had such potential," Imran says, and I can hear the wistfulness in his voice. The loss.

"I'm sorry," I say, choking back a tear. "I wanted to do well for you."

Imran believed in me. Imran gave me an opportunity. For a few short months, he was a far better father figure than the real one I've been saddled with. Imran, at least, tried to keep me away from trouble. He didn't want me near someone who'd already wished. Someone who'd been tempted and gave in to the worst kind of Faustian bargain.

"I wanted you to do well too. I want the Leagues to be the best. That's why we struck a deal with the union to test for granter use. We want our Leagues clean; they don't want their granters used simply for sport. And you were one of the best I'd ever seen. Why did you have to wish for more?"

My brain trips over the last word he says. *More?* I didn't wish for more. I wished for natural-born fire. But then, I'm not going to argue semantics with Imran. The result is the same—I've been expelled. And my family too.

"I wanted to stay in the Leagues," I say, and it's half-true, but it's as close as I can get to a true answer. I had too much want, too much need, and I reached too far. I got greedy.

"It makes me sad to have to do this, Aria. But you have a lifetime ban. There will be no more Girl Prometheus."

But the strange thing is, he says nothing about my family, about the ban for stealing elements earning them a ban too. Maybe he forgot to mention it?

"I'm sorry. I'm very, very sorry."

"I know you are," he says, but there's no reprimand in his tone. He sounds strangely warm, even forgiving as he continues. "And I also know those burns on your hands aren't from playing with fire when you were a kid. I only wish there was something I could do about where they came from."

My chest closes in on itself. They're the most comforting words a man has ever spoken to me.

"Me too," I whisper.

"I'll have to call your father now and inform him. Rules, you know."

"Of course."

The call ends, and I lie on the couch in the living room to wait. My father is probably in his car, driving home from his fishing trip, answering a call from Imran on his cell phone. Soon, my dad will barrel through the door, and I have no game plan. I have no strategy. I glance at my mother. She is freshly made up this morning. She wears mascara. I haven't seen her wearing mascara in years. Jana ran her a bath earlier. Then I sent Jana to Mindy's house.

"You look pretty," my mom says to me as we wait. I look down at my clothes. Shorts, boots, black T-shirt, hair pulled back in a ponytail. I wish I had a sash of bullets to string across my chest, and a gun in a holster on my hip. I can't help but feel I need something to face my father, to face this reckoning. The irony is, I have two perfectly good weapons in my hands, but I won't use them.

"So do you," I tell her, though I wonder if she brushed on eyeshadow and blush for his return from a trip, the good wife welcoming the warrior home, or if she freshened up for herself. I want to make sure her fighting words were real, that she's not going to cave when she sees him, as she always has. I crouch down next to her, take her hands in mine. "What happens when he gets home, Mom? What are we going to do when he freaks out about the Leagues and me?"

"I'm going to tell him to leave," she says crisply. "I'm going to tell him that I never want to see him again. That I never want to be his wife again. That would erase the wish, wouldn't it? *I wish for my wife to never leave me*," she says, bitterly reciting the words that chained her. "If I'm not his wife . . ." She trails off.

A rush of hope fills me. She's right. Like the Lady said, like Taj said, the wording matters. The wish would no longer hold if she's no longer his wife. I squeeze her hand.

"Let's hope so," I say. But as far as I can see, all bets are off when it comes to gaming a wish.

———

The minutes tick, and my ears are trained on my father's sounds. Even after being away for two months, I can pick up the rumble of the engine of his Pontiac the second he turns onto our street several houses away. The car trundles down the road, the engine sputtering. I can hear him well before he slides his car into the driveway and kills the engine. Then the sound of his sandals slapping the concrete floor of the garage, the creak of the doorknob, the heave of his disappointed sigh.

He walks in through the front door and sees me on the couch. His face is sunburned and covered in stubble from being out at sea for so many days. I stand up, and he shoots me a glare. His lips are tight, closed. His eyes narrowed. I wonder if this is how his father looked when he was angry. How his father stared at him before he hit him. Before he taught him how to be a man.

But I don't entirely care *why* my dad is the way he is. There are things we can control and things we can't control. He had a choice. He made the wrong choices.

"Catch anything good?" I'm shocked that I've made the first move, breathed the first words.

"Marlin. This big." He holds his hands out wide.

"Where is it?"

"I'll pick it up later," he answers in the most disinterested voice. "It's being cut."

"Cool. I bet it'll taste great. Maybe grill it."

He tilts his head and stares at me, like he's trying to figure out how I could have this casual conversation with him.

Then he nods several times. "Grilled marlin. Sounds good. You like grilled marlin, dear?"

The question is for my mother. She looks at him sharply. "No. I don't."

I want to pump my fist in the air. Small victory for her, but still, it's a victory.

He ambles into the kitchen, opens the fridge, roots around. "I *wish* there was a beer here," he says. Then he slams the fridge door and looks at me. "I *wish* there was a burger. I *wish* there was ketchup."

His words are biting, but his lip is quivering, and he's going for an old standard. The wounded old dad. "I coached you, Aria. I went to every show. I helped you; we made fire together." There's a hitch in his throat. The crying act. The tears that reassure his black heart that the way he treats me is okay when it's not okay.

"We never made anything," I spit back as I cross my arms. "And who are you to talk about wishes?"

236

He raises an eyebrow, casts a curious look, like he can't possibly know what I mean. I can tell he's ready to play the confused part. But the next words don't come from him or from me. They come from my mom. She's stood up, and she's making her way over to us, wobbly and precarious as she goes.

But determined.

She makes it to the kitchen and points a finger at her husband. "I loved you, Felix. I would have stayed with you forever. You didn't have to wish for it. You didn't have to wish for this." She gestures to her own deflated body, then to her chair.

"You're not making any sense, sweetheart," he says to her, and reaches for her, trying to wrap her in a hug.

She holds off his embrace. "And I'll tell you another thing. Don't you ever put your hands on *my* daughters again."

Fierce and angry, she points a righteous finger at him. Then she takes another step toward him, stumbles, and topples to the floor. I bend down to help her. So does he. We are face-to-face. I reach for her elbow, but he slaps my arm away. "Don't touch her," he shouts. The facade is gone, the mask fallen.

"Don't *you* touch her."

We stare at each other, locked in crosshairs, a face-off finally.

"I mean it," he seethes, and I remember what he's capable of. I remember what's at stake. But then I remember I'm not keeping his secret anymore. The secret has been shared. He has no more power over me.

"No, I mean it. I mean it this time. Don't touch me, and don't touch Jana. Because now Mom knows what you did to me, and Imran knows what you did to me, and if you touch

Jana, I'll call the authorities. I'll make sure everyone knows what you did to me and to her," I say. I don't bother adding that I'll be in some no-man's-land in a few days. I don't bother because I'll tell everyone what he did before I'm taken away. I'll tell everyone to keep him away from my sister. I can't save myself, but I can save her. I can save her with words. I never understood that until now. I never *got* it until now. No one ever wanted to help me. There was never anyone to turn to, no one to tell. So I did what I had to do. I shut my mouth. Now I don't have to be quiet any longer.

He doesn't care though. "Where's your sister? I need to help her. Seeing as she's our only hope. You might as well go join your brother. The two of you belong together." He grabs my chin, and pulls on it, yanking. "You're useless now."

Useless.

I am useless now.

I clench my jaw. I can feel my broken and un-whole heart heating me to record temperatures. My anger stokes the fire, oxygen feeding a ravaging beast, and I'm about to set my own father on fire once and for all.

Instead I use a different weapon. The one I earned. The one I trained. My body.

I don't turn on the burners. I don't light the torches. I take the thing that is still mine—my charred hands—and I grab his throat.

I hold him tight around his flesh, digging the pads of my thumbs deep into the hollow of his throat, hunting for his trachea. He coughs and sputters and spits out my name. "Stop, Aria," he chokes out.

My fingers have found purchase in the back of his neck,

and I will never let up, I will never let go until there's no more air inside him. I am so strong, my hands are so powerful, I have muscles all over my body, and especially underneath the scarred and ugly skin of my hands. My fingers are steel, my wrists are iron, my forearms are merciless beasts that hold my father in place. I may have stolen every last ounce of fire inside me, but I worked for every inch of my strength.

I can do this. I can hold tight until he turns blue. Until he rasps out his last strangled word. I am capable.

Yet . . . I feel my fingers loosening.

Because I'm not him.

I can't do this.

I can't kill my father.

I stop, dropping my hands to my sides, my chest heaving from the exertion, from the shock of what I almost did. What I can't ever do. I will not be like him.

My father slumps to the floor, gasping for breath but fully alive.

I stare at my hands as if they're strange foreign objects, these tools that could have killed him. Now they dangle at my sides as the color returns to Dad's face. He starts to rise and I have no idea what happens next.

Then there's a loud ripping sound. I turn to the screen door.

The snow gator is here and he's lumbering into our house. He looks at me, those big brown eyes as sweet as they were when he let me pet his head. As he turns his long reptilian snout away from me, I understand what happened yesterday on the porch. I understand what the Lady meant. *He'll take care of you when you need him to.*

He spies my father and snaps his massive jaw.

My father does what any Floridian should do. He backs away from the beast. But those fat little gator legs are furiously fast, and the snow gator knows what he wants. He wants a meal, he wants a former fire-eater. My father scurries down the hall to the bedroom, no thought to my mother, no thought to me, and tries to slam his door. But there's no time; the snow gator barges into the bedroom, his snout already pushing the door open. I follow, pressing my back against the hallway wall, and I watch as my father jumps onto his bed. The gator follows, tearing the sheets and covers as he goes. My father jumps off and grabs for the sliding glass door to our backyard, trying to unlock it quickly, terror in his eyes. The same terror I saw in Jana's yesterday when she told the Lady what was happening to her hands.

The snow gator opens his snout as far as it can go and grasps my father's leg, pulling the foot, then the calf into his mouth. There's a sound of twigs snapping, and I cover my face with my hands.

I can't watch. I close my eyes. I hear a crunch, then one final shriek. There's a muffled noise, then silence.

Soon I peer through my fingers from the hallway, dumbfounded, at the armored animal in my father's bedroom who has just swallowed a man whole. The snow gator's belly is distended, like a snake that's just consumed a rat.

I don't make a move. I remain very still. The snow gator stays in place, wriggles a bit, then huffs out hard, and I'm horrified that the snow gator might expel my father, regurgitate him on the newly carpeted floor of the bedroom, leaving me to either put my father back together or clean up the mess.

Neither option appeals.

So I wait.

The snow gator exhales, then shifts one more time, as if he's loosened a belt buckle after Thanksgiving dinner and is now satisfied. He's accommodated his new inhabitant. He waddles a few inches to the sliding door, pawing at it with his big claws, looking longingly at the canal that's not far away. I know what I have to do. I have to give the snow gator a safe escape, just as he gave my sister one.

He is one hell of a cleanup crew, and I will find a way to take care of him whenever the Lady needs me to. I step gingerly into the bedroom, walking carefully by the creature that just ate my father, and I open the sliding glass door for him. The gator glances at me, his eyes soft again.

I lean over to pet his snout. "Thank you."

I stand and he leaves, two hundred pounds heavier than when he entered our house, plodding slowly across the grass of the backyard, slogging his way to the canal, then back to the Everglades, back to the Lady.

It never once occurred to me that he might hurt me too. He would have considered it rude.

30

Reversal of Fortune

I'm not going to lie. I've envisioned my father's end countless times. I've also pictured my reaction. I always assumed I'd be shocked or terrified or knocked into a near-catatonic state, staring at my own hands, staggered that I'd actually done it, amazed that I'd acted on every base desire I'd ever had to incinerate him.

His ashes on my hands, his soot in my throat.

Never have I thought I'd be happy. Never have I contemplated that elation would overcome me after my father's death.

But elation is what I'm feeling because I'm looking at my mother. The same swirling tendrils of smoke and sweet mist that emanated from Taj's hands two nights ago are now cocooning my mother, lifting her up from her chair, swirling her in slow circles inches above the ground. Her eyes are huge, round orbs mystified by the undoing.

The wish no longer has any hold on her. The bonds of it are broken. It simply no longer applies—because only one of them is living—and so it must unravel.

I walk carefully down the hall, at a tiptoe pace, afraid to disturb but anxious to see. Hope fills me up, a breathless wonder at something I've wanted to see for so long. As the smoke spirals her, her body begins to transform. Her flaccid legs are being sculpted again. Her slack, shapeless parts are redrawn by the mist, traced anew as she's returned to the way she was so many years before, the way I remember her when I was younger, when she was chiseled and firm.

Her hair, limp and lifeless, is lifted by the smoke, as if it's being brushed tenderly, then curled and colored into the dark, springy cut she once had. Her face starts to change, as if the pallidness is fading away and in its place are bright eyes and pink cheeks. But it's not a face-lift; she still has lines, she's still her age. Only, she looks healthy. She looks incredibly, remarkably healthy, and it's the most welcome sight in the world.

It's her. And she's well.

Gently, the smoke lowers her to the ground, curves in on itself, and vanishes.

My mother looks down at her legs, then at her arms; she even runs a hand across her taut belly underneath her shirt, astonished at the reboot of her body. She's a fairy-tale character who's been visited by the good witch, by a benevolent godmother, and she's both bewildered and delighted with the transformation.

"You're back," I say, and I run to her. Her solid arms wrap around me, holding me tight. This is the mom I missed. The brave one, the strong one.

I pull back to regard her once more, my hands in her hands. "You're beautiful," I say, and that's how I know my father is really and truly dead, and he's not coming back.

His work has been undone.

"Thank you," she says to me, though I didn't do this. But maybe when I touched the snow gator's head, I activated something, set in motion the animal's instinct. Or maybe the Lady sent him on this mission to right a wrong, to restore some small semblance of justice in the Kilandros family. No wonder she wanted to win the snow gator so badly. He's quite a prize.

My mother looks at the door.

"Go!" I say, encouraging her.

She walks to the door, no longer taking tentative, shuffling steps, but instead walking on strong, sturdy legs. I hold the door open for her, and bask in the sight of my mother walking outside for the first time in years, the sun beating down on her skin. She looks up at the sky, letting the rays coat her face. Then she turns to me, a smile so big and radiant it could warm me for the rest of my days. A tear of happiness slides down her cheek.

It is glorious.

Then I wait. I wait for the Leagues to come for me. I wait for them to wrap metal around my wrists and make a show of me, like they did with Reginald. I'd be a prize to trot before the cameras; a real warning. A top M.E. Leagues performer caught not only using a granter but also apprehended for having stolen the elements. I'd be the perfect elemental artist to make an example of, a warning sign for generations of youth to come.

Here's what happens when you steal.

Here's what happens when you wish.

A future vanished, a lifetime ban from performing. A forever ban for the family.

They have to be coming for me like they did for Reginald. Imran knows what I wished for, so he has to know my stage name wasn't a lie, after all. It was the truth, under his nose from the very start.

But Imran doesn't show. No one shows, except the Division of Wildlife officer the next morning. My mother called the department to officially report my father's death. She is suddenly businesslike and competent as she handles what needs to be done.

Jana and I sit on the couch in the living room while my mother talks to him.

"Then an alligator just broke into the house and ate my husband," she says, reporting the facts, managing to push out a few tears. I think they might be real. I think a part of her is sad. But a bigger part, a more important part, is moving on.

"You saw it happen," one of the officers says to me. He has a mustache and holds a small spiral notebook. "Any distinguishing characteristics on this animal?"

He's ice cold. He acts like a dog. He protected my sister and me. He lives deep in the Everglades with the wisest woman I've ever known. Some might call her a guardian angel.

"He was green," I say. I assume a sad look, like I miss what the snow gator ate. I glance at Jana, my eyes telling her to be quiet. She reads me instantly, understanding the direction. She knows the gator saved me, and saved her, so she doesn't say a word.

The wildlife officer scribbles something in his notebook, then tells my mother he'll be in touch.

She walks him to the door, even escorts him out to his vehicle, just because she can. She comes back in the house. "I don't think we'll be seeing him again," she says, and there's a wink in her voice.

She claps her hands together once, looks from me to Jana. "Now, shall we start packing up the house?"

"Why?"

"I thought we might want to get out of Florida."

"But, Mom, I have friends here," Jana protests, and they continue like that for the next hour, pushing and pulling, resisting and insisting, and there's something strangely comforting to witnessing the exchange. It's the closest thing to normal I've ever seen in my family.

———

That night I take my sister pool hopping. The Markins are back in town, but another family next door to them is gone for a few days, so we sneak into their screened-in pool.

Jana dives in quietly this time, but when she surfaces she has that same bright smile she had the last time we swam together.

"This is how I like to swim," she says when she reaches me.

"This is how you should swim," I say, pushing wet strands of hair off my face. "Race?"

She nods, gives me my head start, and I shoot off underwater. As usual, she beats me. As usual, I don't mind one bit.

"Don't go," she says as we tread water in the deep end.

"You have no idea how much I wish I could stay."

———

Elise bursts through my door and grabs me. I smile and she beams, but we are both sharing smiles of regret. I told her everything on the phone last night.

"I guess my weekend leave was too late," she says. "For everything."

"It's okay. I was always a ticking time bomb."

"This is all my fault."

I shake my head. "It's not your fault."

"I should have swum to shore. I should never have joined the Lookouts. I should have chained myself to your side."

"Stop," I say, and walk into my front yard with her. We sit on the sidewalk, under a small patch of shade from an overgrown palm tree. "You saved my life for many years. Now I have to pay up."

"I would have done this forever."

"It's fine. I mean, it sucks. But it's fine. At least Jana is safe, and my mom is back."

"So you have to be the sacrificial whatever?"

I shrug. I've had the last few years to get ready for this in some ways. I always knew I was living on borrowed time. I always knew I was dying. "It's just the way these deals work."

"The deal sucks."

"Yeah. Some deals do suck. I'll give you that."

She leans her head on my shoulder, and I pet her hair. This may be the first time I've comforted her.

Time marches forward quickly, and when the seventh day arrives, the house is packed, the FOR SALE sign is posted in the front yard, and Jana has barely accepted this newfound authority figure in her life. Jana's only known our mom as helpless. My mother has never set the rules, never made the decisions for my sister. Now she's doing just that.

"It's time for a change, Jana," my mother says.

Jana slams her door, and I'm about to go talk to her, to try to help her understand, but then three figures appear in a *whoosh* in my driveway. Like they sailed through the sky and are floating down on invisible umbrellas.

One of them is Taj, and my heart leaps from my chest. I want to run to him, to touch him, to talk to him, to spend the night on a rooftop. He's back!

But he doesn't look at me. He's aloof, and his eyes are trained far away from me, fixed on some unseen point behind my head. I swallow, and my throat is dry. Why is he looking away from me? Why isn't he happy to see me too? Even if it's only for the exchange. My heart beats too fast, like a hummingbird, and I wish it would settle down.

The man and the woman with him walk toward my door. I try to will him to meet my eyes. To look up, to notice me, to connect with me as he always did. But he stares past me. Only the man and woman look at me.

The man wears a well-fitted suit, dove gray with slim pink pinstripes, and aviator sunglasses. The woman is dressed in a silk blouse, pencil skirt, and sleek black heels. She has long blond hair with a luxuriant wave to it. Are they coming to take me away or to give me a makeover?

"Sorella," the woman says, then flashes a badge inside a wallet, as a cop would do. She uses only her first name, and the badge is gold—real gold, hard metal. It says *The Union of Granters*. "From the Union. Compliance Bureau." She tips her forehead to the gentleman. "This is Barry."

Barry? A woman named Sorella works with a man named Barry?

I open the door and step outside. I cross my arms and glance at Taj, trying to connect silently with him. But the spot behind my head is endlessly fascinating to him, and it aches inside my chest, the way he won't acknowledge me.

Then he meets my eyes, and his are cold and conniving.

Like a blinding light, I get it. I step back, hold on to the doorway, because it feels like I might fall. I'm so stupid, so foolish. I never saw it coming. He was using me all along to engineer his own freedom from the start.

This is the real Taj now. This is the Taj I met the first night. The trickster, toying Taj. The cool Taj who didn't care for his fate.

All the other nights, he was acting. It's like I've been punched in the gut, and I want to double over in pain, to press my teeth into my lips because this hurts so much, knowing he played me the whole time, and I fell for his routine.

Right from the start when he asked me to wait to wish.

He set me up, took me on dates, stretched out the whole ruse, told me granter secrets, provisos, stories about falling in love, stories about payment—about offering oneself for payment. So I could fall for him. So he could be free. He held me off from wishing all the time so he could *buy* time. I bought it all, hook, line, and sinker. I believed it all, from the green light at the end of the dock to the stars above the rooftop, to the hope that stories well told could free you from your fate.

Like a seduction, and I was the one seduced.

Oh, but he was right. He wove fables full of kisses, full of sad eyes, full of dreams for a wisher who'd fall in love with him and free him. He got what he wanted—freedom granted from a fool.

"Some story you told," I say sharply to him, because I never stray far from my store of anger.

He says nothing. His face isn't even stony. Just indifferent toward me.

"You could make your story one thousand and two, don't you think," I say, spitting words out at him. "The granter and the Girl Prometheus. Make an addendum to *Arabian Nights*, because you're just as good."

He rolls his eyes, shrugs his shoulders, and holds out his hands. "Don't tell me you're surprised."

"Yeah. I actually am."

"Well, that's kind of a bummer for you."

"No kidding. And to think I believed you," I say, and my throat hitches, but I won't give in to tears for him. "I believed it all."

"That was the error of your ways, Aria," he says in an admonishing tone. "Because we may be mastered granters, but the real master we serve is the wish to be free. Every day. All the time. Sometimes you do whatever it takes to be free. But you know that, right?"

He's kicking me while I'm down. He's smashing fists and feet and elbows into all the soft parts of me, all the parts that let him in. I should have trusted my instincts all along—the ones that have told me to never trust.

"Can we please get on with this?" Sorella says in an exasperated voice.

Barry flicks a long sheet of paper from his hands, unrolling it, a bailiff before the court about to read off the charges. He lowers his aviator shades.

"According to Wish 5,678,972, made on the evening of August second, exactly seven days ago, you, Aria Kilandros, have agreed to exchange yourself for the granter you received said wish from." Barry looks at me over his glasses. "That would be granter 542, Taj Rahim. It is now"—Barry lifts his elbow in a sharp robotic gesture—"time to collect upon your payment."

Sorella chimes in. "We will take you to your jurisdiction in Manhattan, effectively replacing Taj Rahim from this day forward and placing you in full responsibility for responding to, interacting with, and bargaining on behalf of all granters with any wishers experiencing a need powerful enough to find you on the island of Manhattan. This is your sole jurisdiction, and no other granter shall infringe upon it, and you shall not infringe upon the jurisdiction of any other granter. You will uphold all the rules, regulations, quid pro quos, provisos, and quibbles, recording all wishes in strictest accordance with the Union of Granters forevermore and into perpetuity throughout your servitude, so help you God."

Sorella's face is stony as she reads, but when she reaches the last words—*so help you, God*—she chuckles. "Assuming there even is a God," she whispers, like we're in on this together, as if we're coconspirators.

That makes Barry laugh. "Higher authority," he says with a snort. "As if."

Taj joins in, and the three of them are cracking themselves up with their insider granter jokes. I'm one of them now, or about to be, but the joke is on me.

Soon, the three of them settle down.

"One more item," Sorella adds. "You will be allowed one phone call per month during the times when you're in existence, but otherwise granters are forbidden from seeing their family members. We will escort you to your quarters so that you may begin your new position as granter 892," she tells me. "You will no longer use your last name."

"I'm just going to say good-bye to my mom and my sister," I say, and I try to push Taj and the way he deceived me out of my mind, even though it's my whole and healed heart that hurts more than it ever did. I knew we weren't going to have a happily ever after today, but I thought we'd have a bittersweet good-bye, a moment when he confessed he loved me too. Instead, I am the butt of the joke. I turn to the two people I can truly trust. My mom and my sister. We've been saying good-bye all week, but even so, those preparatory farewells could not have readied me for the real one. I find my sister in the kitchen. A tear is sliding down her face.

I wrap my arms around her, hold her tight.

"Who's going to go pool hopping with me?" There's a hitch in her throat.

"First of all, I hear it's cold in Jersey, so good luck with that. Second, Mom will. She'll swim with you and make it fun again."

"Like you did for me," Jana says.

"Yeah." Then I pull back, grip her by the shoulders, look her in the eyes. "You need to listen to Mom, okay? Give her a chance to be Mom again. Do that for me?"

"I will."

"And whatever you do, have fun. You can do anything. Paint houses, make clocks, travel the world. Weave water or don't weave water. Do whatever you want, Jana. Promise me?" I hold her face in my hands and wipe away one of her tears.

"I promise."

Then I turn to my mom. "Take care of Jana. Don't ever stop. Don't ever go back to how it was. To how you were."

"Never," my mom says, the Mom of old, the Mom of new.

The three of us hug, and I don't know if I'll ever see them again, if we'll ever have anything more than the phone calls, like Taj had with his mom. I return to the door where Barry, Sorella, and Taj are chatting. Taj looks animated, as if he's just been telling them a story, and they both smile and laugh before they look at me. Everything is business as usual for Taj. I want to hate him, but maybe I'd have done the same. I looked out for me before I looked out for him. So who am I to judge him?

Sorella speaks again. "And now we make the exchange."

Sorella and Barry each take hold of one of Taj's wrists, press hard, then let go. I expect him to disappear, to flit away, to flap his arms and be able to fly off into the sky. But he's now been stripped of all powers. He has no more magic. He's human, and when Barry and Sorella take my hands, I feel a surge of warmth and of power erupt in my body, as if my veins are flushed of blood and replaced with something else, something liquid that becomes sweet smoke to bestow the greatest gifts at the greatest price.

"And now granter 542 has been officially relieved of all granter duties from this moment forward. And granter 892 has taken his place," Barry says, then writes down the time, date, and location that I've taken over.

We're gone, traveling at the speed of light through time and space and nothingness. When my feet touch ground again, we've arrived at the sidewalk grate outside the Chrysler Building. Barry lifts it up, and the pair of them walks me through the tunnels—tunnels I can now see clearly, I can now navigate through as if I'm wearing infrared goggles—to the library that used to belong to the boy I fell in love with, the boy who used me to get out of this prison.

31

Reflected Back

I stumble into the library, and I try to lunge for the registry of wishes, still wide open on Taj's desk. *My* desk now. But my breath is racing, and I'm sucking in air through the slimmest of straws, and my neck is squeezed by a thousand mighty hands. The light goes out and the walls close in. The ceiling compresses down on me, as if I'm buried alive. I'm choking as I'm crushed, and then just like that, it's over . . .

———

An alarm goes off. I can't hear it, but I can feel it, all over me. My body has become a rooster, the crow that starts the day. My skin, my senses, my eyes and breath and brain are rattled awake. Not gently, like a nap. But crudely, the morning after a very late night, when all you want to do is slam the snooze button and sleep more.

My legs are heavy concrete blocks weighing me down. My arms are logs. But the alarm is stronger, and I'm pulled awake, yanked from this hibernation into . . .

A loud *pop*, like Bubble Wrap stepped on by someone wearing heavy shoes.

I look down, and the *pop* is me. The snapping sound of my body being reshaped from nothingness into somethingness. I hold my hands in front of me—they're hands, my hands, then legs and arms and belly and face. And I'm all here, after months, weeks, days, or could it be hours of not being here? I don't know, but I lift my feet, wiggle them one by one, getting used to being corporeal again, after being evanescent. Then I notice how I'm dressed. I'm in tailored slacks and a white button-down blouse and a pair of patent leather black flats.

I must look hideous. I'd never dress like this. Where are my clothes? My combat boots, my jeans, my short skirts, and black cotton tees?

I hunt around the library, but they're not here. Nothing's here but shelves and shelves of books extending as far back as I can see. Just like when Taj resided here.

Taj.

His name is a pang in the chest, as the full memory of the last time I saw him collides into me. He made a mockery of me. I was played like a fool, such easy bait. And I hurt so much too. Every organ inside me aches because I miss him. I hate that I miss him. But I fell for him for a reason—he was so kind, and he was so handsome, and he understood me in a way no one ever had. How could I not fall for him? But I was selfish too, just like him. So what right do I have to be mad at him for tricking me to free him? We both played the other. We were both in it for our own needs.

As I search for another outfit, I can't focus on him or myself or the pangs inside me. Because I find myself drawn to the door, and I'm no longer in the library, I'm walking through the tunnels, and it's not absolute blackness anymore. It's bright light, beckoning and clear, and it guides me to the underside of a grate.

That's when I realize why I'm awake, why I'm alive again, what the alarm bell sounding inside me was.

I've been found.

We are found in the wanting.

I've been summoned on my first official call as a granter, and I don't even know what day it is, what time it is, what year it is. But I know this—I'm no longer nuclear. I'm not running at Aria temperature. My blood feels light, my veins flooded with a wispy, smoky granter magic that's so different from the fire I'm used to living with.

I push up on the grate and climb out. It's midday, late after-noon by the sun's position in the sky. It's warm, but no longer hot. I see a group of schoolkids across the street, backpacks slung over shoulders. I see a newsstand and take a quick look at the date on the paper. It's September. Two weeks have passed.

No one notices me, a pristinely dressed seventeen-year-old in New York City, but this is how granters dress. I begin walking south on the avenue, and I bump into a girl a year or so younger than I am. She has a plain face and mousy hair pulled back in a low ponytail. She's got on jeans tucked into lace-up, scuffed-up boots. I feel a stab of jealousy that's quickly displaced by a reminder—as if someone is talking quietly in my ear—that I don't get to have feelings or emotions, because I exist to serve and I've found my wisher.

"Hey. What are you up to?" I ask.

The girl shifts her eyes side to side. "Looking for someone."

"I suspect you're looking for me."

"Why would you say that?" She sounds suspicious.

"Call it a crazy hunch. Or call it my own experience," I say, and though the words roll off my tongue easily, they taste so bitter.

"But who are you?"

That's the question, isn't it?

"I'm the person you think can solve all your problems. Rub my lamp, and I'll give you whatever you want and life will be good again," I say, somehow sliding right into my first day on the job. I feel slippery and smarmy, the snake-oil man in the bazaar. I've become sarcastic too, and I don't like it. The old Aria tugs at my mind, but the granter inside me is in charge now.

"How do I know you're a granter?"

"Ah, the proof test. You want proof. It's so cute. I once wanted proof too," I say, and it's as if I've been plunged back in time, only I'm on the other side now, and I've become the Taj from the first night.

Correction. There was only one Taj. The Taj from all the nights. The facade of Taj. But his bluffs worked on me, so I borrow from his playbook.

I disappear and reappear on the other side of the avenue.

The girl crosses over. "You really are a granter," she says, kind of awestruck. She reminds me of the occasional fans I'd encounter after Wonder shows. That time seems so long ago. I'd only made one big mistake then; I had so many more to make.

I curtsy a thanks, and I find myself wondering where that came from. I'm not a curtsier, I'm not a pencil-skirt-wearer, I'm not super-outgoing-friendly. I'm mad as hell that I'm stuck, but yet I have to curtsy. The curse of the mastered granter. This girl is my master now.

My stomach growls and grumbles. I haven't eaten in ages, but it's not up to me to eat. It's up to this girl, and I'll have to convince her to grab a bite.

"What's your name?"

"Blake Vater."

"Are you hungry, Blake?"

She shakes her head. "No, I just ate."

"So you don't want to get something to eat?"

She shakes her head again. "No. Not really."

"Because I could really go for a sandwich," I say, and I hope Blake is nice enough to suggest getting at least a snack from the corner deli, but she seems preoccupied. "I would love it if we could chat at a deli, please."

"Maybe you can eat later. Because I need something so badly," she says as we stand on the street corner and afternoon traffic rushes by in a flurry of exhaust and honked horns.

"Okay. What do you need?" I ask, and part of me is coldly impressed that Blake is all business in a way I never was. She's ready to dive in, and getting to know her granter doesn't even cross her mind. I'm not a person. I'm a shortcut to her problem.

"There's a boy I love, and he doesn't even know I'm alive."

"Blake, sorry to break it to you. But I should let you know that there are three preliminary conditions and exceptions to wishing. I can't make someone fall in love with you, I can't bring someone back from the dead, and I can't grant you more wishes. So as you can see, we'll have to call it a day," I say, then decide to add a warning all on my own. "Besides, the best way to get someone to fall in love with you is to trick them into it."

She gives me a curious look as she tucks a loose strand of stringy hair behind her ear. "I didn't say I wanted you to make him fall in love with me."

"What do you want me to do then?"

"I want you to make me beautiful, so he'll notice me." She's so dreamy and hopeful, like this is a movie, like she can just rub a lamp and a happy, cheery genie will appear to deliver pizza and earth, wind, air, or fire.

"Really?"

"Yes, really."

I sigh. I want to tell her that it's what's inside that matters. I want to deliver some wise, pithy adage she'll remember forever about beauty being skin deep, and that it's what's in your heart that counts. But honestly, her heart doesn't seem that beautiful either. She couldn't be bothered to take me out for something to eat, and I feel like I'm starving.

Besides, what do I know about love? What do I even know about beauty or true hearts? I know nothing because everything I've felt has been turned upside down.

"You can do that, right? You can make me beautiful, right? I want blond hair, and I want green eyes, and perfect cheekbones, and I want to be thin and tall and have one of those faces that makes everyone look at you," she says in a voice full of a sick and fetid kind of longing.

"Yes, I can do it. But do you really want to?"

"Of course. It's all I've ever wanted."

"You find a granter, and you wish for beauty? You're not going to wish for health or happiness?"

She tilts her head and gives me a sharp and loathing glance. "Do you have any idea what it's like to look ordinary? I bet you don't. But I'll tell you what it's like. It's awful. It's like an awful trap, and I want out of it."

We all have our traps, I suppose. This is hers. "Okay then. Let's talk payment," I say, because this is her wish, her life, her choice. I might as well let this girl know what's at stake, so she doesn't feel used as I was. "Wishes come at a cost."

"Okay. So what would it cost?"

"Your soul. Your love. Your heart. Yourself. You name it. You could give me one of your hands, and we'd be even," I say, and she cringes, but I keep going, and this must be granter magic too, this instant knowledge I have of how she'd need to pay. "Your firstborn child and it'd be a deal."

Blake recoils.

"You could subtract twenty years from your life, and we'd be good then."

"Twenty years?"

I tilt my head to the side, considering. "Twenty years. Yep. That feels about right. Twenty years off your life," I say, and I'm still not entirely sure where the words have come from, but I know them to be true.

"That's how people pay for wishes?"

I nod.

"But what about—" she begins, but can't finish the sentence.

261

I finish it for her. "It's called a Faustian bargain. It's called that for a reason. It's like a deal with the devil." My voice is harsh and clipped, and if I could I'd shake her by the shoulders and slap some sense into her. But she's calling the shots, not me.

She doesn't speak right away. She breathes out hard through tight lips, as if she's considering. I offer a faint wish to whoever is in charge that she'll see the light and walk away. But I believe in nothing anymore, so I don't even know who I'm wishing to.

"Fine. Twenty years from my life. I'll give you twenty years of my life in exchange for being beautiful."

If I were a jackass granter, I'd take the twenty years right now. I'd grant her wish literally, age her up to thirty-five, and make her a beautiful thirtysomething woman in a fifteen-year-old's life. But I am a mastered granter, so I take out the notebook, write down her wish, and tell her, "The terms are satisfactory."

Then I escort her to the nearest park, find a quiet corner, and ask her one more time to make her wish.

"I wish to be beautiful," Blake says.

"Your wish is my command," I say, and mist pours forth from my hands, swirling around her, transforming her limp hair into lushness, her plain face into model features, her short and squat body into a tall, statuesque one. She is gorgeous. She is stunning. She will turn heads. And no one she knows will recognize her.

Her parents won't know she's her. Her classmates will no longer know Blake.

Someday, maybe in fifty years, maybe in ten, someone will

knock on her door, maybe me, maybe someone from the Union, and they will take her life twenty years before she would have said good-bye to this world naturally.

She rushes to the nearest parked car at the edge of the park and looks at her reflection. "I am beautiful," she says, then she runs back to me and gives me a hug. "Thank you."

"I'm still hungry," I say, but she's off in another direction, and I'm forgotten. Because she got what she thought she wanted, and I'm gone now too.

I'm suddenly back in the library, like I was snapped through time and space. I'm weary, though I've had more sleep in the last month than I've had in ages. My feet are heavy, my eyes are so sleepy, but I still have form, I still have shape, so I make my way to the desk, sink down in the leather chair, and pull the registry closer to me so I can enter Blake Vater's name. The registry is open to the last entry made. The *K*s. The spot where my name was entered. I stave off sleep, I fend off hibernation as I run my thumb over the names, searching out mine. I need to know why the Leagues never made an example of me. Why they never strutted me around for stealing—the worst crime, the crime that echoes through your family forever.

I find my entry. I slide my index finger across the ruled line. My name—Aria Kilandros—back when I still had two names. Then the date, then the wish.

I take a sharp breath, bring a hand to my mouth.

The marks are scratchy, as if someone wrote my name while fighting off an invisible hand trying to pen something else. As if the granter recording this wish was resisting all the granter magic, all the granter orders and rules and regulations and stipulations and provisos and quid pro quos, with every ounce of strength inside him.

Because it doesn't say *natural-born fire.*

It says *whole fire.*

Whole Fire.

It's not the full truth, but it's not a lie either.

What it is, however, was enough of the truth for the registry of wishes and enough of a lie for my family to be safe from my stealing. For Jana to have a chance to perform if she wants. For her kids, for the next generation to not be subjected to the League's rules of family banishment for all time. Because *natural-born fire* would tip off the Leagues that I had stolen. *Whole fire* merely suggests I topped myself off and wished for a little more. A small difference in wording, but a big difference in penalties since no one knows I stole now.

Taj recorded my wish, as he had to, but he recorded it in a way that satisfied the granters and gave my family a chance.

He protected them, and something inside me lightens and starts to hope again.

One of his very last acts as a granter was to try to keep me safe.

Then, the choking feeling comes, and it hurts. I'm crushed into vapor.

———

It goes like this for the next several weeks. I'm rousted from the dead of sleep by the greedy, I grant their basest desires for a price, then I choke until I'm obliterated.

Then it happens again.

I grant a man millions of dollars in exchange for his right hand.

Literally—that is what he offers to pay with. I give him a sharp and heavy knife, and he cuts it off himself, handing me the bloody stump one starless night in a dark corner of Central Park. I try to give it back to him, to tell him to take it to the nearest hospital emergency room and have the doctors sew it back on. But then the hand disappears. It's gone forever. He cries in pain, and I imagine he'll keep crying for weeks and months and years to come even as he counts his money with his left hand.

I grant an older woman a job. She's been looking for three years, and she offers me her happiness. I don't know where it goes when I take it. All I know is she'll no longer have it, and it'll be in the same place where that man's hand is, where Blake's shortened life is. In a bank full of horrid desires.

Then I meet a boy who wishes for his sick father to be healthy. His dad has been ill for a year, and the boy offers himself as a trade. I remember the security guard with the sick sister who gave keys to Taj. I ask the boy if he'd instead be willing to give me his most valuable teddy bear, or baseball card, or even a book.

He brings me his entire collection of invaluable first-edition comic books the next day, and I grant his father health.

Then I take the comic books back to my library. I wonder why I couldn't take the hand or the happiness with me. But maybe you can only take payments that aren't beyond measure. Maybe we get to keep only the things that are bartered in exchange for a better life for others, like when Taj kept the keys from the security guard. Maybe there are some noble wishes.

Then again, Taj's parents didn't get to keep him when they traded him for peace.

Maybe there are no good wishes.

But if I could wish for one thing now, it would be for Taj to be enjoying his freedom. For the boy who protected my family to be living his life fully. I miss him. I miss him terribly.

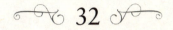

32

The Only Payment

The alarm sounds again, and I rise, rub my eyes, and go through the same motions I went through with Blake and the one-handed man and the job-hunting woman and the boy with the sick dad. I brush my hair, wash my face, grab a new outfit, tsk-tsking the selection in the closet as I snag the least boring of all the boringest skirt-blouse-shoes ensembles.

I open the door, walk through the tunnel, desperate for sunshine and air after this latest nap. I push up on the grate, wondering who I'll see, and there's a hand reaching for me, taking mine, and helping me the rest of the way up.

I'm aboveground, looking at my potential wisher, looking into eyes I know so well.

Taj.

I want to kick him. I want to wail on him with my fists. I want to to yell at him, to ask him how he could have used me.

I want to ask him why he tried to protect my family. I want

to know if he missed me terribly too. But it would be stupid to ask. He doesn't miss me. He needs something, just like I did.

Instead, I fold my arms over my chest and stand against the side of the Flatiron Building. I climbed out of a different grate tonight. I've started to learn the labyrinths.

"You have no idea how long I've been looking for you," he says. "Two months. Every day for two months. I have been looking for you, and it's not as if I didn't know exactly where you'd be. But it took this long to find you, Aria."

"You've been looking for me?"

"Yes. God, yes. All the time. Every day. And I guess it's true—I had to be desperate enough, I had to be at my wit's end before you appeared."

"But why? What could you possibly need from me? Isn't this the only thing you wanted? To be free?" I gesture at him, taking in his new look. He's wearing jeans and a button-down. Not quite the same as his sharp-dressed granter look, but not that different either. Maybe he wasn't that different as a granter and as a boy. But what do I know? Everything I thought I knew about him was a mask.

There's a shopping bag at his feet.

"Yes, and it's great. I'm going to college and I've seen my mom again, and I'm wearing normal clothes, and it's the most wonderful thing in the world. Except—"

I cut him off. "Then what do you want? What could you possibly have to wish for if you have everything you want? You used me. You tricked me into freeing you, and you admitted it at my house. That it was all a story to set you free."

He reaches for me, but I back up.

"Aria, I've been looking for you. Not for me. But for you."

"What's that supposed to mean?"

He dips a hand inside the shopping bag. He takes out my combat boots. The sight of them reminds me of all I don't have, and it's as if he just yanked a bandage off a still-sore wound.

"I brought these for you. I thought you might need them." There's a glint in his eye.

"Why would I need them?"

"Aria, when I came to your house, the reason I lied to you and said all those awful things was because I didn't want the union officials to have a clue. I couldn't let on how I felt about you. They already knew you tried to free me and that it didn't work, so they knew how you felt. I had to act like I'd used you. Like I'd tricked you. That your feelings were all just a wisher's folly. I told you that it happened before, that wishers fell into infatuation. I had to make it seem like that's all that had happened with you. Because if I let on that I felt the same way, they'd have reassigned you. Given you a new jurisdiction and then I'd never have found you."

I hold up a hand in a stop sign. "Wait. Did you say felt the same way?"

He nods and grins, a sweet sheepish grin. The smile of a boy, not the smile of a onetime granter. The boy who kissed me. The boy who looked at stars with me. The boy who believed in the green light at the end of the dock.

Maybe it wasn't an act?

"Yes," he says, and he sounds innocent and shy as he admits it. "*Felt* and *feel*, Aria. It was never just a tale told for freedom. The way I feel for you is a true story. It's real."

My heart is beating fast, and I'm scared and hopeful at the same time. It's so strange to feel this way. "Really?"

"Yes. Really and truly. And more than *like*, Aria. I'm in love with you. And I want to make a wish."

My heart catches and plummets at the same time. Wishes and wants. It always comes down to that.

I assume my best businesslike pose as I reach into my pocket for the small notebook that's magically there, in every outfit, every uniform I now possess. I take it out, flip it open, and begin to take notes. "Let's get down to business. Your wish, sir? And what is it you want to offer in exchange?"

He shakes his head, steps closer, and takes away my notebook. "The only wish that requires no payment," he says, as he drops my notebook to the sidewalk. I watch it hit the ground before I realize my hands are shaking, my fingers are trembling. I can taste something, I can feel something, and it's so perilously close. I want to reach it, but I don't want to miss.

The thing I've wanted most of all, my whole life over. The thing I've sought in different forms, in different shapes, trying on the wrong size, fumbling and stumbling and getting it wrong. But wanting it—always wanting it.

Freedom.

I hope and I wait and I want. There is only one wish that costs nothing.

His lips quirk up, and he speaks again. "You freed me. And now, Aria, I wish you free."

I hold out my hands, and no sweet smoke rises from them, no mist to bring forth desires. Instead I can feel the smoke coursing out of me, mingling with the real elements, with the air surrounding me, then being carried off on a current to become one with the atmosphere. I don't know where granter magic goes when it's drained away, when you're freed of the bonds that come with incredible cosmic power and no free will.

But it's no longer inside me.

My body is mine, my will is mine.

I am safe, finally.

"Your wish is my command," I say as he takes my hands in his, pulls me close, and kisses me. He tastes like oranges, like he did that night we first kissed. Only this is better. Because my heart is healed, all my wish-giving magic stripped away, and he's free too. I am me now, only me, and there's nothing better than this.

Except one little thing.

I break the kiss.

"I hope you don't mind, but I'd really like to get out of these awful shoes."

I take the black patent leather shoes I vow to never wear again and leave them on the sidewalk. Someone will pick them up. Someone will wear them. Just not me.

Instead I pull on my lace-up boots, tying them the way I like. I look down at my footwear, at my worn and beaten-up boots that don't match my outfit. But they sure make this skirt look a heck of a lot better.

"Ah, that's the girl I fell in love with, boots and all."

"Boots and all," I repeat. I take his hand. "What would you say to going to New Jersey with me right now? There are some people I want to see."

"I would say let's catch the next bus."

33

New Life

"Where's my math homework? I can't find it!"

Jana shrieks and runs her hands through her hair, holding it hard.

I place a hand on her shoulder to settle her. "Did you look in your backpack? I saw you put it in there last night when you finished."

Jana unzips her backpack and digs through the mountains of paper inside her binder, like a dog hunting for a bone. "Ah! There is it."

"Dork," I say, rolling my eyes. "Now, c'mon. My first class isn't for an hour, so I'm going to walk you to the bus stop."

"I know where the bus stop is. You don't have to walk me."

"I want to and I'm going to," I say.

She narrows her eyes at me, shoots me a sharp stare.

"Just let me be the big sister, please."

"Fine," she says, then she lowers her voice. "I'm so glad you're back. And safe."

"Me too."

I've been home for a month now, catching up on school. It's not easy, but I find the SparkNotes *are* helpful. I did read *The Great Gatsby* last week for English though, and Taj was right. It's so beautiful.

Then I zip up my coat and tell Jana to put on a hat. "It's freezing outside."

"It's ridiculous here," she says. "It's so cold in December. I don't know how people survive like this."

I love that we can talk about the weather, and the temperature truly is one of the few things we have to worry about.

On the way to the bus stop, Jana chatters about a boy she likes.

"You should ask him out," I say.

Her eyes widen. "Really?"

"Yeah, why not?"

She nods several times. "Yeah, why not?"

"And don't forget. Be home by three. You and mom are taking me to the airport tonight."

"I'll be home."

———

They let Xavi into the visiting room. He sits next to me on the couch. He shrugs at me, an admission that he's sorry we're back like this.

"Hey," I say softly. "It's good to see you again."

"You too."

"How are you doing?"

"The same. Always the same."

I suspect he'll always be the same.

"But what about you?"

"I'm good." Except for my brother being behind bars, life is extraordinarily good. It's also completely different from what I imagined. I always thought I'd have to save everyone—Jana, my mom, myself. In the end, I couldn't save myself. I had to be saved. But then, knowing who to trust and who to love—Taj— was what saved me in the end. He saved me, because I finally let someone know me.

"How's school?"

"I'm finishing my senior year of high school," I tell him. "I started late. I missed the first two months of the school year with that whole granter thing. But I'm making up for lost time."

"And Jana?"

"Oh, you know. She still misses Florida. But she's getting used to Jersey."

He shakes his head and laughs. "Can't believe you live in New Jersey of all places."

"I know, right? But Mom likes the change. We have a small apartment, and she had enough money to buy it from the sale of the house."

"And you?"

"Me?"

"Yeah, you, dork. You."

How am I? I don't perform anymore, and I don't miss it at all. And I haven't gone dark inside like Xavi said would happen. Turns out we are different in some ways. Some people go crazy when they don't use their fire. Some people grow saner. No one's coming to get me, no one's coming to lock me up. I may have stolen fire, but I don't use it anymore. I'd like to say it's my penance, my punishment for the crime, but truth be told, I actually like not making fire.

"I'm happy. I'm going to apply to college. Maybe study English or something. I don't know. Or maybe I'll just be a barista. I don't really know what I want to do with my life."

But I don't have to. Because my life is finally mine.

———

Taj waits for me outside, reading a book. He's sitting on a bench just beyond the chain-link fence that keeps the prisoners inside. I watch him as he flips back a few pages, scans the words for whatever he's looking for, then returns to where he left off. He likes reading even more now that he can take his time with books, now that he *has* time. He doesn't have to race against a clock.

I sit down next to him. "Good book?" I ask.

"Great book."

"I'm going to need to get you a how-to-take-care-of-Florida-wildlife one next."

"Oh, yeah?"

I nod. "Yep. I need to go check on the gator. I promised I'd look out for him."

A deal is a deal, after all.

Acknowledgments

Thank you so much to my agent, Michelle Wolfson, for her tireless and always passionate dedication to my books, to my editors Caroline Abbey and Michelle Nagler for their keen insight into how to make the story better, and to Brett Wright for getting the book over the finish line.

I am ever grateful to the entire team at Bloomsbury for their care and attention to books, especially Lizzy Mason and Cindy Loh.

Hugs and pizza and tea and chatter to my local girls, Cynthia, Malinda, and Cheryl.

Thank you to the librarians, teachers, and fantastic booksellers who share their love of books with readers of all ages.

As always, my husband and children are my loves, and my dogs are my writing companions.

And most of all, thank you to you—the person reading this book. I hope you enjoyed your time with Aria.